A Famished Heart

NICOLA WHITE

VIPER

First published in Great Britain in 2020 by
VIPER, part of Serpent's Tail
an imprint of Profile Books Ltd
29 Cloth Fair
London EC1A 7JQ
www.serpentstail.com

1 3 5 7 9 10 8 6 4 2

Typeset in Sabon by MacGuru Ltd
Printed and bound in Great Britain by CPI Group (UK) Ltd, Croydon CR0 4YY

A CIP catalogue record for this book is available from the British Library.

ISBN 978 1 78816 408 5
eISBN 978 1 78283 643 8

...hed Heart
...den (2021)

7/2022

kfw. 11/22

Please return/renew this item by the
last date shown to avoid a charge.
Books may also be renewed by phone
and Internet. May not be renewed if
required by another reader.

www.libraries.barnet.gov.uk

For Carol, greatly missed

1

Dublin, 1982

Father Timoney rang the doorbell a third time. Listened to the soft *bing-bong* resonate somewhere deep in the house. A figurine of the Child of Prague in his big frock stood in the narrow window beside the door, dead flies scattered at his feet. The nylon curtain hanging at the statue's back shut off any view of the inside.

Most likely the sisters had gone away and not told anyone. He had noticed they hadn't been at mass lately; his congregation was so sparse, of course he'd noticed. If he'd thought about it, he might have assumed they'd followed the rest of his migratory parishioners over to Holy Trinity, where the heating functioned and the brass chandeliers shone bright in the dark mornings. Or they could have gone off to visit a relative, a sick relative. Often women did that.

But their niece, a small punky-looking one, had arrived at his door, saying she hadn't been able to reach her aunts for a month, and no one would answer the door. It was nine o'clock last night when she'd shown up, distraught and melodramatic. 'You are their shepherd,' she'd said, clutching at his hand. A sharp waft of alcohol came off her breath. He told her to go home, to leave it with him.

He had asked his housekeeper, Mrs Noonan, for her advice – she knew so much more about the people around here. He hadn't even known the keys to their house were among the hoard in the hall cupboard, until she told him.

He took the keys out of his coat pocket now, the brown label written in Father Deasy's fussy hand. *The Misses MacNamara*.

Still he hesitated. There would be a simple explanation. And yet he realised he was rehearsing the sequence of events that led him to this moment, as if noting it to tell someone later.

He took a breath and slid the key into the lock. When he turned it, the door opened easily, but juddered to a stop as a little gilt chain tightened across the gap, a chain someone inside must have slotted in place. He looked over his shoulder, along the cul-de-sac spattered with yellow leaves. Nobody about. He should have asked young Jimmy to come with him, but it would be spineless to go back to the parish house and get him now.

He put his face to the gap, about to call *Hello there*, but inhaled a waft of heat so thick it stopped his voice; a swampy warmth bearing a bouquet of chemical flowers and there, like a wire running through it, a very specific smell.

Despite the many bodies he'd prayed over and delivered to their rest, he had met this smell only once before, ages past, down by the railroad near Sandymount. Hunkering in the long grass on a hot day, hiding from the older boys, the thread of a strange odour – redolent of mutton and sweat – had led him to the body of an Alsatian dog wreathed in broken bricks, the rising flies unveiling a pale-pink crater behind its plush ear.

One hand against the door now, his heart began thumping. Why did it have to be him? Why did the Lord – or was it the world – try him so? Another priest would have had the wit to call the police. To not be the lone one standing here, knowing he had to press on, because every action on this earth is witnessed.

Father Timoney took a step back, then threw his bulk at the neat white door, bruising his shoulder against the wood. The chain held.

He flung himself again and heard a metallic 'ping' as the chain gave way. But he couldn't halt the momentum of his body and fell through the opening gap, landing on his knees on a spill of unopened post, sliding forward on layers of glossy paper and envelopes. He braced his hands against the grimy carpet to stop his face meeting it. When he raised his head, he was in the doorway of the living room, and there in an armchair she sat, facing him. One of the sisters. Her head was bowed, she was swaddled in shawls, but the hands braced on the chair arms were not like hands at all, but the dry claws of a bird.

2

Francesca nodded her way past the doorman guarding the revolving door of the Gramercy Hotel. 'Hi there, how are you?'

He acknowledged her passing with only a slow bat of his eyelids. He used to be chatty with her. She ducked straight into the bar area and took the first stool at the long bar, shielded from the foyer by a room divider paned with coloured glass. It was wonderfully old-fashioned here, unchanged since her first days in New York – what – fifteen years ago? No, can't be.

She pushed up her sunglasses and shucked off her rabbit-fur jacket, let it fall over the back of the seat. She loved these bar stools. They were like the bastard love-child of an armchair and a high stool. They swivelled. They had buttoned upholstery. If there was a pub in heaven, it would have bar stools like these.

It was the kind of thing she loved about the States. They had no fear of luxury. In Dublin it was seen as a bit soft to be sitting at all while you drank. Sitting was for geriatrics.

She placed a newspaper on the shining counter to mark her domain, then sauntered over to where the guest breakfast was laid out. Yesterday's bagels, cream cheese, a jug of thin orange juice, big metal urns of coffee. If she had paid the fifty dollars a night to stay here, she might well have complained about this sparse, unmanned buffet.

The other breakfasters were a mix of business people and tourists, planning out their days over diaries or guide-books. Two stocky women in casual clothes bent over a map of Manhattan. The Russian girl who occasionally cleared the tables appeared, and Francesca moved away, bearing her two bagels and coffee back to her corner.

The newspaper was yesterday's, just a ploy to look occu-pied. It was turning into a very lean week. An unforeseen taxi fare the previous evening had almost cleared her out – some men were badly brought up, in that respect. At least he had paid for the dinner. There were two days to go before payday, and since the entire company had accepted shares of the box office rather than a wage, she was worried it wouldn't add up to much. During every performance she looked into the auditorium and counted the empty seats. *A matter of faith*, she told herself. The play could take off yet, it wasn't *so* bad. Or her agent might call with news. That second series of *Honeybun* might be commissioned. There was no end to the good things that could happen.

Which reminded her. She reached for her jacket pocket and pulled out an envelope. She didn't particularly want to read Rosaleen's holy nonsense, but it *had* been her birthday recently and there was a chance her sister had fallen into the old habit of sending her a bit of money.

She'd picked up the letter from the mail office on the way to breakfast. The bastards were holding it for the 82 cents owing on the postage. Rosaleen had scrawled 'airmail' on the envelope, but neglected to stick on the right stamps.

6

Francesca had been tempted to abandon it rather than pay the extra, and asked the official if she could hold it – more than one sheet of paper, possibly a bit of folding money – before handing over her dimes.

Rosaleen's handwriting on the envelope just about broke her heart. It was still the well-behaved hand of a convent girl, but seemed to have gained a trembling quality. Like the writing of a feeble old lady, not her bright-smiled big sister. How could Rosaleen grow old when she herself felt so unchanged?

A line from a play came floating out from that part of her mind where years of memorised lines lay in a jumble. *I was not in safety, neither had I rest … then the trouble came.* What was it from? No. Gone, so much gone.

'Excuse me?'

She mustered her dignity and turned, expecting the sharp-featured waitress, but it was one of the lady tourists.

'Sorry to bother you, but my girlfriend and I thought we recognised you.'

Francesca gave a modest shrug.

'Where would we have seen you?'

Jesus! The guessing game. The woman's 'girlfriend' gave a little wave from the table.

'Do you go to the theatre?'

'Don't get the chance much. We're from Virginia. You *are* an actress, though, right?'

'I am that,' said Francesca. 'It might have been a film. Perhaps *Dark Flows the Bann*?'

'Hmm,' said the woman, puckering her lips. 'Can't say it rings a bell. How about TV?'

'Well, I've just been in a series called *Honeybun* – about a girl who runs a bakery.'

The woman twisted to shout across the room, '*Honeybun*?'

'That's the one!' said the woman at the table. Everyone in the room was watching now. 'You're that old downstairs neighbour – Mrs O'Leary.'

'She's not old, she's—'

'This is so exciting,' said the woman at her side. 'Dianne thought she saw Lionel Ritchie yesterday, but it was just some black guy with a mullet.'

With an eager smile, Dianne padded up to join them. 'I didn't mean *you're* old. It's the make-up they do, ain't it? You are just *gorgeous*.'

'That hair!' said the first woman and reached out to take a strand and show it to her friend. 'Is it natural red?'

No such thing as a free breakfast, after all. But Francesca smiled and gave them a printed flyer for her play, said she'd love to see them there. They couldn't visit New York and not go to the theatre – it was unthinkable. If they showed, it would boost her wages, by … oh, a dollar at least.

The women headed off for the top of the World Trade Center, and Francesca took her sister's letter from under the newspaper, where she had automatically tucked it.

There was no money inside, just three battered pages of pale-blue writing paper, one of them torn nearly across, as if the letter had survived various ordeals before even reaching the envelope. She couldn't face reading it over breakfast. The agitated script, the wrong stamp – little signs of Rosaleen not quite managing. She hoped Berenice was

8

taking care of Rosaleen, was being kind to her. She'd tried to phone them a while back, to catch up, but the number kept ringing out. She could do without the worry right now.

Francesca took a last bitter swig of coffee and a chew of bagel before gathering her things. She pulled her sunglasses down to hide her eyes. As she reached the revolving door, someone called from the reception desk, 'Ms Mac-Namara!' and she turned automatically.

It was one of the junior managers, looking like a young undertaker in his dark suit. He curled a finger.

'My car is waiting,' she said.

'It won't take a moment.'

She sighed and approached the desk.

'Breakfast for non-residents is six dollars.'

'I did not partake of breakfast,' said Francesca. 'I was obliging two of your guests, who wanted information about my play. Those ladies from Virginia?'

'Don't know 'em.'

'It's very disappointing. This petty harassment. The Gramercy always had such a reputation for supporting artists. International actors ...'

She gestured towards the bronze wall plaque to Siobhán McKenna, another flame-haired Irish woman, whom a previous management had obviously treasured during her great Broadway triumphs.

'Very disappointing,' she repeated and headed for the door.

'Well, you ain't no *Shee-bawn* McKenna,' said the man.

Francesca kept walking away, delicately raising her middle finger in an over-the-shoulder farewell.

3

Vincent Swan took the call from Deerfield Garda station, wrote down the relevant address and scanned the office for someone to bring with him. Young Colin Rooney was eating a sandwich with his mouth open and reading the sports pages, a tempting target.

'I've got a car signed out.'

He swivelled towards her voice. Detective Garda Gina Considine was already getting up from her desk. One week in the unit, and keen as a razor.

'Okay, so.'

She swung her jacket off the back of her chair and jangled a set of car keys at him.

'You can drive,' said Swan.

'Taking your life in your hands there,' commented Ownie Hannigan from his den in the corner, half hidden by a buttress of filing cabinets and a fug of smoke. Swan ignored him, but some of the other men obliged with rote chuckles.

They headed out from Garda Headquarters onto the North Circular. The radio was playing some dreadful chirpy pop, so he twisted the knob and hit RTÉ1. A woman with a drawling voice was discussing food. The third time she said *luscious*, he hit the button again.

Gina Considine side-eyed him. 'Can I ask what we're going to?'

'An old woman, dead in her home. Found by her priest.'

He looked out of the side window. They were waiting at lights near Phibsborough Cross, entering his home turf, and his eyes automatically sought out his father's old shop. The sign on the gable wall was still visible – just – the white letters faint on the red bricks now:

HARRY SWAN
FINE FURNISHINGS

Considine was following his line of sight. 'He's got the same name as you. A relative?'

'I can see why you were promoted to the detective unit.'

She looked uncertain how to respond.

'Sorry,' he said. 'I didn't mean to sound sarcastic.'

The lights changed and she drove on, obeying his directions wordlessly. It was the thought of his father that made him irritable. Harry had been a spectacularly bad businessman – filled his shop with gilt frou-frou when the style was sleek and modern, then changed to sleek and modern when the middle classes were all for stripped dressers and Victoriana. His father never listened to anyone's advice, least of all that of Swan's mother. And now he was two years dead, and his mother still heartbroken for the old bastard.

They passed by the end of his street and pulled onto the busy road towards Glasnevin. When he spotted the ugly church of St Alphonsus coming up on the far side, he pointed to a slip road and Considine turned off.

'It should be around here.'

They drove past a fenced lot where the remains of a garage canopy stood like an outsize dolmen, then an expansive car park around a modern pub with an attached run of three motley shops. There was a metal pedestrian bridge linking the shops to the church across the road. He couldn't see any houses nearby.

'Two Rowan Grove,' recited Considine, as if that might make it appear.

Swan glimpsed a small terrace veiled by a line of trees on a rise behind the pub.

'Up there.'

As they got closer, he could see they were fairly new houses – narrow, boxy things squeezed onto a strip of land in front of an old stone wall. A patrol car parked by the kerb confirmed it was the right place.

There were no fences or gates dividing the strip of grass that ran in front of the five houses. Simple slab paths ran up to each door. Every house had a large plate-glass window to the right of a small porch, but the overall proportions were mean. Outside number two stood a tall Garda sergeant and a moustachioed younger man in a brown bomber jacket.

'Ready?'

Considine flashed a quick grin. 'I am.'

Swan recognised the sergeant and managed to pluck his name from some hinterland of his brain as they approached.

'Flaherty, isn't it?'

'Yes, sir, and this is Detective Sergeant Clancy.'

Swan shook the younger man's hand.

'Darren,' said Considine crisply.

'You should get some tape up,' Swan said. 'Tie it to the lamp posts, if you need to.'

'We didn't want to go over the top, you know,' said Clancy.

'What's worse,' said Swan, 'looking stupid or messing up an evidence chain?'

'We're thinking it's probably natural causes.'

'I'll keep that in mind.'

He noticed Considine studying the ground, a wry twist to her lips.

'I'll call the station,' said Sergeant Flaherty. 'They'll send some up.'

'What else do I need to know before we go in? Where's this priest?'

Sergeant Flaherty jerked his thumb towards the church across the road. 'Back in the presbytery. He was apparently alerted by the women's niece that she couldn't contact them, and came to investigate. There should be two women, y'see – sisters – but there's only one. One of our Guards is with him.'

'Make sure he stays there until we get a chance to see him.'

Sergeant Flaherty reached for his walkie-talkie. Swan squinted over at the church. It looked like it had been built in the 1960s, with a steep green roof that rose asymmetrically to a single pinnacle. The adjacent bell tower was like a concrete lift shaft topped by a slab on four thin legs, a metal cross with a drunken tilt stuck on top of that. Plain and unlovely.

'How long did the pathologist say he'd be?' asked Swan.

'Eh, he didn't say,' said Clancy.

He had the impression that Clancy hadn't asked, that urgency was not a factor. The young detective was not the one who had called in the murder squad, Swan reckoned. Flaherty, more cautious and more experienced, would have been the one who asked for a second opinion.

Now it was down to Swan to make a decision as quickly as possible. The right decision. If Swan called it in as suspicious, the forensics team and enough back-up to scour the neighbourhood would be there within the hour. Call it wrong, and Superintendent Kavanagh would take a flame-thrower to him for unnecessary expenditure. Back at the Depot, the talk was more of budgets than of crime these days.

'Right. Let's take a look.'

'Sir ...' Clancy was practically squirming. 'The priest. He opened the back door and windows to let in some air. We left them like that.'

'You come with us, so. Show Detective Considine exactly what he moved or touched. Flaherty, will you try and check in with the pathologist?'

Swan led the way across the threshold, noticing the splintered frame where a small guard chain had been forced. A holy-water font hung beside the door, pearlised pink plastic bearing an oval picture of the dove of the Holy Ghost. The little square of sponge lying inside the bowl was shrunken and convex, dry as bone. Straight ahead, through the kitchen, he could see the open back door, but the house still breathed a foul warmth. Letters and leaflets

15

were scattered down the hall, a few stamped over with grey footprints. Swan hopped over them neatly, then watched that Clancy and Considine did the same.

He nodded them towards the kitchen. 'See if you can get it back to how everything was, without leaving prints.' Considine glanced into the living room as she passed and he saw her falter, then keep going.

Swan stood in the living-room doorway and made himself look methodically from left to right, to take it all in, ignoring what screamed for his attention in the armchair.

The room was low and long, running from the front of the house to the back, where sliding patio doors framed a view of a modest garden. The room was untidy, yet staid, the furniture of an older style than the house. There were two green damask armchairs and a few dark mahogany pieces; nesting tables, a big standard lamp with a fringed shade, a Victorian sideboard that was much too large for the room. In contrast, the fireplace surround was modern, made of a kind of pale marble, and the flame-effect fire had been pulled out so that it was tilted to face the armchair with the body in it. The carpet was scattered with serious-looking magazines and books with plain black or dark-red covers. A grey plastic bucket sat in one corner.

Finally he turned his focus to the figure in the chair, hunched and ancient-looking, an Incan mummy dressed in grandmother's clothes. The wrists sticking out from thick jumper sleeves were thin as broomsticks, the hands skeletal, skin the colour of leather. Her upper body was wrapped around with a knitted shawl or blanket. She wore a tweed skirt, and the legs visible below the skirt were as emaciated as her arms, shinbones sharp inside wrinkled nylons. Knobbed ankles disappeared into fluffy pink slippers, incongruously bright.

They had described her as an old woman, but the hair on her head, though lank and matted, was brown, with only a few strands of grey twisting through it. It hung forward so that it hid most of her face. Perhaps she wasn't so very old; it was the clothes and thinness that had made them think so. His own mother was far greyer than this woman at – what? – sixty-five or -six, she must be now. The thought of his mother tugged momentarily at his attention, a guilty, sinking feeling wrapped up in it.

He stepped over a pile of books and balanced a hand very lightly on the chair arm, squatted down to get a better look at the woman's face.

It was still a face, just. Skin stretched over a skull. The lips shrank back from the long teeth, the eye hollows retreated deep into shadow. Her skin looked terribly dry, the surface minutely wrinkled, like gauze.

Desiccated. That was the word. He looked down at the pamphlets and papers spread around the woman's feet. A stapled journal called *The Bugle of the Revenant*, with a hovering angel on the cover, caught his eye.

Considine leaned in the door, Detective Clancy at her shoulder.

Swan stood up, wiping the palms of his hands together to rid them of the feel of the chair.

'The lads here unplugged that fire after they checked her,' said Considine, 'and the priest moved some bin bags in the kitchen to get at the door.'

17

Her voice was steady, and her eyes darted about the room as she spoke. They fixed on something behind him and he turned to follow her gaze. Above the mantelpiece, a photograph of Pope John Paul II saying mass at the Phoenix Park hung in a cheap gilt frame. There was an empty picture hook two inches above it, suggesting that the pontiff had recently ousted a larger picture to gain his place. Below the mass scene, a heavy wooden clock overhung the narrow ledge of the mantel. To its left stood a black crucifix with an abstracted figure of Christ attached, swaying from his nails in a sickle of pain. On the right was a framed photograph, five children sitting on a low country wall, an unremarkable hill swelling in the background.

He turned back to Considine. 'You've got the names of who touched what?'

She nodded. 'Is it a goer?'

'Probably not. No obvious signs of interference. But I want to see what the pathologist says. Any word on that, Detective?'

'I'll get on to it,' Clancy hurried out the front door.

'I could have a look upstairs,' said Considine, waiting for Swan's nod before she moved.

He bent to examine the family photograph. It looked like it had been blown up from an older, smaller snapshot – everything was slightly blurred. Four teenage girls and a younger boy. The girls' identical buttoned-up coats and heavy boots were reminiscent of the 1940s or 50s. The back end of an old dark car butted into the frame on the left. Three of the girls had their hair in plaits, with big bows on the end. The fourth and smallest girl, maybe eleven or twelve years old, wore her thick hair loose, curls lifted and blurred in the wind. She faced the lens with a confidence that set her apart from her sisters – bright eyes and a bold smile. The boy, sitting a little apart, sulked in a short-trousered suit. A pale rosette on his lapel indicated that this was his first communion. A family jaunt, in honour of the sacrament. Swan looked at the figure in the armchair, then back at the photograph.

She could be one of those girls. Perhaps even the lively one. It could have been a simple heart attack or stroke. A thing that happened unnoticed. But why unnoticed? They'd need to track down the sister. But the woman's thinness was disturbing, he'd never seen such a thing. Could she have starved? But what was there to stop her walking out the door, if she was in need?

He looked again at the stuff scattered around the chair – a few crumpled tissues, but no teacup or glass, no sign of any sustenance taken. He was vaguely aware of Considine's feet moving around above him. A handwritten page poked out from a prayer book and he bent to coax it out delicately by a corner:

… you say God burdens no branch with fruit too heavy. But I cannot stand the pain Bernie. I want to be in heaven but this way is too long and too awful. How soon will he come for us?

She knew she was dying; someone else knew it too. Swan's pulse quickened.

He was heading for the door when he heard Considine

stumble above him, and a weird exclamation. Before he could call to her, she was racing back down the stairs. She stopped cold at the sight of him, her voice breathless when it came.

'I found the other one.'

4

Francesca walked south, towards Union Square. The sun was battling to heat the autumn air back to summer levels. The bagel sat heavy in her stomach, the fur jacket heavy on her shoulders. Passing Union Square Park, she flicked her eyes away from the cardboard sarcophagi of homeless sleepers. *There but for the ...* She should go back to the apartment and change into lighter clothes, but couldn't face the horror of Elliot, Máirín's boyfriend, again.

'Haven't you got work to go to?' she'd asked when he walked through her space to put some coffee on.

'I'm on vacation,' he said, 'and I promised Mo I'd fix up those curtains for her. If you want to help, you can hold the end of my pole. So to speak.'

She didn't dignify that with an answer, just tightened the belt of her robe. He was gross. And he was spending more and more time in the apartment. Máirín's apartment, sure, but Francesca did pay rent for the privilege of a pull-down bed in the space that also served as a passage between Máirín's room and the kitchen and bathroom.

A few mornings back, she'd been carrying her clothes to the bathroom to change when Elliot waylaid her, to tell her how beautiful she was without make-up on.

'I can see your freckles,' he said, leaning close. 'You actually look younger this way.'

She should just come right out and tell Máirín he was a letch, but a woman in love was seldom looking for an honest opinion. Their inevitable break-up couldn't come soon enough.

In Barnes & Noble she picked *Variety* off the rack and took it to an armchair. Barbara, her agent, would call her if anything interesting came up, but it had been such a patchy year, and it was good to keep an eye on the landscape. It was professional. But reading other people's rave reviews proved no balm, and the interviews with up-and-coming actresses were unspeakable.

On the announcements page, her ex-husband's name caught her eye. Jay was named as one of the producers of a forthcoming blockbuster, some sci-fi thing. She stealthily tore out the column that he appeared in and folded it into the pocket of her jacket.

She reached for *Vogue* next, even though she knew it would only make her feel poorer. Some cheapskate had already peeled back all the flaps on the perfume ads. Still, Francesca tipped the page to her nose and inhaled, thought about what she would buy, once the money came in again. Thought of the thousands of dollars that had run through her fingers in LA, during the good times. She couldn't help smiling, though tears were a ready alternative.

She got her purse out and stacked up a few dimes, then got up and went out to a sidewalk payphone.

'Buttermeyer Sandler?'

'It's Francesca MacNamara – can I speak to Barbara, please?'

The girl put her on hold. She should really find out the girl's name, that would be politic.

After a minute the girl came back.

'I'm sorry, Barbara is out at meetings all day.'

It was an amateur lie – why check, if she wasn't in the building?

'Please tell her I'll call tomorrow.'

Francesca re-entered the bookstore and took the escalator down to the restrooms. She took her time in front of the line of mirrors, applying powder, fluffing out her hair and pulling it round to one side, so that the long curls fell down over one lapel. She inspected her parting. Little glints of grey were starting to show at the roots.

'All will be well, all will be well.'

She had always managed to manage. She would continue to manage now. Leaving the bookstore, she headed south, crossing Washington Square and walking down Macdougal Street until she reached the Gotham Cinema.

Máirín was raising the shutters on either side of the old-fashioned ticket booth when she arrived. Her friend smiled. 'You're looking very Faye Dunaway today.'

Francesca pulled a pose – hand on hip, profile to sky. She had met Máirín back in Dublin, long ago, when she was appearing at the Abbey, and Máirín was front of house there. When Francesca fled to America, she never intended to end up hanging out with the other Paddies, but there it was. A woman in need has to fall back on her people.

She helped Máirín roll out the big popcorn machine

from the foyer. The Gotham was a sweet old place, playing double bills of vintage films to village nostalgists and idle students.

'I had this weird dream last night,' Francesca said.

'Yeah?'

'A half-naked man was at the end of my bed, then a light went on and he pissed like a horse for – oh – about ten minutes.'

'Did he not close the door? Oh, he's a pig.' But Máirín was smiling like it was a joke.

'It's just so … squalid.'

'Mmm,' said Máirín, loading a new ticket roll into the machine inside the booth. 'You're not wrong. It's an awful squeeze with three of us. I do realise that. I'm sure Elliot would prefer not to have to walk through your bedroom – but what choice has he?'

'You could go to his place once in a while!'

'His place is in Jersey.'

Two skinny, bleached-hair boys came up to the booth and bought tickets.

'It doesn't start for ten minutes.'

'That's okay,' said one of the boys, giving his companion doe-eyes, 'we like sitting in the dark.'

'You two are the cutest,' said Máirín. 'Aren't they the cutest, Fran?'

'Yeh, cute. What's on today, anyway?'

'Bette Davis week. Look, Fran. The thing is …'

Francesca turned back from watching the boys disappear down the red corridor.

'Elliot's agreed to move in with me.'

'I'll bet he has. But, Máirín, really – you just said it's too small for three.'

'And you said you were going back to California two months ago! Don't make me feel bad, I need to make this relationship work. I need the apartment back.'

'I'm in the middle of a run. If this play takes off, I'll be able to afford my own place. You wouldn't kick a girl while she's down?'

'Ah, Fran. We all deserve better than we get. Why don't you go in and watch the film and have a think about it. Popcorn on the house?'

Francesca sat well to the front of the small auditorium, where she wouldn't have to look at the boys canoodling, or worse. A few more single souls came in. None tried to sit near her or initiate contact. She sat in the cool dark, ate her popcorn and watched *All About Eve*, feeling a sharpened empathy as Anne Baxter schemed to take Bette's place.

If Máirín really did kick her out, she *could* go back to California, throw herself on the mercy of Jay and his new wife, stay in their pool house and wait for the right script – any script – to come by. He owed her, and not just alimony. She always assumed she'd go back to Dublin one day, trailing clouds of glory, with money enough to buy a small red-brick house near the canal and choose her roles. Not limp back because she was so broke she was eating popcorn for lunch.

As the credits rolled and the house lights brightened, she remembered Rosaleen's letter. She wiped the oily chaff of popcorn from her fingers and placed the box at her feet. There were minutes to kill until the next movie – *Hush* …

25

Hush, Sweet Charlotte – and she might as well be occupied.

She opened the fold of pale-blue pages. The writing was difficult to make out at first; the letters seemed to collapse on themselves:

Dearest Frances,

I think of you lots and trust God is looking out for you in these dreadful times we live in. I hope you've got work you like and the love of friends at the very least, now that you are divorced. I do not think divorce is a sin. Don't tell Bernie I said that. It's difficult to live with people. You say you have to use your talent where people can appreciate you, but I miss your dear face. There are things I can't tell you in a letter—

After this, something was started and crossed out. The next section was in different ink, just as hard to decipher. Francesca mouthed the words as she struggled through them:

Bernie says I am stubborn, but it is she who is. We used to agree. We saw eye-to-eye, she used to say. We prayed together every day. But the road she has me on is so hard, and I don't know if I can stand it, even with Jesus holding out his arms. There is no one to talk to. Madeleine doesn't come to visit any more

The writing stopped abruptly and started up again on another page:

If I could get you the money, would you fly home to see us? I need to talk to you. Sometimes it is not Jesus I hear. Sometimes I think it is Satan, lord of lies. I've been begging Mary to help me.

Francesca felt a cold dread. *Satan*. Things wheeling out of control in her sister's head. More fragments of writing followed, completely illegible, like scraps of tangled thread thrown on the page.

She swiped quickly at her eyes with a paper napkin. This wasn't good. Not good at all. Rosaleen didn't sound right in the head, and if she'd fallen out with Berenice, that was going to be hard to resolve. Berenice was as stubborn as a boulder, always had been. Francesca would have to make an expensive call to Phil and nag him to go and see his sisters, to step up to the plate for once and sort it out. Her niece Madeleine obviously couldn't be relied on, sweet as she was.

What a blighted family. But no matter how far away, they still pulled at her. Rosaleen's letter scalded her heart, but how could she fly home now, like this? That would feel like the end of hope.

5

'I don't know why they didn't look under the bed in the first place.'

Considine couldn't keep a shade of pride from her voice. *And why should she?* thought Swan, seeing as the local division had known that two women resided in the house, but failed to find the second.

Terry O'Keefe, the pathologist, was down on his hands and knees, his bald head almost touching the carpet as he peered beneath the bed, his forensics overalls straining over his substantial rump.

'Dear God,' he said, panning his torch into the dusty gloom.

Swan had already seen what O'Keefe's torch was now illuminating: the empty gaze of a second emaciated woman, lying with her back to the skirting board, knees curled up, hands protectively clenched in front of her mouth. Red rosary beads snaked from her grasp, like a string of blood drops. Her pale hair lay in strings over her devastated face. It was hard to avoid the impression that she'd been hiding under the bed.

One look at her had been enough. He ordered Flaherty to call in to the Depot, tell them that DI Swan had decided there were grounds to investigate and to send out more bodies to assist, and a full forensics team.

Swan looked down at the single bed that concealed the woman – the grimed yellow sheet, the thin pillow and the flung-back continental quilt sprigged with a pattern of spring flowers. Lying on top of the quilt, half hidden by a fold, was a pad of blue paper, scribbled all over, many pages coming loose. He also noticed sticky flecks staining the pad and the duvet around it.

He took a biro from his pocket and lifted the quilt where it rose in a bump. Underneath was a child's stuffed toy, a brown corduroy monkey, its flock worn away to beige patches here and there, stubs of thread where its eyes should be. The ends of the paws were matted and dark, as if dipped in something. The forensics boys had work to do. As if his thoughts had called them into being, he heard a shout from downstairs.

'Detective Inspector Swan. We await your pleasure!'

It was Bob Corcoran leading the team, that was good. He could get along with Bob.

'Up you come!'

Considine offered to leave. The little bedroom wouldn't hold them all. There was a narrow bed on either side of the room, one of them stripped back to the mattress. Beyond the beds, a window framed a view of yellowing trees beyond the back garden, and below the window a china chamber pot, a bucket and a plastic mixing bowl had been lined up, each holding stinking puddles of amber urine. A ramshackle wardrobe filled up the remaining wall, preventing the bedroom door from opening fully.

'Could you find a phone, Detective Considine, check who they're sending out to us and direct a couple of them to the priest's house for statements.'

'Isn't he very bossy, now?' Bob Corcoran was attempting a kind of flirtatious ingratiation.

'He's my boss,' said Considine shortly, and left them.

Bob waggled his eyebrows at Swan. 'Nifty little assistant you got there, you old rogue.'

The likeability of Bob Corcoran was plummeting.

'Terry needs to get a look at a body lying under this bed.'

Bob's expression changed to blank professionalism.

'I'm thinking you could photograph everything,' said Swan, 'then place this bed on top of the other one, for however long Terry needs. And I need copies of all the written material soon as you can. Doable?'

'Okay,' said Bob, 'But the photographer has started downstairs.'

'I'll begin downstairs, so,' said O'Keefe, rising laboriously to his feet.

'Ah, the old bones,' said Bob.

O'Keefe threw him a dirty look.

Before leaving the house to the technical team, Swan looked into the front bedroom. It was larger and fancier than the one the body lay in, with matching dressing table, wardrobe and double bed of old burred wood. Walnut, he decided, his father's expertise rising to the surface, furniture in the blood. He popped his head into the small and very dusty bathroom at the head of the stairs, and a boxroom piled with more furniture – elaborate dining chairs, a large folding table, a hallstand.

Down in the living room O'Keefe was already circling the dead woman in the chair, talking into his Dictaphone. Bursts of white flash lit the room.

Swan went to the kitchen and looked at the pile of black bin bags. He nudged one with his toe and heard the crackle of paper. If they contained food waste, they would smell a lot worse than they did. They were knotted at the top, so he'd have to wait to discover their contents. He stopped in front of the window over the sink and looked out at the back garden. To call it a garden might be to honour it unduly. It was just an overgrown patch of weeds and fallen leaves lapping around the shaft of a rusted rotary dryer. The side fences were high, made of vertical overlapping boards, and the old stone wall at the back was even taller, maybe eight or nine feet. A rowan tree in the next-door garden dangled bunches of vivid red berries over the fence.

At the front of the house, the small cul-de-sac was growing lively. Apart from the forensics team suited up beside their van, three boys on bicycles slalomed past, curious about the cordoned-off house and the vehicles parked on the verge. School must have finished for the day. They stared at Swan as they passed, rising on their pedals. Sergeant Flaherty and the pale strip of a Guard were standing by the patrol car. He went to join them.

'If any reporters turn up, see if you can keep a lid on it. Story is: there is no story, no suspicious circumstances. If they suggest gas, for instance, don't deny it.'

'There's no gas in the house.'

'I just want to keep it all mundane, if possible.'

Although he had called in the deaths as suspicious, there was a strong chance they would turn out not to be. He could do without the attention of the press for now, while he tried to figure it out. The cycling children circled each other in the turning space at the top of Rowan Grove.

Swan had been around their age when Mick Foster called him over in the playground to look at 'dirty pictures'. You didn't refuse Foster. Swan had expected naked women, lewd body parts or disturbing acrobatics. It took him a good minute to work out what he was looking at. It was like a nest of chicken bones. But the bones had human heads and black, empty eyes. So many eyes. When Foster ran off, jeering, the awful image was locked in Swan's head. Years later he saw that same photograph in a television documentary and learned it was Dachau, but by that time he had grown the necessary defences – defences that now functioned so well that his thoughts were moving on to his dinner, and the need to tell Elizabeth he would be late for it, once again.

He caught sight of Considine coming across the pub car park and started down to meet her. The old stone wall that the back gardens of Rowan Grove butted up against continued down to the main road and around the corner, containing a stately mass of trees, the source of all these drifts of leaves. He couldn't quite recall what was behind the wall; it was easy to get mixed up between the colleges and convents and old folks' homes that formed a large proportion of the northern suburbs. The geography around the new road further disoriented what knowledge he had.

Considine was hurrying up the pavement to him. She had a small packet of cigarettes clutched in her hand.

'Been to the shops too?'

She shoved the box in her pocket. 'Sorry.'

'Doesn't matter. It's all research. I've left the house to Forensics. Let's go back down here a bit.'

He led the way to the low wall edging the pub car park, and passed a hand over the top of the wall before sitting down.

'I don't mind you smoking.'

'Thanks. It's just … you know.'

'I do.'

She pulled the packet out again, unzipped the cellophane, cracked open the top. Swan looked back up the quiet little road. The street lights came on, glowing pink as they gathered strength. There was one light on in the house at the furthest end of the terrace, but no signs of life in the rest of it. The door-to-door team would be out soon; hopefully, people would be coming home from their work.

Considine had her fag lit and her notebook out, smoking and writing. It was a shame she smoked, and he was just about to voice that when he caught himself. He wasn't her da.

'Who's coming out from the unit?' he asked instead.

She twisted her mouth to blow smoke away from him.

'Just Colin Rooney. Everyone else is suddenly too busy. I told him to meet us down at the presbytery. The guy from here – Detective Clancy – offered to help us out, but I said we'd manage. That okay?'

'You don't like Clancy. What's that about?'

'It's nothing.'

She looked down at her notebook, furtive. Maybe there was some romantic history between them. He waited.

'It's just … he was the stupidest cadet in our year at

Templemore. The others used to call him "The Brain". That's how bad it was. And he's a detective sergeant already. It's amazing.'

'You'll get there soon enough.'

'But he got there quicker.' She took a deep drag on the end of her cigarette, then tapped it out vigorously on the front of the wall.

'So were you the smartest in the year, Gina?'

'That wasn't what I meant.'

'Focus your smarts back on this. What happened up in that house?'

'I think they might have got isolated, socially. The niece raised the alarm, but she can't have seen them recently or she would have known they were in trouble.'

'I looked round the kitchen,' said Swan. 'Nothing. Practically nothing. A pickled-onion jar with an inch of vinegar in it. Not a bite of food in the place. Their bodies are so thin – I don't think that's just decay.'

'If they had no food, why didn't they go and get some?'

'Maybe they were ill. There were telephone sockets, but I didn't see a phone, so it's possible they couldn't call for help, though you'd think they could always bang on the wall. These houses don't look too stoutly built.'

'Looks like no one's home on either side tonight. Maybe it's always that way.'

The cold of the wall was starting to leak into his bones. He stood.

'There was one thing,' said Considine. 'Clancy says the priest said the back door was unlocked. When I closed it over, I did notice there was no key, no bolt.'

'It wouldn't be easy to get in or out of that garden. Maybe they felt safe enough with it unlocked.'

'What's over the wall?'

He suddenly remembered.

'I think it's an old folks' care home. Dementia.'

'Not the ideal witnesses.'

'I doubt anyone witnessed anything through that wall,' he said. 'They probably don't even know Rowan Grove exists.'

'I wonder if the women had some kind of wasting illness and just didn't get help.'

'It's not often you see a person waste away while hiding under a bed.'

They strolled back up the hill to the house. A dark mortuary van passed them and parked up on the pavement, as near to the front door as possible. Considine stopped walking and looked at Swan.

'How long did the hunger strikers take to die?'

She was giving voice to the same half-formed ideas that were in his head. It was just a year since the Long Kesh hunger strikes were called off, and the seething unrest and mixed loyalties were fresh in his mind.

'Bobby Sands lasted sixty-six days, I think.'

'More than two months. Christ!'

'Less if you drink nothing, I think. They say it's agony.'

They walked on in silence. As they reached the house, O'Keefe came out of it. His face had a rinsed look to it, tender and tired.

'We're ready to move them.'

'Any signs of interference? Wounds?'

'Not to the eye. But they're both so emaciated, I think you could have killed them with a strong breeze. Things are looking fairly quiet for me – I can start the post-mortems day after tomorrow. Any preference for which lady goes first?'

'I don't mind.'

A patrol car sped up the hill and pulled into the kerb beside them. Sergeant Flaherty was driving. He wound down the window as the car came to a stop.

'Your Detective Rooney just phoned from the priest's house. The niece has turned up there, he says. In an awful state.'

The drive took all of two minutes, most of that spent waiting for a gap in the traffic on the big road. As Considine worked the clutch and craned her neck, Swan studied the church. The lack of upkeep undermined the original ambition of its architect. The concrete walls were stained by swags of dampness under the eaves. The wood cladding on the porch had started to warp and spring out of a strict geometry. The windows – narrow strips of stained glass running from roofline to ground – were veiled with grime.

The priest's house was oddly situated in the corner of the church car park, a rather dull bungalow, with no greenery to serve as a boundary or to soften the look of it. Considine parked right in front. The woman who answered the door to them was in her fifties, lean, with a harassed expression, her blonde hair held in a tight 'set' of curls, in a manner Swan remembered his mother sporting in the 1960s.

'They're all in the kitchen,' the woman said and began

to lead them there, but Colin Rooney was already coming up the hall to waylay them, a panicked look on his face.

'Thank you, Mrs Noonan,' said Rooney, 'thank you.'

'I'll put the kettle on again, I suppose,' said Mrs Noonan in a bleak voice.

Rooney was looking shifty and noticeably flushed. They waited until the housekeeper was out of earshot.

'The thing is,' Rooney said, 'I thought the niece already knew. I thought that was why she was here. So it wasn't handled as well as it could have been – the breaking of the sad news.'

'That's unfortunate. Did you get a statement from the priest and housekeeper before she arrived?'

'I did, yes. From the priest,' said Rooney, keen to make amends.

'Give me the short version.'

'He's only been in this parish since May, didn't know the ladies that well. Confirms their names as Rosaleen and Berenice MacNamara. Doesn't know when he last saw them, but thinks it was in the summer.'

'Anything else we need to know?'

'The priest got the brandy bottle out, and the niece is taking a good deal of comfort there.'

The kitchen was warm and smelled of cigarette smoke and fried food. It was a big room, but relatively gloomy, lit only by a band of light between brown wall cupboards and brown countertop, bouncing off garish orange tiles. Swan looked up at the ceiling light; it had no bulb in it.

'It's broken,' said Mrs Noonan, appearing at his elbow, noticing, defensive.

The priest had been seated at the table with his back to the door, but turned in his chair as they entered, revealing a plump, anxious face, small eyes behind large glasses. Across the table from him sat the niece, presumably, an elfin mite with a cap of auburn hair, kohl-rimmed eyes and whitened face. She could have been twelve, she could have been twenty-five. Both of her hands held a small glass to her chest, as if hiding a treasure. She wore some kind of outsize jumper, accentuating her slightness.

The priest stood and offered his soft hand. Introductions were made.

'I'm very sorry for your loss,' Swan said to the girl, 'and for the shock of it.'

She wiped a tear from her cheek in what felt like slow motion.

'Thank you.'

'You've both been through a great deal.' Swan addressed the priest, 'I understand you've already given a statement to Detective Rooney. Thank you for that. Perhaps we could avail ourselves of another room in your house for a short talk with Ms ...'

'Moone,' The girl said. 'I had to change it for Equity. They already had a Madeleine MacNamara, and Moone sounds – you know ...' She circled a hand through the air and took a swig of brandy. She looked woozy.

On the priest's prompting, Mrs Noonan agreed to show them to the living room.

'Just give me a minute to straighten it for you.'

'Thank you,' said Swan. He caught Considine's attention, indicating with a jig of the head that she should remain in the kitchen, where he hoped she might work on the housekeeper and priest in a friendly way, getting information Rooney might have missed.

The living room was overheated and poorly furnished, with two old couches and a wooden coffee table marked all over with white rings of hot beverages past. A full ashtray sat in the middle of it, and the corner television ticked sporadically, as if it had just been switched off.

Swan and Rooney sat on one of the sofas and Madeleine Moone took the one opposite, kicking off her little slipper shoes and curling into the corner, neat as a cat. People had odd reactions to sudden bad news, Swan knew, but something felt off-key about her coy weepiness. Perhaps she had been drinking before she arrived. The glass was still clutched in her hands, although it looked quite empty.

'Madeleine,' said Swan, 'do you want us to call someone to be with you while we talk?'

A shake of the head. 'I have no one.'

'Can I ask how old you are?'

'I'm nineteen.'

'How much do you know about what we found at your aunts' house?'

Her mouth trembled just a little before she answered. 'They're … dead.'

Swan softened his voice. 'Can you talk us through what happened last night, before you came here to see Father Timoney?'

She flicked her eyes between his face and Rooney's.

'I came out to see Auntie Rosaleen – I hadn't seen them

for ages, the phone wasn't working, I'd been busy.' She looked up at the ceiling. 'Oh God.'

'Take your time.'

'I rang and I knocked. No one answered. But I could see a light on upstairs ... I thought maybe Berenice had fallen asleep with it on. D'you think they were dying and could hear me knocking? I can't bear it.'

'So this was what time, Madeleine?'

'Only eight or nine. I was at rehearsal, then I came out here. I was worried, so I came here to find out if the priest had seen them.'

'So when *did* you last see your aunts?'

She shook her head for a time, her mouth open, tears shining in her eyes. Swan could also see, out the corner of his eye, Rooney leaning forward, about to intervene, and flicked out a warning hand in front of him.

'It was my birthday,' she said finally. 'I bought a Bewley's cake, so we could have a little celebration. And some balloons. Rosaleen loved birthdays. She was like a big kid, you know. Berenice used to call her an *innocent*. But she was the sweetest person on this earth. There was not one bit of harm in her.'

'When exactly was this?'

'June. The twenty-first of June.'

'That was four months ago. You really had no contact since?'

The girl twisted on the sofa.

'I had a row with Bernie. Everyone was always falling out with her.' She pressed her fingers hard against her eyes, as if to stop the tears. When she looked up, her eyes were

41

reddened, kohl smudged on fingertips and cheeks. 'Wait. I talked to Rosaleen in August. I phoned to tell her I got some work. She said Bernie was out at the shops, so we had a good chat. Bernie called me about a week later to say their phone was broken – which was weird, like, because she was phoning – and not to worry if I couldn't get in touch. And then I was just so busy.'

'Who else used to visit? Your parents?'

'I don't have parents. My mother, Theresa, died a long time ago. I'm an orphan.' She said it with a note of mockery, yet something forlorn carried with it.

'I'm sorry for the assumption. Is there other family?'

'My aunt and uncle. They don't visit. Fran's in the states. My Uncle Phil lives here in Dublin, but he and Bernie haven't spoken in years.'

'What about your aunts' friends?'

She shrugged. 'I don't know. They're very holy. I think all their social life is the church, and things like that. That's why I came to see the priest when I couldn't get an answer. I should have come sooner.'

'Madeleine, your aunts had been dead for a while. I don't know if there was anything you could have done.'

He'd said it to offer some comfort, but it made her start weeping in earnest, shoulders shaking. Rooney moved to her sofa, handed Madeleine a tissue from his pocket, pressed a hand to her shoulder. He was not entirely useless. The girl looked very pitiable, but Swan couldn't let her go just yet.

'Just so I understand: why did you fall out with your Aunt Berenice back in June?'

It came out like a wail. 'She wouldn't let us have this tiny party. She put my cake in the bin. It cost me three pounds, and I never even got a slice. She said it was indulgent nonsense. So I called her a bitch, and then I was out on my ear.'

And though she was crying still, the remembered anger lit up her eyes.

'And why did you come back here tonight? You could just have called Father Timoney.'

He thought she hesitated a moment too long for such a simple question. The crying increased in volume.

'I was just *so* worried!' she sobbed, and threw herself unexpectedly into Detective Rooney's arms. His mouth opened and shut like a goldfish's.

'All right, said Swan, 'we'll leave it there for now.'

6

Francesca arrived at the theatre with a deli sandwich in her pocket and an hour to spare before curtain up.

A new review from *The Village Voice* was pinned to the noticeboard. It was favourable, but didn't single her out, so there was no need to get a copy.

She wondered if Rosaleen was still keeping the book of all her press cuttings. It was a long time now since anyone, even from the Irish papers, had asked to interview her. Rosaleen's strange letter came back to her – the religious fervour that ran through it. It gave Francesca a feeling of suffocated panic.

She would call them tomorrow – she could chance using Máirín's phone. Máirín was always calling her mammy in Longford, she mightn't notice it on her bill. And what the hell, it sounded like she was getting kicked out anyway.

In the dressing room she arranged her hair into a modest bun. She was playing the role of inspirational teacher to a prodigious Latino boy-poet, whose family wanted him to stifle his gift and follow his father into construction. It was a plonking, didactic kind of play, set in Queens, the place where Manhattanites thought 'real people' lived.

A knock came on the door.

'Enter!'

She was expecting the young director who assailed her nightly with ideas for how she might disport herself when she was onstage, but not in the action, which was actually most of the play. The day before, he'd asked her to 'make the listening more interesting, but not distracting?'

But it wasn't the impossible director. It was Boris from the stage door, saying she had an urgent phone call.

'Are you sure?'

'I am so sorry,' said Boris.

Fear was already prickling her scalp as she picked the receiver off Boris's desk. A half-eaten Danish pastry lay on a square of greaseproof paper beside the phone, and this was what filled her vision, as Máirín spoke on the other end of the line.

'... your brother Philip ... trying to get you all day ... didn't say what happened ... both your sisters ... yes, both ... so, so sorry ...'

'I have to go now,' Francesca said, wanting Máirín to stop talking. She needed to get back to the dressing room. She had so little time to get changed into her costume.

'You have to get back to Dublin,' said Máirín. 'I'll ring the airlines for you.'

'I'm due onstage, I'll sort it out later.'

The Danish pastry had nuts scattered on top of it – pecans, she thought they were. One had fallen off the pastry and lay alone on the paper. She could feel Boris at her elbow, leaning in as if to catch her. The director was rushing towards them.

'Francesca? Boris just told me. This is unbelievable, awful.'

'Don't worry, I'll be okay to go on.'

'No, I'll get someone to read in for you.'

'Really,' she said, 'I want to go on.'

She had never meant anything more. On the far side of the play lay some terrible shift in her life. A black disaster. Just for a few more hours she could resist it. Just for a few more hours she could be where she was meant to be, on a New York stage.

7

'Go in peace to love and serve the Lord.'

Father Timoney spread his arms and offered his empty hands to the small congregation. They struggled to their feet and started to shuffle out of the pews. One by one they bobbed in his direction, turned and headed for the door.

There were more attendees than usual for morning mass – at least thirty. Word of the MacNamara sisters had got round, he supposed, and the saddened and the curious had swelled the ranks. *My lost lambs.* He had mentioned them in the intercessions: *pray for the souls of Rosaleen and Berenice MacNamara, taken from our midst.* That made it sound a bit like a vanishing trick. Some of the women below stared at him very intently at that point, knowing he had been the one to find them, hungry for emotion. No, that was not fair. He must not be so critical of people.

He stood with downcast eyes and noticed that the two bowls of artificial flowers on the altar were starting to look dusty. He would have liked real flowers, as they had had in Cavan, but Mrs Noonan said they couldn't afford real, that this was more practical. Other parishes had women who actually vied with one another to adorn their churches with flowers.

Matt Cotter, supposedly his main lay helper, scuttled

up from his aisle seat to the altar, affecting a reverent half-stoop.

'Sorry, Father, I need to get back to the shop. Will you manage on your own?'

Timoney nodded briefly, keeping the solemnity of the altar. He turned around and bowed towards the sanctuary lamp, a minimal cylinder of glass on the end of a long chain. Cotter's footsteps sounded down the aisle. Palms pressed together, tucked to his chest, Timoney walked slowly to the sacristy, though there was no one watching now. With Cotter absenting himself – as usual – he would have to return for the chalice, the bells, the offertory vessels, the good candlesticks. Mrs Noonan was always going on about break-ins and robberies, reading out every atrocity from her lurid daily paper. She thought him a country bumpkin, someone who couldn't imagine the wiles of the Dublin poor. He had given up pointing out that he had once been one of them.

It was an unfriendly barn of a church, there was no way around it. An unfinished buttress out the back of the building was where they should have built on the new seminary that the church was meant to be part of. The changes of Vatican II and the slump in vocations had put paid to that plan, along with whatever heating system the architect had envisaged. St Alphonsus became a sub-parish of Holy Trinity, the congregation made up mainly of those not hardy enough to go elsewhere.

The cold concrete walls bore the imprint of the wood that had formed them, ironically, it seemed. The stained-glass windows were coloured in pale blues and yellows, the cheapest glass colours, in an angular pattern reminiscent of shattered nerves. Timoney suspected the diocese would have liked to bulldoze the place, if it wasn't for the unwelcome symbolism of such an act.

It had been early summer when he first set eyes on it, so he didn't notice the leaks and draughts, half blinded by the excitement of coming back to Dublin after so long down in the country. He had been gripped by the intoxicating idea that he would make a difference here, among the multitude, in a way he had not done in Cavan. He had missed the important detail that he would no longer be a 'real' parish priest, but an auxiliary one; that resources and responsibilities would be controlled by Father Geraghty at Holy Trinity.

St Alphonsus was yet another test of character, it seemed, one problem on top of another. And now these deaths – the taint of neglect, of no pastoral care. How he wished he had been the one to notice the women's absence. He dreaded the coming winter in this place.

In the relative cosiness of the wood-lined sacristy, he removed his outer vestment and hung it in the wardrobe. He took a plastic tray and went out again to the altar, loaded it with the silver, glass and gold. A creak alerted him to the main door opening, a wave of light shattering the silhouette of the person entering.

'Hello?'

The figure of Father Gerry Geraghty cohered in the centre aisle and strode to the bottom of the altar steps, genuflecting solemnly. Geraghty could have been mistaken for a prosperous businessman instead of a priest, his coat deeply black, a silky maroon scarf crossed at his throat, concealing the collar beneath.

'I think we need to discuss what happened yesterday,' he said, brushing a swoop of hair to one side with a practised gesture.

Timoney nodded to the sacristy, let Geraghty follow him there. Carrying the laden tray made him feel like a waiter.

'Still no altar boys,' observed Geraghty. Timoney remembered being assured at the time of his interview that this was an issue the parish would take care of, yet as with so many things, the lack had somehow become his own fault.

Geraghty watched as Timoney opened a drawer, took out a dust cloth and wiped the objects before he put them away, his fingers feeling fat and clumsy.

'There's a lot to be said for doing a thing yourself, seeing it done right,' Geraghty observed.

'Not that I have much choice. Mr Cotter seems far too busy to help these days.'

'Noel. I can see you're upset, and no wonder. It was a dreadful thing to come across these ladies. Did you really not notice them missing?'

'With respect, the same could be asked of yourself. Weren't they always up at Holy Trinity for Devotions?'

'I meant no blame in what I said. Please don't look for offence. I'm here to offer support, that's all.' Father Geraghty picked up the chalice, stared intently at its surface, tilting it to the light as if to show up any flaws. Timoney itched to grab it, but stopped himself; he must try and listen to the words Geraghty said, not find other meanings behind them.

'Thank you,' he managed. 'I do hope this tragedy can bring the congregation together, that good can come from bad.'

'Ah, good man, that's the spirit. But if you feel troubled at all, you must talk to me. You must open up.'

Timoney was visited by a strange vision of Geraghty leaning over him, studying the pink convolutions of his gaping stomach.

'All the same, I think – when we have time to look back, to reflect on these sad events – we may well come to the conclusion that we should not be keeping parishioners' spare keys in the presbytery. Too much a blurring of the boundaries. Legal implications and all that.'

'I didn't even know they were there. Father Deasy was the one—'

'Again, it was not a criticism, Noel. Though a better knowledge of what was where wouldn't go amiss. You have been St Alphonsus's priest for – what – half a year now?'

Timoney turned away and went to the wardrobe to remove his alb. There were two small spots of purple on the end of one white sleeve – wine splatter. He should rinse it right away, in cold water, but couldn't face another menial task in front of Geraghty. He pulled a hanger through the neck and shoved it into the wardrobe, took out his normal black jacket. Geraghty stood waiting. Father Timoney felt suddenly conscious of his unpolished shoes. He had hardly slept, then at dawn had fallen into a deep, wonderful blackness. He woke in a panic only fifteen minutes before mass was due to begin.

'There were quite a few more at mass today,' he said.

Geraghty nodded 'At Holy Trinity too. It's to be expected.'

'I thought maybe a special mass on Sunday in their memory, involve the family ...'

'Excellent. Only I've organised something at Holy Trinity for tomorrow evening.'

'Something?'

'I thought a little prayer vigil, or a memorial mass, as you say. The choir will do a lovely piece, it will all be very fitting.'

'But *this* was their church—' He stopped himself. He was sounding petulant.

'As you said yourself, the Misses MacNamara often attended Holy Trinity. No one would be expecting you to give a lead on this, given the shock you've had. But I don't think we should wait until Sunday, we have to be responsive to the public mood.'

'I see.'

'And I would like it if you could be at my side. If you're up to it.'

Timoney nodded dumbly. Father Geraghty looked up, cast his eyes around the room until they focused on one particular spot.

'Oh, now, that one is quite bad.'

Timoney turned to see what he was talking about. A patch of damp spread like a tongue down one corner of the concrete, from where the walls met the ceiling. He had been aware it was there, but it now it had a bloom of bright-green mould.

'Ah, yes.'

'We can't let moss grow on us, Father, can we? Vigilance is an important quality in a good priest. Noticing what goes on. Do you know you can practically see the Mac-Namaras' house from the front of the church? Well, you can. Those poor women, dying under our noses. No one missing them. No wonder people find it shocking.'

Timoney didn't answer. There was nothing he could say that Geraghty wouldn't twist.

'You'd be wanting to get Mrs Noonan's boy onto that.'

Timoney stared up at the damp stain until he heard the sacristy door close.

8

Superintendent Kavanagh shuffled the crime-scene photographs into a single pile and held them out across the desk for Swan to take.

'It's weird, I'll grant you that, a dreadful sight. But I'm not seeing murder. It's more likely illness, or some kind of neglect. Were they very old?'

'Not at all – the emaciation makes them look it, but this one,' he found a photograph of the body beneath the bed, 'was only forty-nine. The one in the chair we have as sixty, or thereabouts.'

'And no signs of break-in or interference?'

'There's a couple of anomalies I think we need to look at.'

'Oh, we love an *anomaly*, don't we, Swan?' Mockery was part of the deal with Kavanagh; that and a simplistic caricaturing of his detectives to help him tell them apart. Swan was stuck in the role of a kind of finicky pedant, lacking muscle. Grossly unjust, but there were worse labels going round: the coward, the loose talker, the alcoholic fuck-up.

'We have to consider why one was concealed under the bed. And they left a lot of handwritten material to go through.' Swan drew out a photograph of the living room to show him again, pointing out the scattered sheets of paper on the floor. But the superintendent had already lost interest, eyes sliding to the door like a suggestion.

'Seeing as I can't put you on anything decent for the time being, you can have a few days on this case. That doesn't count tomorrow, when you need to show up for this tribunal thing, mind. I don't need to tell you what we've been up against this year – armed gangs all over the place, and drugs like never before. The border leaving us short-staffed. Don't get me started on the border. This show pony was the last thing I needed.'

Swan supposed he meant 'show trial', but he wasn't about to correct Kavanagh, who was now giving him the hard stare from beneath his wild brows.

'I'll keep you informed, sir.' Swan gathered his files quickly. A few days was something to work on, a start.

The 'show pony' had been trotting on the horizon for some time. The Owens Tribunal had been set up to investigate historical allegations of police brutality within a now-disbanded unit. Now the director of public prosecutions had allowed an 'extension of the field of interest' to include a more recent case brought against the Gardaí by a republican gangster called Brían DeBarra. He claimed he'd been knocked about in custody to force a confession. Swan had been one of the detectives interrogating him over the course of three days. His contact with DeBarra had been minimal, but all three detectives involved had been summoned to give evidence, a process he hoped they could get through swiftly.

He was almost out of Kavanagh's office when the superintendent barked him back. 'Swan! I'm relying on you to take the bad look off the other two.'

That could either have been a compliment, he thought, as he walked along the top corridor, or a condemnation of his colleagues. There were always more things in motion behind the scenes than a mere detective inspector could understand. He paused to look out of a window. The morning had grown darker, against the proper order of things. Sooty clouds seemed to touch the tops of the yellowed trees in Phoenix Park, and he felt the cold draught of some non-specific apprehension.

Considine was at her desk, head bent almost to the table as she wrote on a pad, her desk lamp making a bright spot on her dark hair. She looked up as he walked over.

'I wasn't sure where you were,' she said.

'Kavanagh.' He put the file of photos on her desk. 'He says we can have a few days. You could have come in with me, but you weren't here.'

Considine looked away quickly. 'I was down at the morgue for the identification.'

'Right. Was it their brother?'

'It was. Philip MacNamara. He managed to ID both of them, though it was pretty tough on him. The one we found under the bed, that's Rosaleen, the younger one. He was sure because of her hair and a pendant she always wore. The downstairs one was Berenice, he said – because of the hair, and the clothes – but I'll check their dental records for certainty. O'Keefe will start the post-mortems tomorrow.'

'What was the brother like?'

'He didn't have a whole lot to say for himself. Works for the ESB as an engineer. Says he hasn't seen his sisters for a couple of years. He implied it was because he lived on the south side, though that sounds a bit lame, doesn't it? He said they "weren't close". He informed his other sister in New York last night – she's on her way back for the funeral. I did tell him it might be a while before they could have a funeral. Anything your end?"

'The Guards at Deerfield are going to follow up all the regular attenders at St Alphonsus and Holy Trinity, to try and pin down who had the last contact with the women. Not a lot from the door-to-door – as we feared. No one living in the end house on the left, it's an un-let rental property. The others in the row are rental as well; various landlords, Flaherty says. Mostly young working couples and the like – no one around in the daytime. Those who did notice the sisters described them as "quiet".'

'Kept themselves to themselves,' said Considine.

'Bingo! The uniforms did get hold of the two fellas that rent the house on the right, late last night it was, and one of them confirmed that someone of the same description as the niece was there on Tuesday night. Yelling through the letterbox, banging the door, he said. This was about half past eight, and it fits with her going down to the priest's house after. They couldn't confirm whether lights had been on or not. They're not home much, both work in bars in the city. Deerfield will send over copies of the statements, if you could look out for them.'

Considine opened the file of photographs and started to lay them out on her desk.

'The post-mortems will throw us something, hopefully,' said Swan. 'And we need to get a read of the letters.'

'Tech Bureau agreed to us photocopying them. My powers of persuasion. Rooney's doing it now. Gloves and all.'

'Rooney? I didn't think he'd stoop.'

'I think he wanted to sneak a look – everyone's talking about it.'

Swan cast his eyes about the office. A few detectives on their phones, nobody obviously earwigging. 'Any other early snippets from the tech boys?'

'I caught Bob just before they set off back to the house. He said they found a purse tucked away in a drawer in the kitchen. It had cash in it – six or seven quid, he said, and one of those Bank of Ireland Pass cards.' As Considine talked, Swan picked up the photographs one by one, let his gaze wander over their detail.

'We need to get hold of their bank statements.'

'And they haven't found a key for the back door yet, so the priest was right about it being open. Front door had only a Yale.'

'If someone else had been in the house, could they have gone out the back way? The front door had the chain across, when the priest found them. So no one left that way, not recently.'

'Which leaves us with the possibility that one woman killed the other, then committed suicide,' said Considine.

'Lurid, but probably not likely.'

Considine shrugged, picked up a photograph that showed the body in the armchair. 'Well, this one would be the murdered one, wouldn't she?'

'And the other hid from what she'd done? I thought the

other way round – the one in the armchair was to blame, and that's why the one upstairs was hiding from her.'

Swan picked up a photograph of the front bedroom, the one he'd briefly looked into. The bed was neatly made. Above it hung a pendant light with a white shade circled with a design of flowers – glass probably, perhaps plastic, but in the photograph it was a dull grey, no inner illumination.

'The niece said she saw a light on upstairs. This is the only room on the front of the building, and that light is off.'

Considine took the photograph from him and quickly rearranged it with two others showing the same room from different angles. The central light did appear to be unlit in all of them, as did the little bedside light.

'Madeleine was there – what – Tuesday? Two nights ago. These women were in no state to switch anything on.'

'A bulb could have blown. Deerfield guys could have made a mistake and switched it off.'

'Maybe.' Swan lifted one of the photos for a closer look. There was a heavy wardrobe in one corner of the room. One of its doors lay open, showing a long mirror on the inside. Hangers hung on the rail, but no clothes.

'Were there clothes in the bin bags downstairs?'

'I think so – clothes and household stuff, they said, but Forensics haven't had a chance to look in all of them yet. The women were either throwing their stuff out or thinking of moving somewhere new,' said Considine.

He liked the way she kept throwing possibilities towards him, rather than fixing on one interpretation, the way other young recruits like Colin Rooney might.

The office door opened and Rooney himself came in – whistling some nonsense until he caught sight of Swan. He carried a thick wedge of photocopies. Swan noticed Considine slipping the crime-scene photographs back into their folder.

'I did two copies of everything, though that collator yoke is a bloody nightmare,' said Rooney.

'It's appreciated,' said Swan. 'What do you make of it?' He should give Rooney a chance to contribute, at least.

'Eh … seemed to be a lot of prayers written out, religious stuff. Many mentions of God and the holy family. A lot of them seem to be letters, but there's pages of just scrawls. Like a child did them.'

Rooney put the pile down on Considine's desk.

'I've divided them into three. The biggest lot is from the upstairs bedroom. These, under the yellow sheet, are from around the body downstairs; and these last few, with the pink divider, are what they found in the hall.'

'The hall?'

'They'd become buried under all the post,' said Rooney. 'But you said to copy anything handwritten, right?'

There were only five or six handwritten pages found in the hall. Swan scanned the first page, then the others. The writing was clearer than what he had seen on the notepad upstairs, and each page was a letter, addressed to *Dear Bernie* – the sister found downstairs. Swan recalled the narrow gap between the banisters on the upper landing and the slope of the stairs.

'Christ! Rosaleen was writing to her sister. Posting them from upstairs to downstairs.'

'And there they lay,' said Considine. 'Presumably unread. Do you think Berenice was ignoring them or didn't know they were there?'

'There was one tucked in the missal, beside the arm-chair,' said Swan, 'so she read at least one. It mentioned being in pain, so she knew her sister was suffering upstairs.'

'So creepy – any word on the post-mortems?' asked Rooney.

'Tomorrow,' said Considine, a little too firmly.

'Thanks for your help, Colin,' said Swan. 'Could you perhaps check in with the brother, see if he has any letters from his sisters to compare these with?' When Rooney was out of earshot, Swan said, 'All one big team, Detective, all one big team.'

'Sorry,' said Considine. She looked annoyed as much as repentant.

He picked up the pile of photocopies, feeling the heft and his own hungry anticipation of reading them. So many words from such a slight body, as if she had emptied herself out onto paper.

'The tech guys also trusted me with the family photos.' Considine opened the bottom drawer of her desk, took out an evidence bag with something bulky inside.

It contained two big photo albums, grimy with finger-print dust. The first was full of small old photographs in sepia and black and white, including a version of the one that had been framed on the mantelpiece: the five children standing in a row.

'So the eldest one here must be Berenice.' He pointed to the tallest girl, a young woman in fact.

'And the blonde one,' Considine bent over the album with him, indicating the girl with a shy grin in the middle of the line-up, 'must be Rosaleen.'

She pointed at the other two in turn. 'Theresa – Madeleine's mother – and Frances, the youngest girl. She looks lively. And the communion boy must be Philip, who I met this morning. I see he was fairly miserable as a seven-year-old too.'

Swan flipped to the back pages. There was only one colour shot in the whole book, a Polaroid of a family group standing in front of what looked like the door of the house at Rowan Grove. Three sisters in a row, and an adolescent Madeleine Moone in front of them, shoulders held rigidly still by the hands of the woman standing behind her. They worked out that must be her Aunt Berenice. On the left was a blonde Rosaleen, still something of the child in her middle-aged face. The red-haired woman on the right wore sunglasses, and was lifting her arm in a blur of motion. Frances, they presumed.

'Looks pretty recent,' said Considine.

'You can just make out cardboard boxes in the hall behind them. It was probably when they moved in.'

'The brother said they bought it in 1976 – so six years ago.'

Swan lifted the second album, fringed with yellowing folds of newsprint sticking out from its pages. He was expecting it to be full of holy pictures or gospel tracts, but he opened it at random on a grainy newspaper image of a glamorous young woman. She was waving from some aeroplane steps, wearing a pale trouser suit. A patterned scarf blew back like a streamer from her neck and her long hair flew in the same direction. Something familiar about her. Underneath the headline 'Fairytale Bride', he read: '"Francesca MacNamara, star of the forthcoming film *A Fairytale for One*, waves goodbye to fans at Shannon Airport en route to Palm Springs, where she will marry Hollywood producer Jay Santini."'

The date on the corner of the newspaper clipping was 1966. So Frances had become starry Francesca. He turned back a few pages and there was a glossy magazine ad, an unexpected frisson of recognition. So that was how he knew her.

It showed a girl with long red hair looking out of the window of a dark room. The window was small, but threw an unlikely amount of light over her gauzy nightdress. The line of her hips and breasts was tantalisingly suggested, and Swan experienced a brief and nostalgic twinge of arousal. He had scissored this same ad out of *Spotlight* magazine, and kept it for months among the books in his bedroom at his parents' house. In terms of what titillation was available in the 1960s, this was hardcore.

A chortle from Considine broke his reverie. She intoned the title with mock solemnity: '*Dark Flows the Bann*. Sufferin' Jay, is that not a bit perverted?'

She was pointing at the disembodied face that loomed out of the darkness behind the girl's shoulder. His craggy good looks were accentuated by dark curls and sideburns, not to mention the Roman collar visible at his neck, the white rectangle smudged and burning in the dark.

Swan smiled. 'Before your time. It became known as

Dark Flows the Banned after the bishops got it taken out of the cinemas. A huge hit in America, apparently – you know, lots of sea views and repressed desire.'

Considine reached over and flipped back another page. 'It's all the same woman, isn't it?'

Swan flicked quickly through the rest of it – theatre and film reviews, society pages, magazine articles. Francesca's public profile seemed to have tailed off recently. The last cutting was two years old, an interview with the *RTÉ Guide* in which she said that she was concentrating on the theatre now, inevitably referenced as her 'first love'. There was no mention of Jay Santini. She was still a very good-looking woman, thought Swan, more interesting than in her twenties.

Considine was nudging him to turn the page. Swan gave her a glower, for her cheek. He was enjoying himself, he realised, and working with Considine was no small part of it. She was spirited, and smart with it.

The final pages had a few cuttings featuring Madeleine, following in her aunt's footsteps. There was a picture of a stage show, young people pretending to be gangsters and flappers and policemen. 'The graduating class of the Evelyn Roche Academy present *Bugsy Malone*.' Then a list of names, with 'Madeleine MacNamara' underlined. He wouldn't have recognised her without the prompt – she wore a heavy Cleopatra wig and had adopted a cutesy pose, hands clasped under her chin and one foot kicked up in the air behind her. The last cuttings were small reviews of plays with a 'Madeleine Moone' mentioned, but no photos.

'Shall we go through the letters now?' asked Considine.

Swan looked at his watch. The morning had slipped away.

'I'll look at them later. We need to get out to Deerfield.'

'How long is Superintendent Kavanagh's few days, do you think?'

'Remember, I'm not here tomorrow. I'm up at the Castle. Maybe we can stretch it out to a week.'

'I forgot about the tribunal. It seems such a waste of—'

Swan put a hand up to quieten her.

The office was empty except for one desk in the corner, where hunkered the hefty silhouette of T. P. Murphy, also due to appear before the tribunal. He was probably beyond earshot, but was holding himself suspiciously still. The tribunal was not a subject for discussion in the office.

'So. This afternoon,' he said, holding Considine's eye. 'Forensics should still be at the house, but you could work with Deerfield on that congregation list and start tracking them down, see if we can't get a last sighting date ...'

'Did you see the papers on the way in? They're mentioning carbon-monoxide poisoning.'

Swan was pleased that the bait had been laid and taken. 'Well, that's all right, isn't it? The press won't be in your way.'

'My way? Sounds like you're about to abandon me to it.'

'I feel certain you'll get on fine without me, Detective.'

9

Dublin airport was bigger than Francesca remembered, the distance from gate to exit further. On the other side of a glass wall, fluorescent squares shone down on a duty-free shop and an ersatz Bewley's café – the bentwood chairs looking odd on the endless carpet tiles. Everything looked odd, the time shift and sleeping-pill fog making her feel drunk, but not pleasantly so.

As she stepped onto an escalator, she passed under a lit billboard featuring a crowd of attractive Irish youth smiling down. She missed whatever words were there to make sense of it. Perhaps it was aimed at business travellers, an offer of our freshest and brightest. *Take us, we're eager to get out.* Just like she had been.

Waiting in the baggage hall, she listened in on a joking argument between two middle-aged men beside her.

Ah, go on.

Swear to God.

Ah, stop.

Her ears hoovered up this jovial codology. She might pretend to care little for her country, but their rhythm tugged at her marrow like an old sweet song. She leaned heavily on the handle of the trolley, praying for the belt to start moving. She needed to change some dollars to get into town. Maybe she should call Phil first to find out what was happening, what was needed of her.

Máirín had booked the first flight available, paid for it with her credit card. Francesca was caught between genuine gratitude and the mean suspicion that this served very well Máirín's desire to get her out of the apartment. It was easier to think about trivial annoyances than think of what lay waiting for her out there in Dublin – the impossible news. Being made to face it.

She had gone onstage after the phone call, despite the director begging her not to, but was persuaded to come off at the interval, sweating with tension after missing two easy cues. Back at the apartment, Máirín and Elliot had been waiting, wide-eyed. Her flight was already booked. Then she had phoned Jay in California to try and get some money. She was forty-three years old and had eighty dollars to her name and no credit – nothing for an emergency.

'Good God,' Jay said when she told him. 'It's unbelievable. Both of them? What happened?'

'They won't tell me. That's why I need money to get back to Ireland, Jay. You owe me fifty thousand dollars in alimony.'

'I'm bankrupt! My lawyers told your lawyers.'

'Jesus, Jay – I know you're working. I saw it in *Variety*.'

'That's just smoke, you know the game.'

She reminded him of the one time they had stayed with her family, back when they were engaged. How Rosaleen had adored him. She cried freely down the line until Jay crumbled. She wasn't sure if she hated him more than she hated herself.

He promised to wire a thousand dollars to her account right away. Máirín had found her suitcase and started her packing by the time she came off the phone.

'The flight's at midnight. Don't worry about your other stuff, I'll take care of it.'

'I'm paid up to the end of the month – why wouldn't you?'

Máirín gave Francesca a look designed to convey infinite patience. 'You're just upset.'

Francesca dressed in a black dress and matching jacket, in mourning for every bloody thing, and wrapped her hair up in a wine-coloured scarf. She pushed on her big shades and pecked Elliot and Máirín on their cheeks. Brave chin. Taxi to JFK. She made herself look straight ahead, not back at the lit-up skyscrapers. This was not a farewell scene. She would be back in no time.

A blurt of buzzer brought her into the moment, and the baggage belt chugged into motion. The two joking men insisted on grabbing her heavy case and wrestling it onto the trolley for her, making quips about the kitchen sink and the boundless needs of women. She pushed through the customs channel, and the frosted doors whooshed open to reveal a crowd of staring people behind a barrier. A swarm of confusing faces. The tears were starting up again. She dipped her head and pushed firmly for the gap in the waiting crush. She almost missed the light voice crying, 'Fran! Fran!'

Running footsteps behind her, a hand on her sleeve.

'Auntie Fran!'

She turned and felt her heart clench. 'Theresa?'

The young woman stepped back in shock.

Francesca had meant to say *Madeleine*. She wasn't so addled as to think her dead sister was living again, but that chin, those dark eyes.

'Shit. Madeleine! I'm sorry. Oh, look, you're *lovely*.'

In Francesca's mind, Madeleine had remained as she was the last time she saw her, caught in the awkward transitions of adolescence. She was still tiny, but now had the poise of a dancer and the dark-red mouth of a burlesque act. Her choppy hair was a vivid copper, and she wore an outsize tweed jacket. Madeleine stared back at Francesca, no doubt making her own adjustments, then suddenly closed the distance between them, lashing her arms about her aunt and pressing her face briefly into the softness of her chest.

She tipped her face up. 'I'm so glad you're here. I can't believe it.'

'How did you know I'd be on that flight?'

Madeleine released her, reached for the luggage trolley.

'A friend of yours in New York phoned Phil, and he left a message at mine. She must have thought he'd pick you up; she doesn't know what a self-involved bollix he is. But I'm here! Sorry, didn't mean to sound like it's a celebration. My head's completely fucked.'

'I'm glad you're here. I've been flying all night and we'd a long wait in Shannon. "Fucked" is right. Where are you parked?'

'Parked? I don't have a car. I thought we could get a bus. Or a taxi, if you want.'

'Bus is fine. It's not so many stops to Deerfield.'

'You want to go to their house?'

'I thought … I thought that's where I'd be staying.'

Madeleine stopped in her tracks, halfway out of the doors of the arrivals hall. People pressed behind them, tutting and harrumphing. Francesca caught her niece's elbow and forced her out onto the pavement, steered her to the side of the building.

'What is it?'

'I don't know how much they told you. You can't go to Rowan Grove. The police are there still. I thought maybe you'd come and stay with me. I'm in a flat.'

'Why are the police still in the house?'

'They don't know how they died. Until they know, they won't leave.'

'Wasn't it some kind of accident?'

'They don't know, I told you.' Madeleine clicked the brake bar of the trolley up and down in an agitated way.

'I don't know what to make of that.'

'They asked me a lot about their "state of mind".'

A wave of tiredness overtook Francesca, along with the sensation that there was a kind of void near her, some bottomless thing that she must neither look at nor fall into. She put a hand on the trolley and pulled it towards her, a support.

'Your flat will be just fine. Thanks.'

The bus into town passed through Deerfield. Francesca noticed the concrete church coming up on her left, and she looked in the opposite direction to catch sight of the house, as did Madeleine. The boxy little terrace sat behind trees now. Just a glimpse and they were past. The idea that her sisters would commit suicide seemed ridiculous, but she had not been in touch with them much in the last few years. Rosaleen had not sounded happy in her letter, it was true, and Bernie always had her black depths. Francesca had never seen Bernie joyful, not even as a girl, and now she never would.

'Where are they?'

'The police took them away. Uncle Phil had to go to the morgue. He had to say it was really them.'

'That must have been awful.'

The bus crossed the Royal Canal, past the usual pubs and bookies. The red-brick buildings pressed in closer as they entered the city centre proper, doorways with fanlights and pillars appearing. Francesca was aware of a fizz of anticipation rising in her, despite the circumstances.

Madeleine stood up to pull the bell cord; she could scarcely reach it.

'This is us.'

Together they wrangled the suitcase onto the pavement, and Madeleine led the way up a side street, to stop by the steps of a tall Georgian tenement.

'What floor are you on?'

'Guess.'

'God, I know what that means.'

'We'll take turns.' Madeleine grabbed the suitcase and bumped it up the steps.

The front door opened onto a bare hallway with a grand staircase curving up to a half-landing with a high arched window. The walls had been painted a dark green decades before, but were scratched and flaking now, patched with pink plaster where repairs had been made. A hole in the ceiling revealed the fragile lathes to which ornate cornicing had once clung.

'I didn't realise there were still places like this,' said Francesca. 'You're living in an O'Casey set.'

'It's cheap.'

'You don't say.'

'The flat itself is fine.'

But it wasn't. The floorboards had draughty gaps between them and the furniture consisted of odd, crooked things, probably scrounged or found on the side of the street. The bathroom was a disaster. Madeleine told her there were two other residents – boys – indicating their closed doors. She took Francesca to the kitchen, which smelled of old fat and damp tea leaves, to demonstrate which rings on the cooker worked and which ones were broken. As if Francesca was suddenly going to take up cooking in this awful place. She found tears stinging her eyes and flicked them away quickly, but Madeleine caught her doing it and stopped mid-sentence.

'I don't know what I'm thinking. You must be exhausted. Go on into my room and I'll make a pot of tea.'

Madeleine's room was large and low-ceilinged, two dormers providing light. Yellowing Sellotape sealed over cracks in the little panes, but there had been attempts to cosy it up: scarves and throws spread over things, a straining after the bohemian. The one or two good things in the room – a circular table, a gilt mirror with a fancy bow carved on its frame – were already familiar, flotsam from the old family house in Fairview.

The room was possibly bigger than Máirín's whole apartment in New York, but the only bed was a mattress in one corner. It raised the obvious question of where she would be sleeping. And she really needed to sleep.

The door swung open and Madeleine came in with a tray.

'I just realised that you might want to stay at a hotel or something. Don't be polite with me, I couldn't bear that. If you'd rather be somewhere else.' She put the tea things down on an old tin trunk that sat in front of a battered sofa.

Francesca didn't want to spend money on a hotel, and she couldn't think of anyone else she could – or wanted to – impose upon.

'This is just perfect. I'm not sure I'd like to be on my own right now.'

'I'm glad,' said Madeleine. 'That's just how I feel.'

'But I don't want to take your bed.'

'I can sleep on the sofa, here. It's not so bad.'

Although Francesca kept smiling, something must have shown on her face, because Madeleine quickly added, 'Or I can sleep in Derek's room; he stays with his girlfriend most nights.'

'We'll work it out ... Madeleine, love?'

'Yeah?'

'There's a bottle of duty-free in my case. Will you root it out and we can have a nip with our tea – I'm not used to Dublin weather any more.'

'Sorry. I'll put the bar-fire on. I don't feel the cold so much.'

'Not through all those layers of men's clothes. Did you strip some squire?'

'No, I borrowed them from the costume room. The jumper's cashmere, can you believe it?'

'What costume room?'

'At the Olympia. The girl doing the costumes for our play works there. I'm in a play!'

'Well. That's great.'

Madeleine clicked open the case, prodded at the layers of clothes to find the bottle. Francesca had assumed that her niece had given up her early acting ambitions. It was a career to be wished on no one, let alone flesh and blood.

When they were settled on the sofa with tea and whiskey, Francesca asked, 'So. When is the funeral?'

'We don't know. Maybe not for a good while.'

'But Phil said I had to be here right away. He was insistent. I thought there was something urgent happening. I didn't even have time to pack properly.'

She looked at the jumble of mismatched clothes lying in her open case. A bright-pink summer blouse tangled round a gold strappy shoe caught her eye. She didn't even remember putting them there.

'The police say they can't release the ... the ... *bodies*.'

Madeleine's scarlet lips began to tremble. She was still so young, really, under the make-up. A girl who had already lost her mother, her grandmother and now the aunts who had tried mothering her in their turn. It wasn't fair. It wasn't real. All Francesca wanted to do was sleep.

Instead she put down her whiskey glass and held her arms out. 'Shimmy over here and give your old aunt a hug.'

10

The morning arrived windless and mellow, with the kind of side-slanting autumn light that makes you look up and notice buildings you'd usually ignore. Swan paused on the cobbles of Dublin Castle to run his eye over the ranks of windows, the polite hatchery of Georgian panes. A seagull glided across the square blue sky. Once the very centre of British rule, the castle was now pressed into multiple purposes for the Republic – municipal, touristic and bureaucratic. Today the Owens Tribunal was due to convene in one of the stuccoed salons.

As Swan approached the double doors, a black-robed man he recognised as a barrister for the Gardaí waylaid him.

'They're going through preliminaries at the moment. You'll be called, when needed.' He directed Swan to a side corridor lined with expensive chairs in brushed chrome and bright-green tweed. 'Might be a while,' added the barrister and hurried off.

Far down the line of chairs, his colleagues T. P. Murphy and Ownie Hannigan broke off their conversation, waved a greeting. Swan opted to sit at a distance, pantomiming the weight of his briefcase and the unavoidable amount of work inside. A smile and a helpless shrug. Hannigan shook out a newspaper and disappeared behind it, while Murphy leaned forward, elbows on thighs, fondling his hanging tie in a meditative way.

Swan believed Brían DeBarra's charges of brutality against the unit were nonsense, invented to clear himself of looking like a grass to his comrades, or out of some false bravado. But if there was room for doubt, it would be in the actions of these two jokers. Hannigan and Murphy were genetic Gardaí, both born into police families, loyal to the force, but contemptuous of politicians, journalists, the director of public prosecutions, internal reformers – all considered terrible meddlers with no understanding of the real job. They were nostalgic for the era of Lugs Branigan, when a clip on the chin could be used to end a brawl, and a judge would turn a blind eye to the resulting bruise. Hannigan and Murphy didn't particularly like Swan, thought him a boss's man. In turn, he didn't much respect them. They were lazy and incurious, would take the first plausible explanation and run with it, find the facts to fit the theory.

Swan hardly ever joined in the revels at the Garda Social Club, had never felt completely at ease among the volatile dynamics of men in groups. His refusal was interpreted as a notion of superiority. But he didn't feel superior, he felt flawed, as if he was missing out on a commonplace skill.

He took out the photocopies of the writings from Rowan Grove. He'd hoped to have them read by now, but when he finally got home the night before, he'd found his wife facing his mother over the dinner table. He'd forgotten she was coming. A dish of lasagne was set between them and an almost empty bottle of wine. It should have been a heart-warming sight, but both women appeared relieved at his entry.

'Sorry. Sorry! I couldn't phone, you know how it is.'

He kissed his wife's head, and his mother's cheek. Protested that cold lasagne would be just fine. They were more than a year married now, but still these two women – the dearest in his life – had not found common ground. Or he was the only common ground, and that was the problem. His mother had 'views' on the dangers of marrying out of your class, awful outdated stuff that he'd managed to persuade her from ever voicing. She might be less restrained about expressing her desire for grandchildren. She could be sentimental when she drank, something that used only to happen at Christmas. But nowadays his mother had a wine rack on her kitchen counter. His father – a heroic pub-goer – used to blame the EEC for this decadence. *They'll drown us in their bloody wine lakes.*

'What are you working on that has you out so late?' asked his mother.

'We don't discuss Vincent's work at dinner, Eileen, the things he has to deal with … We'd rather keep them on the other side of the front door.'

'Is that right?' His mother pressed her lips together. Swan knew he'd have to hear her thoughts on this ban somewhere down the line. She'd always loved any scraps about criminals and their bad doings.

Swan skimmed through the pages now, scanning for dates or names. The writing varied wildly in style throughout. Some pages were neat, cursive, the words keeping to straight rows. On others, the lines slid up and down, the writing switching from capitals to lower case on a whim, the biro line jiggling, as if the paper had been vibrating. Sometimes the letters grew in size and separated, as simple and emphatic as those in a primary-school copybook. A few sheets were just tight tangles of overlapping lines, like something done by a person miming the action of writing – no separate words, no real letters.

Using the empty chairs beside him, Swan sorted out the photocopies, according to the clarity of the writing. Those found downstairs with Berenice MacNamara were the most legible – early in the ordeal, he guessed, when the sisters could move about. The most chaotic pages had been found in the bedroom, closest to Rosaleen's body. The more he studied them, the more he became convinced that they were all by the same hand, the variation due to some kind of disintegration of sight or dexterity. He looked up and caught Hannigan and Murphy staring at him.

'Jaysus, I hope that's not your statement to the court,' said Hannigan, his newspaper descended to his knees.

Swan laughed briefly. 'It's just casework.'

'Is that the Deerfield women?' asked Murphy.

'Yes.'

Murphy liked to keep an eye on his colleagues' work, often preferring it to his own.

Hannigan folded his paper and tossed it onto the seat beside him.

'I'd say now, that must have been a dreadful sight.'

Swan said it was, but did not oblige them with details.

Murphy shook his head for a sorrowful moment. 'Mind

you, if there's anything to be gained from this inquiry lark, it's not having to work. You shouldn't be doing cases while under suspicion.'

'I doubt they'll keep me long.'

Hannigan snorted. 'We've been off for two weeks now. Sitting around. No overtime, either, so we're out of pocket, to boot. They keep saying they'll get to our bit, but the lawyers are stringing it out. Budging up their fees.'

Hannigan and Murphy had handled the questioning following DeBarra's arrest. Swan had stepped in for one afternoon to help out. He'd hardly spoken, just backed up Hannigan in the interview room for a few hours. Murphy had been at a doctor's appointment. He was a martyr to many invisible ailments.

Murphy leaned back, stretching his arms along the adjacent chair backs, giving the swell of his striped belly an airing and his mauled tie a rest. In the silence they could hear the drone of a lawyer's voice pressing through some argument in the main room. Hannigan went back to his newspaper. Murphy let out a theatrical sigh and wiped a finger and thumb down his drooping moustache.

Swan went back to his pages, stacking them together in their new order, and settled into the chair, angling his body away from his colleagues. He riffled the pages one final time, enjoying the anticipation.

He looked at his watch and began:

Dear Bernie,
You often say God's will can be hard to divine. But then you say you know what he wants better than me. It's not

true that I am weak in spirit. I can pray and look into my heart as well as you.

What if we've taken a wrong turn? Father Deasy used to say the devil is a clever fellow, and it's not beyond his power to pull the wool over our eyes and lead us into mortal sin, thinking it was Jesus we were following.

Don't be angry with me. When you explain it makes sense, about renouncing the world and the flesh, like we were baptised to do. Jesus fasting forty days and forty nights and the imitation of Christ can never be wrong. When I am on my own in the night, I don't know. I imagine you are talking to someone downstairs – that I'm the only one to starve. You see the ideas I get? They are bothering me more than the pain in my belly.

You could come and sleep up here. We could pray for guidance. Only the thought of Mammy and Theresa waiting in heaven keeps me going. And Daddy too, but I don't remember him at all now. If we are committing a mortal sin and are kept out of heaven, then I will never see them again, and I'll never see the ones left here.

Come and talk to me, please.

Rosaleen

So that was their plan: to fast like Jesus until the world and the flesh were thoroughly rejected. But to the point of death? That was clearly suggested. A devout suicide – a paradox, in that the method of their leaving would be a sin and might prevent them from getting into heaven. But why was she writing to her sister rather than talking to her?

The next letter was similar. This time Rosaleen was asking if she could come downstairs:

> ... I promise not to prattle or to try to change your mind.
> Just call out to me to say yes and I will get myself down somehow; you don't even have to help me this time, I am weak, but I can get up to go to the lav myself, so I'm sure I can make it down to you, if you let me. I die of loneliness.

It was like a child writing to an angry parent. Also, it sounded as if Berenice was stronger in the physical sense, too. She had helped Rosaleen upstairs or down at some point. Swan put a little question mark in the margin. The next two letters were just variations on the same theme. They referred to some kind of falling out between them, and again there were pleas that Rosaleen be allowed to come downstairs to join Berenice. Again, suspicions featured:

> ... I wonder if you are eating things downstairs. Laughing at me, calling me nyeve like you do, you wouldn't fool me Bernie, you woud not be so cruel? It would be a comfor if you came and talk its so hard. I dont want this. Are ye there at all?

The handwriting was beginning to slip, the spelling too. The pages following this one lost legibility rapidly, just the odd word jumping out among what still appeared to be entreaties, to the Lord and to Mary and to her sister downstairs. Some lines of prayers. Mentions of angels and Jesus looking down on them. There were fragmentary complaints about her physical state – *my arms hurt – my heart is too fast* – but these took second place to Rosaleen's agonies of abandonment. And wasn't it awful that her end bore out those fears, hiding alone in the shadowed space between floor and bed?

What was missing from the pages was an explanation of why she could not escape the radical path they had embarked upon. Did she fear her sister that much? What purpose could override the body's howling needs?

There was one letter addressed not to Bernie, as the others were, but to 'Fran' – presumably the glamorous Francesca. This one strove for a more everyday tone, but Swan couldn't decipher all of it. Something about a phone not working. Something about a wrong address: *Have you moved?* Then mentions of prayers or praying, before it trailed off, unsigned. *Phone?* he wrote in the margin. They never did find one at Rowan Grove, though the niece mentioned a broken phone also, so the sisters had one once.

'Will they let you off for a coffee?'

Considine was standing in front of him, her mac collar turned up against the world and her belt pulled tight.

'How'ya, Gina!' Hannigan called from down the row. 'This fella treating you right?'

'No complaints, Ownie – and yourself?'

'Oh, don't start me.'

'I won't so. Just need a word with the boss.'

Swan got to his feet.

'Be sure and hold my place,' he said, but Hannigan and

Murphy just looked at him. His attempts at joking usually went this way, a tune he couldn't sing. Swan put away the pages and stuck the file under his arm.

They walked in silence to the self-service café. Considine offered to go up to the counter, while he found a table by the window.

'Didn't expect to see you so soon in the day,' he said, when she came back with the coffee.

Considine raised a mildly offended eyebrow.

'I only mean, I thought the post-mortems would last longer than this.'

'He could only do one. He was called away to something else before he could start the second.'

'Which one did he do?'

'Downstairs. Was that what you wanted?'

'It doesn't matter.'

'Your face says it does.'

'No. It's just that I'm reading what Rosaleen, upstairs, was writing. She mentions starving, says she doesn't want to starve. Just wondering if there might be anything physical to back that up – injuries, signs of restraint. There was no lock on the bedroom door, was there?'

'No.'

'Well, it will have to wait. Tell me about the sister.'

'I made sure to get to the morgue early, but of course O'Keefe was there first. I think it's true he sleeps there. He had them both out, and God, they were a sight. Did you ever go down to the crypt at St Michan's – we went there on a school trip, would you believe? Well, that's what they reminded me of, those dusty old skeletons. Can you imagine thinking it was a good idea to send schoolgirls to look at dead bodies? Did you never see them?'

'No. But I did see a saint in a glass coffin in Venice once.'

'Well, that's put me in my place. When were you in Venice?'

'I think we need to refocus our discussion here.'

Considine smiled, looked down at her notes.

He didn't want to say he had been to Venice on his honeymoon, it was too personal. It had been a perfect week of lazing and strolling and beauty. He had been surprised, though, at Elizabeth's insistence on lighting a candle in every church they passed. He hadn't even realised she was religious in that way. Maybe she'd been asking God to smile on their marriage. In a huge church near the railway station, a boxed cadaver on the altar had taken him by surprise. St Lucy. Supposedly uncorrupted by death. Her face was hidden behind a gilded mask, the body by heavy red robes, but the fingers that stuck out from her embroidered cuffs were like cinnamon sticks.

Considine took him through the main points of the post-mortem. Although O'Keefe hadn't yet opened the second body, he was willing to say that Berenice, downstairs, had died before Rosaleen. His rough estimate was that she had been dead for three or four weeks. Rosaleen had died perhaps a week or ten days later, but he would confirm after the post-mortem. So they had died somewhere between mid-September and the beginning of October, at least two weeks before their bodies were found.

'What got him most excited was that Berenice MacNamara's stomach was so shrunken. He'd never seen the like.

He was cock-a-hoop. No signs of any poisoning, including gas poisoning. The lungs were possibly congested, but the other organs appeared clear. No marks to the body. He's waiting for some tissue tests to be done, but says all that he saw supports starvation as the cause of death, or possibly pneumonia aggravated by starvation. So – no signs of violence or interference, that's the main thing.'

'Unless they were prevented from eating.'

'What makes you think that?'

Swan tapped the file of photocopies. 'If Rosaleen was having her doubts, why is she writing about it, rather than making a break for it? She fears her sister, but she's also paranoid about Berenice talking to someone downstairs. It could be nothing, but if her sister actively starved her, or someone else knew what they were up to, there could be charges.'

'Have you come across anything like this before? Ever?'

'No. Not outside of jail or a protest. Then it's for a cause, and for an audience. There's a reason this kind of thing doesn't happen at home.'

'Only it does,' said Considine.

'What do you mean?'

'Anorexia. I'm not saying this is anorexia – these women don't fit the usual profile, and they looked reasonably healthy in their previous photos.'

Swan felt foolish that he hadn't even thought of eating disorders.

'Well, what comes across from the letters is that at least one of them didn't want to die.'

'There's still the second post-mortem to go – as long as

Kavanagh doesn't decide to pull the plug on us completely,' she said.

'The post-mortem will go ahead, whatever happens.'

When Swan and Considine had returned to Rowan Grove the previous afternoon they'd been dismayed to find there were no longer any forensics technicians at the house. It was shut up and taped, not even a local Guard outside. At Deerfield station, he phoned back to the Technical Bureau and got through to Bob.

'It wasn't our call. Superintendent Kavanagh asked for a progress report. I told him everything was photographed, and evidence taken from around the two bodies, and he said he'd be happy with that. We were needed at this Enniskerry robbery – three sites involved in that: the bank, a car-crash site, a cottage where one of them held off the Guards with gunfire—'

'But I'm not happy, Bob. The way you tell it, you've only really been in two rooms.'

'It's not my call, Swan. We live in far too interesting times. I've got the basics – you're covered. And anyway ...' Bob tailed off.

'Anyway, what?'

'Well, you were there yourself. Just a couple of harmless ladies. Died of neglect.'

'I thought you lot were all about empirical evidence.'

'We've still to do the fingerprint work, and lab tests on the clothing. If there's something to find, we'll get to it eventually.'

Swan pushed his empty cup and saucer away.

'That coffee was awful,' said Considine.

'Was it? I must give you some money.' He handed over a pound note and she took it, without making any fuss or protest. He liked that. 'What are you doing this afternoon?'

'Kavanagh's pushing some admin onto me – collation of statistics for the press office, would you believe? But I can bang through that easy enough. Why?'

'See if you can find an excuse to drop by the tech labs and get our friend Bob a bit more excited about this case. Ask him about the lights being on a few nights ago. Ach, you know what to do. He's pretending he's snowed under with this Enniskerry thing, but they could do more, if they wanted.'

Considine set off through the café, the sound of her brisk steps enlivening the sleepy place. She pushed through the swing door just as the police solicitor was coming through the other half of it. He instinctively stepped out of her path before heading for Swan.

'Am I on?'

'There's been an adjournment. There's a chance they'll be back before lunch, but only slight. You okay to hang on here?'

Swan went up for a second cup of coffee and a scone, then returned to his pile of papers. If he thought of all the things he'd rather be getting on with, he'd go mad.

He rubbed his face and settled down to it, focusing on lines that he hadn't been able to decipher on his first reading, copying them out onto some scrap paper, feeling it out. A passage he hadn't managed before began to give way to his efforts.

This is not what we agreed. It can't be what God wants. I want you to tell them to bring food.

At least that's what it seemed to say. The fourth-to-last word definitely began with a *t*, followed by a zigzag waver, but 'bring food' was clear enough.

Even in her drifting state, Rosaleen would hardly believe that God or his angels could go to the shops. But if the 'them' she referred to was mortal – someone in the house – they could bring food. It was a concrete request, surely. *Tell them to bring food.*

Swan chewed on the last of the dry scone. Rosaleen could have easily been saved, if anyone had known of her predicament. She wanted out of the situation. This wasn't holy martyrdom. He wasn't sure what it was.

11

The girl's voice was a thing of wonder, radiating pure as light around the vaulted space of Holy Trinity.

'*Panis angelicus*,' she sang; he'd always loved that one. '*Pauper, pauper, servus et humilis.*' It shifted something in his chest, a feeling that made Father Timoney want to run from the altar to some small private space. She stood at the front of choir loft, her fringe and long, straight hair framing her pale face. Only he had this clear view of her performance; Father Geraghty and the altar boys were occupied with giving out communion. He would have been happy to give out communion too, but there was only one ciborium set out. The congregation shuffled forward in a double line, heads bowed. The marvellous curve of the ceiling framed the choir like an embrace, creamy white plaster with a pattern of indented squares edged in gold. And hanging from the ceiling's highest points, those many-limbed brass chandeliers – the ones Mrs Noonan said cost £5,000 apiece. Enough money to fix St Alphonsus's leaks, and Holy Trinity had three of them.

Oh, but that music; the way the rest of the choir supported the young soprano with deep, almost murmuring harmonies. The gentle power of their human voices made Father Timoney feel contrite. Contrite about his resentment of Father Geraghty, his envy of the chandeliers, the flower-bedecked altar, all those material things that mattered nothing against the priceless souls of these lost women. All through the mass he had let himself lapse into self-absorption, his uselessness fully on show as he shadowed Father Geraghty like a handmaid, echoing his moves.

'If only you'd arrived earlier, we could have given you a reading or something,' Geraghty had said.

'If you just mark something in the book, I can—'

Geraghty dismissed this with a wave of his arm, lace cuff swinging. 'Don't you worry.'

Father Timoney had been sitting by a bedside at the nursing home all afternoon, holding the soft hand of an old woman. She had pneumonia; they weren't expecting her to last, they said. He watched her fall in and out of sleep, her pale fingers clutched around his. Sometimes she woke and called loudly for her mammy. Once she fixed him with an angry stare. Or he thought it angry, until he realised that what it was really was empty – blank as a hen's. She didn't seem ready to release the world, or his hand, despite her frailty. She reminded him too much of the dead women, and he was glad to uncouple from her as she fell into another sleep, telling the staff he had to be at the memorial mass.

The upshot was that he had hardly time to pick up his vestments and swipe a wet comb through his hair before trekking the mile to Holy Trinity. He had wanted to show he was part of the parish, one of the team. Again he pulled his mind back to the women, the dead women, not to where he stood in the pecking order. He had to get beyond himself.

When mass was ended, he stood beside Geraghty

outside the church door and shook the hands of the congregants, many of whom wanted to share their thoughts on the deaths of the MacNamara sisters. He was listening to a small woman with strange teeth when he overheard Geraghty beside him, saying, 'It was a random tragedy, that's the direction the police are thinking. Carbon monoxide was mentioned.'

Timoney wanted to butt in and contradict this. What he had seen was nothing to do with gas. Geraghty hadn't been there. But the woman in front of him had noticed his distraction and suddenly stopped whatever she was saying.

'I'm trying to tell you something,' she said.

'Apologies, my dear.'

'You have such a sad face on you – there's no need. Berenice and Rosaleen are rocked in Jesus's arms. You should understand that, of all people. They're home and happy.'

She smiled briefly, and Father Timoney realised that the odd thing about her teeth was that they did not quite join her gums, some kind of ill-fitting denture. That was a shame for her. Now that he considered her properly, she looked a bit of a soul altogether, hair going in every which direction, wearing what appeared to be a child's duffel coat, although she looked to be in her late twenties or thirties. He never found it easy to tell, with women.

He put his hand out to touch her sleeve.

'Thank you for your words,' he said with as much conviction as he could manage, and moved his eyes to the church doorway in anticipation of the next person, but the doorway was empty. The cream-and-gold interior glowed like a palace.

The shabby woman turned away without a goodbye, went off to join a group of other women clustered by the doorway of an adjacent building. Father Geraghty was taking his time chatting with a comfortable-looking couple. He had the woman's hand in both of his, and she looked at him with liquid eyes. Timoney waited. He wondered if Geraghty was deliberately delaying, just to keep him standing in the cold and dark, but that thought struck him suddenly as typical of his skewed mind just now – overly critical, resistant to the good in people, alive to their superficial faults. Like that woman's teeth. A true man of God would not even have noticed them. He looked again at the cluster of women gathered around the entrance of an annexe attached to the side of the church. They seemed to be heading indoors, but each one was trying to urge the others ahead of her, impeding any progress by politeness. As they progressed inside, he recognised the stiff blonde curls of his housekeeper in the lit hallway. She might have said she was coming, offered him a lift.

'Father?' Geraghty was looking down at him. The couple had departed.

'Sorry,' he said automatically, inanely.

As they started back inside, he asked, 'What's in that part of the building?' He indicated the annexe the women had entered.

'Oh, yes, meeting rooms, youth club, the like. Did we not show you? It used to house a primary school. So important to have facilities for the community.'

'What's going on tonight?'

'It's the women's prayer group, I think. A very devout,

well-organised group. I think they enjoy having a forum of their own, and I don't mind at all. I always say, Noel, that it's women who rule the world, they just let us think we do.'

Timoney chuckled, as was expected.

Father Geraghty led the way into the church and down a side aisle. He seemed in a mellow mood. Timoney took his chance.

'I've been meaning to talk to you about fundraising. You've done such a brilliant job here with Holy Trinity – I thought we could all get together for a bit of a push. For St Alphonsus, I mean.'

Geraghty stopped by the sacristy door, new varnish gleaming on the grained wood. 'Do you know now, Noel – you don't mind Noel, I hope.'

'Of course ... Gerry.'

'I sometimes think I have the best parishioners in all Ireland. The way they worked their hearts out on the fundraising. And we did get good grants. A clever lot, they are, but perhaps we need to give them a bit of a break. Recharge the fundraising batteries. Perhaps you could look to your own congregants for now.'

The sacristy hummed with activity. The two altar boys were putting things away, wiped and polished. A young lay helper with a big boyish head offered to take his vestments.

'It's all right, they're my own,' Timoney answered and snuck off into a corner to disrobe. He regretted asking about the fundraising. Holy Trinity would have been easy to raise money for, but St Alphonsus was such an ugly place – which of his elderly and impoverished congregants would give up time to save it? An architecture student wandered in one day to declare it 'a classic of 1960s modernism', but no one else seemed to share his admiration.

Father Geraghty offered him a lift home, and though his pride would have liked to refuse, his back was suffering, after most of the day spent sitting in one awkward position. Geraghty's car was a family-sized saloon, comfortable. Cello music seeped from the speakers.

'You don't drive yourself?' asked Geraghty, pulling away from the kerb.

'I've never been very mechanically minded.'

'I thought it might be because of your health. Mrs Noonan mentioned you had chronic back pain. Very debilitating, I imagine. You never mentioned it to us – you mustn't be so stoic with your brothers.'

'I manage.'

'Still, though, a car would be an advantage.'

'I like to think you meet more people on foot, rather than shut away in a big car.'

He shouldn't have said 'big' – that made it rude, directed. Father Geraghty didn't reply, just turned up the music a notch. There was no more talk until the car drew up to Father Timoney's bungalow.

'So you've been chatting with Mrs Noonan? I hope she has no complaints.' Timoney found himself adding a foolish laugh.

'Well, she often drops by the parish house to check up on us.'

The parish house was a fine double-fronted Victorian house where Father Geraghty and three curates lived. It was where Timoney assumed he would be staying when he took on the job. So many things he should have asked. He imagined them sitting around a fire at night together, watching the golf or chatting to visitors.

'She has a good heart, Noel,' Geraghty was saying, 'though mostly kept well hidden.'

Timoney smiled and nodded, as if he too had seen kindness in her. Geraghty leaned over him and opened the passenger door. Dismissed.

As he put his key in the door, he noticed a light in the sitting-room window. Mrs Noonan couldn't have beaten him home yet.

When he arrived in Dublin, his housekeeper was presented as a great advantage of the post. Flattered by the idea of being cared for, he had not paid enough attention to the proportion of parish finances that this service absorbed, or how little space he would have to himself. And her grown-up children seemed to come and go as they pleased, especially Jimmy, who doubled as the church handyman.

Father Timoney stood in the front hall and listened to a television chattering behind the closed door. The smell of cigarette smoke pervaded.

Gathering himself, he swung open the door, and there was Jimmy Noonan on the couch, his arm around a brassy-looking girl. The girl immediately shifted to create a gap between them, smoothed her skirt.

'How'ya, Father,' said Jimmy, saluting him with his fag, eyes sly. The girl murmured a greeting, then pretended great interest in the programme, her painted mouth slack.

Timoney nodded a few times, but could think of nothing to say. He stepped back into the hallway, closing the door but not loosening his grip on the handle.

Should he order them out of there? That would probably be an overreaction. Or would it? Jimmy was a handsome boy, it was natural that there would be girls about him. He remembered how the dead sisters' niece had goggled at Jimmy when he passed her at the front door, the night the trouble started. Attraction was part of life. Birds and bees. But it shouldn't be part of the life of a presbytery.

He should go back in there, take up his rightful space. Get a conversation going with Jimmy about mending the roof. Man-to-man. Talk to the young woman, set the tone. He was boss of this house.

But instead he turned for his own room. It wasn't even past eight o'clock, but he just couldn't summon up what was needed, couldn't face anything but bed.

12

Rosaleen MacNamara was the focus of the morning. She lay on one of the porcelain slabs in the old morgue, light falling gently on her from the dirt-misted skylight. O'Keefe was uncovering her gradually, folding the sheet back in precise stages as he chatted to Swan and Considine. With the first fold, her head emerged, her eyes open and milky. Someone had twisted her long hair into a fine coil in the angle between neck and shoulder. O'Keefe was expanding on the subject of starvation for their benefit – always an air of the headmaster about him.

'You'd think we'd know all about this kind of process, what with famines and so on, but there are fewer pathological studies in the records than you'd think. If it *is* a case of acute starvation, we can expect death caused by heart failure, if some opportunistic infection didn't strike first. In layman's terms, the body cannibalises itself. Once all the glycogen is used, it breaks down the fat stores, then turns on the tissues.'

O'Keefe turned the cloth down another fold and the woman's torso was revealed, the skin stretched tight over the struts of the clavicle, the breasts lying flat as pockets on the prominent ribs. Swan snuck a glance at Considine. She looked collected. Rosaleen MacNamara's resemblance to a skeleton, to simple skin on bone, somehow made the sight less stomach-churning than the usual run of bodies, with their gaseous swellings and lurid bruising. The emaciation made her look not just aged, but distant.

'Would she have been able to move about, do you think?'

'Not in the final stages, I don't imagine,' said O'Keefe. 'She would have been terribly weak, and most likely blind.'

'So she was under that bed for some time?'

'The darkening here' – he pointed down the body's right flank – 'comes from the blood draining towards the floor post-mortem, but there aren't pressure sores on her side, which I'd expect if she had been stuck there for days. People can gather themselves to do extraordinary things *in extremis*.'

'Like get under a bed?'

'Well, I was going to say the brain would be affected too. She would have been confused – probably hallucinating. It could be green monsters she was avoiding, not an actual threat.'

'When does the blindness happen?' Swan was thinking of the deteriorating handwriting of the letters.

'The corneas would go fairly early on, maybe a month or so in.'

O'Keefe turned down another fold of sheet. The woman's exposed stomach dipped in an extreme hollow between ribs and hip bones, a suggestion of lumpiness under the thin skin. Her arms lay like sticks by her side, her hands still curled into loose fists.

'What's fascinating is the mummification – you saw that?'

'I'm not sure. Did I?'

'They're so well preserved, air-dried, as it were. It doesn't often happen in temperate climates, but the lack of fat, coupled with the effects of central heating, probably accounts for it.'

He pointed to the woman's feet and hands, darkened and tobacco-dry.

'I've seen one case before – a starved child, God help us – where the stomach was distended, though the rest was emaciated. We don't have that here; perhaps these women starved over a longer period. Her sister's organs were extraordinarily small, even the heart had shrunk – just another muscle, of course.'

Swan noticed a dark indentation around one wrist. 'This mark here. Is that where the rosary was wrapped around? It must have been very tight.'

O'Keefe came round to his side for a closer look. 'Well, it depends. As it was round her wrist when she died, this kind of impression could be from contact with the skin as it changed post-mortem, not necessarily from its tightness. Also, the skin is more delicate than you'd usually find. I would expect that. If it *is* starvation.'

The pathologist folded the sheet down her legs in silence, turn by turn, flipped it into a neat square with a practised move. He placed it on a side counter and gestured his assistant forward, a young lad whose thick red hair was bagged up in a hairnet. He was holding a big camera to his chest with exaggerated care. Swan couldn't remember seeing him before, but O'Keefe went through assistants at a rapid rate.

They waited as the boy photographed the body in its entirety and its parts. He leaned in close for the markings on the wrist, when O'Keefe told him to. The camera looked heavy, and the lad appeared nervous.

'Are you shaking?' said O'Keefe. The boy looked up anxiously. 'Get the tripod, *amadhán*.'

Minutes passed as the boy struggled to attach the camera to the tripod head at the suitable height. There was always a feeling of slow time at the mortuary, the sense that no one was going anywhere. Beyond the walls the traffic thrummed, the city rushed through its day.

'Get these,' O'Keefe was saying, and Swan moved round to see what he was pointing to. On the side of Rosaleen's left arm and left leg there were dark marks, purple bars, set at different angles.

'Is it bruising?'

O'Keefe angled his head this way and that, then grabbed hold of her wrist and bent the arm up, putting the hand by the chin. Two marks aligned into one straight line. He placed the arm down and slipped a gloved hand under the knee, pulled the left leg up, so it folded into the body. Again, the dark bars on calf and hip aligned.

'It's the bed slats, isn't it?' said O'Keefe, a note of triumph in her voice. 'She was tucked in tight.'

He put the woman's foot back down on the slab, but hadn't extended it fully. When he stepped back from the slab and motioned his photographer in, the heel slipped forward and the leg straightened itself. Mere gravity at work, but it gave Swan the chills.

He looked at Considine, and she grimaced back.

O'Keefe pointed out the marks for his assistant, then mumbled into his little Dictaphone machine – *pressure contusions on upper left arm, forearm*. He toured the body slowly, describing all that he saw there. Next, they turned her over, and documented the marks of pressure sores on her back.

Eventually O'Keefe set aside his Dictaphone and pulled his instrument trolley over to the side of slab, the sound of rattling metal bouncing off the tiled walls.

Swan gave Considine the nod to go.

'We'll leave you to it, Doctor. Call you this afternoon, if I may. A timeframe, obviously, would be a great start.'

But O'Keefe barely acknowledged their leaving, busy as he was tearing strips off the new assistant, this time about the arrangement of instruments on the trolley.

Swan hardly ever stayed for the cutting and weighing, the slicing and packaging of organs, not since his first few years with the squad. While the marks on the exterior body were legible, the interior was best left to science. But really he could not bear the weighing of soft things in scales identical to those in a butcher's shop, and the bagging up of the remains to place into the chest cavity like so many giblets. There was no need to get used to that.

Stepping out onto the butt-strewn pavement, Swan tilted his head back, breathed, took in the blank white sky.

'There's winter in that wind,' he said.

Considine was by his side. 'Why did we not stay? I stayed yesterday, and it was really interesting.'

'It's quicker to read the reports.'

They crossed the road to where he had parked, running the last bit to avoid a bus swooping out of Busáras.

As he started the ignition, Considine said, 'O'Keefe didn't encourage me to stay, mind. Kept staring at me like he couldn't understand who I was. So then I had to stay.' She laughed.

'I know it can't be easy for you, being the only woman in the unit.'

'Ah, will you stop with your pieties.'

'I think you handle the old guard very well.'

She took out a cigarette to fiddle with. 'I used to know a brilliant dog trainer, a posh old bird. She had this mantra: *Reward the good, ignore the bad.* I find it works pretty well on men too. I never get annoyed, so they give up baiting.'

It was more honesty that Swan had asked for. He couldn't work out whether she was telling him because he was an exception, or because he wasn't.

The crime-scene tape had either snapped or been snapped and now snaked loose and fluttering across the grass verge at Rowan Grove. There were no curious onlookers, no signs of life at all. The soft swooshing of traffic on the main road behind was all that broke the silence.

'Heard anything from that lot?' asked Swan, nodding at the house to the left.

'Been empty for six months. Apparently it was rented up until April, the neighbours say. We're trying to trace the couple who left, just in case they noticed anything. Maybe I should find out how much they're asking for it. This sort of thing would do me nicely. A proper house, but small enough for one.'

'Wouldn't you be lonely on your own?'

It was an unthinking bit of chat, but as soon as he said it, he realised he'd stepped into territory he didn't particularly want to be wandering in. Start asking someone about their private life and you didn't know where it would lead. She might even expect confidences in return.

'I'd love a bit of loneliness. A bathroom you could use when you pleased. I've been sharing with two other girls in Rathmines for years now. Loneliness would be a luxury. How much would it cost to buy one of these, do you think?'

'I haven't a clue. We'd better get on.'

Considine led the way up the path and put the key in the lock. She looked back at him before turning it.

'I've been in the Gardaí for eleven years now – *eleven*. Good record, steady promotions. First woman in the murder squad. You'd think I could afford a little place like this, now, wouldn't you?'

'Well, prices are mad these days, right?' He didn't want to get into it.

She pushed the door open for him, gave a mock-acquiescent swirl of her hand.

The place was much as it was when they first saw it, but smudges of grey fingerprint powder on various surfaces added a new layer to the general grime. The living-room doorway still framed the view of the armchair where Berenice MacNamara had sat, the cushions dark and dented.

'The windows are big and light, and I like the stairs.'

The stairs were the open sort – treads of bare polished wood, contained by a screen of floor-to-ceiling wooden bars, stylish but probably not that easy for an ill woman like Rosaleen MacNamara to negotiate.

Swan removed his coat, folded it into a rough bundle and placed it on the bottom stair. He put on the thin gloves from his jacket pocket and handed a spare pair to Considine.

'A brilliant breakthrough could be right before us, and they'll give you a massive promotion.' He started to climb.

Behind him, Considine said, 'Don't worry, I'll shut up now.'

He paused in the doorway of the front bedroom, the most likely source of the light that Madeleine had claimed to see.

The bed faced the window, a paisley eiderdown placed neatly on top. When he pulled back the covers, he saw the bed was made up neatly with sheets and blankets, not the modern continental quilt that Rosaleen's bed had. It looked as though it had not been used in a while.

The light switch and surround had not been dusted for prints.

'You can do the honours, but don't use your finger.'

Considine drew a biro from her coat pocket and pressed the switch with the retracted point. The lampshade filled with light. Swan went over to the bedside cabinet and pressed the little switch attached to a reading lamp. That also worked, as did the light in the hallway.

'So how did the light that Madeleine saw get switched off?'

'The boys next door said she was drunk, and they're bartenders, so should know,' said Considine. 'How reliable is she, really? She could have been looking up at the wrong window.'

'I suppose it's possible.'

'I'm going to check all the other switches and doors – see which ones they've dusted,' said Considine.

In Rosaleen's bedroom, the light switch and door had been dusted for prints and he could see the blurred ovals and smudges of various finger marks on the wall around the plastic square, but the switch itself showed only smears, as if wiped by a cloth.

Swan went to the window and glanced down into the back garden. The tall weeds were beginning to fade and droop. Winter would soon flatten them. The pegs hanging on the rotary dryer were rusting at the hinges, but every back garden in the row looked similarly neglected. The garden of the empty house to the left was turning wild, brambles arcing through the long grass. The three to the right were shabby but under control, just spaces for bins and plastic garden furniture, the odd crippled bicycle.

He turned and viewed the room anew from the window. He was bothered by that little chair beside the dead woman's bed. They had pulled it aside to reach her, but it had been angled close to the bed, suggestive of a visitor, though perhaps just a place for a book or alarm clock. He placed it where it had originally been. It was delicate and old. Mother-of-pearl flowers set into dark wood and the seat made of woven cane, a trellis spanning air. Swan eased himself down onto it with care. It creaked, but held.

The wall over the bed was hung with a scrappy montage of holy pictures, scapulars and a poster of a sunlit field of wildflowers, with text from the Bible over it – the one about the lilies of the field, how God cares for them though they don't raise a finger. The fate of the MacNamara sisters gave the lie to that.

He examined the bedhead – it was padded, velvet buttons dimpling the material. Careful not to strain the chair further, Swan leaned over near to where Rosaleen's head would have been. The thin curtains were pushed open to their full extent, the view made up entirely of sky and the tops of trees. He imagined looking at that view day after day. Rain against the glass, stars and moon at night. All blurring, as her vision failed.

Considine stuck her head round the door.

'Here's a thing. They've done the obvious bits – front door, back door, here, but no sign that they did anything in the kitchen, or the back garden. The bin bags are still lying there. Shall I give them a ring – check where exactly they got to?'

'Do that. And ask if they've got anywhere with the prints they do have.'

'I'll use the payphone in the pub. It's got a discreet booth.'

She left. Swan looked again in the open wardrobe, although he had checked it on his first visit. No clothes hanging there, but shoes and a few hangers lay in a muddle on the base of it, an old belt from a towelling dressing gown snaking among them. He closed the wardrobe door with a gloved hand.

He wandered around the living room next, inspected the shelves built into the alcove beside the fireplace. Three volumes lay on the otherwise-empty top shelf, a *Good News Bible*, an old volume called *Six O'Clock Saints* and what looked like a child's communion missal, bound in plastic mother-of-pearl. The lower shelves were home to a scatter of ornaments. A couple of them were holy – a cherubic angel, a flattened bust of the Mother and Child – but most were the kind of random junk that his mother used to fill various cabinets with, in the belief that something given as a gift could never be discarded. A brass wishing well and a slender-horned antelope. A line of elephants of diminishing size. Someone had taken the largest elephant and propped its front legs up on the back of the antelope, so that they appeared to be copulating. That was odd – a dirty joke in a pious house. He wondered if the Technical Bureau had caught it in a photograph, if it hadn't been someone messing about in the aftermath of the deaths.

There was a stack of pamphlets and magazines on the lower shelf, similar to the ones that had been scattered around Berenice MacNamara's feet. He picked up the topmost one – yellow stapled cover, photocopied text on the inside. The title was *The Visions and Revelations of St Catherine of Siena*. The back cover stated that this publication had been produced by 'The Acolytes of Siena, 2 Rowan Grove, Deerfield, Dublin 7'. The very address in which he was standing. He hadn't noticed a typewriter or reams of paper anywhere. Maybe someone else produced it, and the MacNamaras were just the correspondence address. Swan was skimming through the arcane contents when Considine returned.

'You're not going to like it.'

'Well?'

'It's like they weren't going to tell us, just put it all in the report – like in a month's time, no rush at all.'

'Are you going to tell me or not?'

'No prints on the front or back door – doorknob and all around wiped clean. They haven't done any work on the prints they got, because they're waiting for Pathology to give them the sisters' prints for elimination, and they need the priest's too. But that mightn't happen any time soon.'

'Why not?'

'After talking to Bob, I phoned the office and Rooney was having a panic. Kavanagh's been looking for you.'

'No … he said we'd have a few days.'

'It's not the days is the problem. You and Hannigan and Murphy are pulled off all active duties, Rooney claims. And we're to mothball the MacNamaras until after the inquest. Apparently Kavanagh talked to O'Keefe, and he's happy there was no interference.'

'We don't even have half the facts! And far too many people happy to walk away, save a bit of money.'

'If one sister was coercing the other,' said Considine, 'there might not be anyone else involved. You know what families are like.'

Swan looked down at the cheap brochure he was holding and realised his hands were shaking. If Considine hadn't been watching, he would have wrenched it to pieces. How could a case like this just be discarded?

He put the brochure on the shelf slowly, deliberately. Gathered his calm.

'There are anomalies. The light going off, the wiped switches, the open back door … And what about this?' Swan pointed at the elephant mounting the antelope.

Considine snorted. 'You did that.'

'I did not. And you could do with sharpening up, Detective Considine, and getting your attention away from your accommodation troubles and back in the room.'

'I apologise,' she said tightly. 'When we get back to the office, I'll check the position of the elephant in the photographs. I doubt the MacNamaras would do anything like that, though I know a lot of jokers on our side who might.'

'Which was exactly my point. We'll leave everything just as we found it, lock the door. It will be here waiting, when we persuade Kavanagh to change his mind.'

A sudden flurry of movement in the garden made them both jump. A jackdaw had landed on the rotary dryer, setting it moving with a grating squeal. Beyond the wall, the first leaves were falling from the chestnuts, spinning down. Time was moving on, and they had nothing.

13

What a bloody family! They hadn't even reached the church, but already they weren't speaking. It was no wonder she had emigrated. Maybe the funeral crowd would take their silence for sadness. Phil was wearing exactly the same sulky mouth he wore as a boy. It nearly made Francesca smile.

'*Two* hearses?' he'd exclaimed when he arrived at the morgue and looked at the undertaker's gleaming convoy.

'I don't think there's such a thing as a double hearse, Phil,' she'd said. 'Nice to see you, too.'

'Hello, Frances, you're looking well.'

Madeleine screwed up her face. 'Maybe you could ask them to slide one coffin on top of the other, or on their sides maybe, and the three of us could go on the roof rack. That would be nice and cheap.'

Francesca pressed her hand on Madeleine's shoulder, but the girl shrugged her off, looking away as if there was a sudden interesting something on the other side of the road.

Phil tried to appeal his case, hands held out. 'I was just surprised – I hadn't thought it through. Two hearses and a limousine. Right. I'm adjusting.'

'You're a real peach, Phil.'

Francesca nodded to their chauffeur, and he opened the back door of the limo for her. She slipped into the cream leather interior and waited for the others to follow. Philip's two teenagers, Jennifer and Jason, were hovering nearby, lanky and wilted-looking, but he shooed them back to the family's red hatchback.

'Go keep your mother company.'

Phil was wearing a charcoal suit that wasn't too bad, but the jacket he wore over it was baggy, more like an anorak than a proper coat. Francesca was surprised to see her baby brother with greying hair. He had thickened out too – not fat, exactly, just solidified. His air of discontent was unchanged, however. Their mother had loved Phil with an unreasonable passion. People would have you believe that there was no limit to the praise you should give a child, but Phil provided the counter-argument. Their mother had treated him like a prince, got his sisters to serve him at table, never taught him to look after himself or that there might be any need to. Life after boyhood had proved a great disappointment.

He had his face turned to the car window now, probably nurturing equally hostile thoughts about her. They were all each other had now, the only MacNamara siblings left.

Madeleine sat opposite, on one of the little pull-down seats, fiddling with what looked like an old binocular case that she was using as a handbag. Under her little bouclé coat she was wearing a black satin dress with layers of pointed gauze for a skirt. Another borrowing from the costume room. She looked sweet, and a bit eccentric. Although the day was dull, Francesca wore her sunglasses. If she felt like weeping, the glasses would hide her eyes. If no grief came, they would hide that too. There was always the chance there would be press there.

116

As they followed the hearses out to Deerfield, she watched people on the pavements stop and bless themselves. The kind of old men who wore hats removed them. She felt a temptation to play it up, to raise a snowy handkerchief delicately to her cheek. This glibness was just nerves. She could have done a funeral scene in a play or film, no problem, but maybe that *was* the problem. Now that it was happening for real, she didn't know how to be.

'It's just that I'm the one having to put the money up front for all this,' said Phil suddenly. 'We don't even know if there's any money in their account to cover it.'

'Phil. I'm going to pretend that it's grief making you act this way and not sheer meanness. Of course there's money.'

Madeleine giggled. She was rolling a cigarette on her lap, shreds of tobacco falling into her skirt folds.

'Oh, Maddy, don't do that!'

Madeleine looked right at her, took a box of matches out of her bag and lit the cigarette. Francesca rolled her window down, let the cold air flow in and buffet them. Madeleine squealed.

'For God's sake, Frances!' said Phil.

There were only five cars parked outside the church when they arrived. Francesca realised she had expected a crowd, but couldn't think now why she had. Her sisters had led a quiet life.

The undertaker came over to the limo. 'I am sorry. We seem to have made better time than I estimated. Would you care to wait in the car?'

'For how long?'

'Ten minutes should do it.' The old man had a practised

smile, kindly but professional. A flash of red passed behind him as Phil's wife and kids drew into the car park. Phil practically leapt out of the door to re-join them. They were his preferred family now.

She noticed a priest emerging from a sad-looking bungalow in the corner of the car park. His face stretched into panic when he saw the cortège already there.

'That's Father Timoney,' said Madeleine, as they watched him hurry round the back of the church. 'It was him that told me. Him that found them.'

'Let's get out of here.' Francesca opened her door and pulled Madeleine with her. The idea of sitting in the car, doing nothing and being looked at, was suddenly unbearable. She walked towards the main road, Madeleine at her heels.

'Where are we going?'

'I want to take a look at the house.' In the two weeks she'd been in Dublin, she hadn't found the heart to come out and see it. Besides, the police still had the keys.

She put an arm round Madeleine's shoulders as they crossed through a gap in the traffic. The most direct way to Rowan Grove was across the pub car park. As they reached the low wall that edged the road leading up to the terrace, Madeleine stopped dead.

'We can see it fine from here.'

'The trees have grown a lot in six years,' said Francesca.

It could be a nice house, she thought, *small, but handy enough for town*. Warmer than Madeleine's flat. If she was forced to stay in Dublin any longer.

Madeleine sat down on the wall, facing away from the

house. Francesca was remembering how hectic it had been, moving her sisters here, when it was bought. How many times had she driven her little hire car up and down that road? She'd had a gap between movies, had flown to Dublin and almost broken her arse with positivity throughout all the tears and the to-ing and fro-ing. Her sisters heavy with grief for their dead mother and the loss of the only house they had ever known. Madeleine a sullen and silent adolescent. She had done her best for a week. It had felt so much longer.

She sat down next to her niece. Gazed across tarmac and cement, the random strew of ugly buildings – garage, pub, shop and church, with too much space in between them. And the road roaring in the middle. Nothing good to rest your eyes on.

'Roll me a cigarette, would you?'

Madeleine didn't look round, just took the tobacco pouch out of her bag and extracted a thin, fluttering paper.

'Do you remember that week I moved you in here?'

Madeleine stole a look at her as she loaded tobacco into the fold of the paper, like she was trying to judge what might be required.

'It was shite,' she said. 'I couldn't believe how small my room was. Or the house. Bernie was on top of me the whole time I lived here, you know. Nothing she enjoyed better than giving out. I spent more time here than in the house.'

'What, right here?'

'More or less. Or in the doorway of the pub, if it was raining. There were always a few other kids hanging round.

Sometimes you could get a grown-up to get you a bottle or can from the pub.'

'The pub? You were thirteen.'

'Ach, it was six of us to one bottle of cider, type of thing. Pretending to be drunk. We called ourselves the Lazy Acre gang. Don't know who came up with that – makes you think of a cornfield or something. Ridiculous shite.'

'I'm glad you had friends, at least.'

Madeleine laughed, a bitter edge. 'They weren't *friends*. That age, don't you remember? It's like combat. Girls judging you, and the boys just *at you*. If someone fancied you, they'd do something like trip you, so you fell on your face, then everyone would laugh. And that bastard Mr Cotter, he stills run the shop. He used to sell us single smokes, then threaten to tell our parents. He took me into the back room once, after I tried to shoplift a Curly Wurly. I'll never forget it.'

'He didn't … did he touch you?'

'No, he didn't. It felt worse than that. He insulted me. For hours, it felt like, watching me crying: *You're a useless smear of shite, and your mother was a slut.* Sadistic aul' bastard.' Madeleine concentrated hard on rolling the tobacco, adopted a lofty tone. 'And that's not even my worst story.'

Francesca wanted to go right round to Mr Cotter's shop and give him what he deserved. 'I'm sorry I wasn't around more.'

Madeleine gave a half-smile that might have been forgiveness or mockery.

'Was that why you went to live with Phil, because you were unhappy?'

'No, Bernie sent me. Long story. She thought I was in special danger because of – and I quote – my *illegitimacy*.'

'Maddy—'

'I don't like being called *Maddy*. Just so's ya know.' Her eyes were shining with tears, but there was ferocity in her voice.

'You should have said.'

'Fair play to Phil and his wife, they did put me up until I turned sixteen. They didn't like me, their kids were young, but they did it.'

She licked the paper quickly, little cat tongue, and offered the thin white cylinder between thumb and forefinger. Francesca looked at it for a confused second, then took it and put it in her mouth, allowed Madeleine to light it. Maybe she shouldn't have taken a Valium, as a terrible heaviness had come over her. As the smoke filled her lungs, her head went woozy and the world lurched in front of her eyes. When it steadied, she noticed Phil over in the church car park, looking their way, his hands flapping impatiently.

'We were never kind to each other, when we were kids,' she said. 'We weren't a kind family. Except Rosaleen. Rosaleen didn't even know how to be mean.'

'Rosaleen was the best,' said Madeleine.

They were sliding out a coffin from one of the hearses now, smooth as a drawer opening. Francesca dropped the cigarette onto the tarmac and stamped on it quickly, reached for her niece's hand.

'Let's get this over with.'

14

Swan and Considine sat at the back of the church, waiting for the funeral mass to begin. She was fidgeting, rubbing her hands together.

'This place is bloody freezing,' she muttered.

Two and a half weeks had passed since the women were found. Far too soon to be letting the bodies go, but the case was no longer a murder case, just an investigation of suspicious death, a matter of paperwork and laboratory samples.

The big church was only a quarter full, mostly women. Swan scanned their coated backs: bowed shoulders, a few woollen hats and old-fashioned headscarves. The dead sisters were women like this, ordinary and devout. Good at making themselves invisible, tucked into the corners of things. *Don't mind me*.

The central doors scraped open, and the squeak of trolley wheels heralded the first coffin, steered by two tall pall-bearers – professionals, not relatives, by the look of them. The next coffin followed, wheeled by two more hired boys. Swan looked towards the door and saw the family group outlined in light, Francesca MacNamara to the front, with long curling hair and sunglasses. She entered the aisle, head held high and steady, walking like a queen.

Drawing to her side, the little niece cast nervous glances over the congregation, saw Swan and looked away quickly. Following them came the brother, presumably, his wife and two teenagers. Swan noticed how the people in the rows in front of him stared at Francesca, their eyes drawn to her, and only her.

As the monotony of the mass got under way, he checked his watch, though he had nowhere else to be. He had been temporarily posted to the computer department, but all work had been suspended there because of some technical problem with something called a 'mainframe'. He had never felt more useless, professionally speaking.

'I'm not happy about this, of course,' Kavanagh had said, formally relieving Swan of his investigative duties. 'Hopefully we'll all be back to normal soon.'

'I don't know anything about computers.'

'Well, maybe you can come back as our electronic information expert. Moving with the times, and all that.'

The Owens Tribunal rolled on, slow as a glacier, pulling in more Garda personnel and lawyers as it travelled. Someone – he suspected the DPP's office – had leaked the internal report on Brían DeBarra to a *Sunday Tribune* journalist, resulting in an article about alleged 'aggressive methods' within the unit. It was accompanied by a photograph of a bunch of his colleagues, including Hannigan and Murphy, smoking outside Mullingar Courthouse during a case last year. There was an additional photo – one he'd never seen before – of himself in some woods with uniformed Gardaí about him. It was from the aftermath of the Zanotti kidnapping. He was looking straight at the cameraman with an annoyed expression, one that reminded him of his mother in a mood. *Named in report*, said the caption. In the context of the article, he looked like a very angry man. Which was ironic, since back then everything was fine. Zanotti had been rescued unhurt, and Swan himself was deliriously newly-wed.

He tuned back in to Father Timoney's rather uninspired sermon, about reaching out to neighbours in times of trouble. As if that was the key to these women's deaths – their neighbours' indifference, rather than some delusional death wish.

Superintendent Kavanagh had been unpersuaded by Swan's careful arguing of the oddities of the case – the position of Rosaleen's body, the open back door, the absence of prints, the light seen in the upper bedroom, the paranoid letters. The pathologist's report was clear: the women had died of starvation, there were no signs of injury or coercion. In time, there would be an inquest and closure. For now, Swan was to sit in front of a black screen and input information that was apparently too important for a mere secretary to see.

The database was Kavanagh's pet project, his legacy bid. Swan's role was to repeatedly stub his two fingers on a keyboard to create the strange green language of forward slashes, arrows and tabs that would make all the information cross-reference itself with itself. Whenever he started to get into the swing of it, up would pop an ERROR notice, which meant phoning down to the technical department (not to be confused with the Garda Technical Bureau) and waiting for some young buck to come upstairs and enter whatever four-number code would undo the damage.

Considine nudged him. The mass was ending and the priest was thanking everyone for coming to remember 'two precious souls'. He announced that the burial would be at Glasnevin.

'You going?' she whispered.

'I'm heading home for lunch, but it's on my way.'

'You'd do anything to stay away from your new friends in the boffin department.'

'It's more like the typing pool. Actually I'm off until the weekend.'

'It's well for some.'

'Aren't you supposed to treat me with enormous respect, Considine?'

They were starting to move the coffins out. He intended to scan the congregation as they passed, see if there was anyone who stood out, but found himself watching Francesca MacNamara again. That was the very definition of a star, he supposed: someone who drew the eye. She walked with her arm around Madeleine, and the girl was weeping in great gulps. Francesca's eyes were hidden behind dark glasses, but she didn't appear to be crying. Her head turned to glance over at him as she passed, and he felt rebuked for all the questions he had not managed to answer.

Outside, a mill of people lined up to shake the family's hands.

'I'd go with you to Glasnevin,' said Considine, 'but Kavanagh's got me loaded with work. With you three off, there's no shortage. Enjoy your days off, though.'

Hannigan and Murphy had been assigned to old cases, tidying up loose ends, confined to the office, but still part

126

of the unit. The fact that Swan had been singled out for exile unnerved him, even though Kavanagh tried to make out it was some kind of tribute to his intelligence. It was donkey-work, but the regular hours left him plenty of time to spend at home with Elizabeth, plenty of time to think. But the thing his mind kept returning to was the reluctant death of Rosaleen MacNamara.

As the crowd thinned, he approached the family line. Shook hands with a truculent-looking woman whom he had identified as the brother's wife – *very sorry for your trouble*; then the brother, a put-upon-looking chap.

'I'm Detective Swan,' he said slowly and deliberately, watching Philip MacNamara's face, but his expression didn't change from the slightly scatter-eyed look of the bereaved and exposed.

Beside her uncle, Madeleine turned her head, alert.

'I've been working on your sisters' case. I hope we can talk, in due course.' Swan shook the man's hand, took a side step to face the niece, bumping lightly against someone who was talking to Francesca MacNamara, the last in the line.

'It was good of you to come,' said Madeleine, 'and thanks for your help in getting my aunts back to us.' A spasm of emotion crossed her face for a moment, and she inhaled audibly.

'Not at all,' he said, 'not at all.' He hadn't even been consulted. He would have fought it, if asked, but Kavanagh just wanted to bring it all to a close.

He was suddenly aware that Francesca, now alone, was studying him. He took a step towards her, offered his hand. It felt like giving in to something.

She slipped her hand into his and left it lying there a moment. He could barely make out her eyes through her amber lenses.

'Vincent Swan,' he said, and a mocking voice in his head commented: *Vincent, is it, now?*

'Hello.'

Her hand slipped away, tucked itself back in her opposite jacket sleeve.

'This is the detective I talked to,' said Madeleine.

'Oh, right,' said Francesca. 'I wanted to ask—' She hesitated, glanced towards her brother, who was busy consulting his wife about something. 'When will we be able to access the house, do you know? Only I'm still staying with my niece here, and we're finding ourselves on top of each other.'

Her voice rolled in lovely modulations, her accent still Irish, but not like anyone he knew. An accent from somewhere with castles and wolfhounds, tied up with a black velvet band.

'I can find out for you,' he said evenly. 'I thought you lived in the States.'

'I do. But I can't go back at the moment, can I? Not until things are settled.'

'Where can I contact you?'

'I'll be at my niece's, as I said. But they only have a payphone in the hall.'

'I'm sure we have the number.'

'It might be better if I contact you.' Her manner was imperious.

'Garda Headquarters.' He handed her a card. 'That's an

old extension,' he pointed out. 'Just ask the switchboard and they'll find me.'

The cars were waiting, the hearses running their engines discreetly. She tucked the card up her sleeve. He felt that he should say more.

'I know it must be frustrating, but it is vital that we establish the sequence of events that led to their death. The circumstances are quite unusual—'

She lifted her sunglasses then, gave him a hard look with her strangely familiar grey eyes.

'But the house is just lying empty. Surely you have everything you need by now, *Vincent*.'

The brother was trying to get them to move to the limousine; Francesca ignored him. Swan returned her gaze.

'I'll do what I can.'

Francesca nudged her niece's shoulder, getting her moving towards the car. As she passed, she brushed close to Swan, her mouth so near, he could feel the warmth of her breath.

'I know you will.'

He watched her walk away, amusement rising in him. His old pin-up. Wasn't she something?

At the graveyard Swan kept a discreet distance. The funeral crowd had thinned to the immediate family, Father Timoney, his housekeeper and half a dozen women from the congregation, probably friends of the sisters. He could ask the priest who they were later, tried to memorise their faces for now. He was just gathering information – nothing wrong with that.

All the women wore the same closed, pious expression. A couple were dressed in good black coats, others wore more everyday things. One looked to be well into her eighties, her jaw working away at nothing in a spasmodic way. Beside her, a smaller, younger woman in a duffel coat stood absolutely still, her eyes closed. He kept watching, but she never moved, not a twitch. Her stillness had the effect of separating her from the people she stood among, as if she was not wholly present.

The pall-bearers walked stiffly to the wide grave with the first coffin. Four to carry one coffin, they did not need their full complement today. They placed the coffin on a stand and unfurled the straps to lower it in with.

He heard the gravel crunch behind him, and a tall man appeared at his side. When Swan turned to acknowledge him, he noticed the collar. The priest blessed himself and pressed his thumb to his lips briefly, before addressing Swan.

'An extraordinary tragedy.' He had a politician's voice.

'You knew the women?' said Swan.

'Are you from the newspapers?'

'Detective Inspector Swan.'

'I thought you might be. Father Gerry Geraghty. I'm based over at Holy Trinity. Parish priest. I decided we'd keep the funeral low-key, leave it to Father Timoney. If we can be of any assistance, do ring my office, though I understand that the circumstances are not suspicious …' He kept looking down on Swan, expectantly.

'There'll be an inquest. In time.'

'Well, do keep us informed,' said the priest.

Swan said nothing.

Over at the graveside they were lowering the second coffin. Father Timoney, prayer book in one hand, bent forward to take a pinch of earth from the pile beside the grave, about to perform the gesture that people both feared and relished, the sound of the first clay rattling off the polished wood.

But instead of rising, the priest stayed bent, one hand pushing into an earth mound, the other, with the prayer book flapping in it, reaching back for his hip. His face was growing alarmingly flushed. He managed to turn his neck to say something to Philip MacNamara, and Philip moved to the priest's side, put a hand to his shoulder, about to grasp and lift.

'NO!' Timoney practically screamed it.

'Oh, for God's sake ...' Father Geraghty strode over to the graveside and crouched down to talk to Timoney, who remained in his strange right-angled stoop.

At practically every funeral Swan had been to, there was a moment like this, where the sorrowful dignity of the occasion threatened to tip into farce. The one short pall-bearer, the dog lifting its leg. Once he had even seen a distraught mourner trip over a roll of fake grass and bring down the widow with him, both of them almost tumbling into the yawning grave. It seemed that Father Timoney, on this particularly tragic occasion, would add the rogue element.

Swan watched Father Geraghty call forth the pall-bearers to assist the distressed priest away from the graveside, invite the mourners to add earth to the grave, if they so wished, and say a little solemn something to round things off.

Swan turned away and headed through the gravestones for home. He lived just outside the walls of Glasnevin, on a little square of houses facing a pub popular with mourners and known as The Gravediggers'. Benny the cat was on his front windowsill, curled up like a bun. He could make even granite look comfortable. The yellow eyes opened as Swan unlatched the gate, an expression that, to a stranger, might look like disgust.

'Same to you, Brother,' said Swan, coming down the path. Benny jumped off the sill and waited for Swan to unlock the door so that he could precede him.

'Vincent?'

Elizabeth's voice came from the kitchen, high and strained. He set his shoulders and headed down the hall. 'I got away early from work, so I thought I'd—'

'It's not working.' She was sitting at the kitchen table in a smudged overall, looking dejected.

'What is it, love?'

'It's all wrong. The yellow is horrible, it's too bright.'

Swan had spent every evening of the week papering and painting the kitchen with her. He brushed buttercup gloss on all the cupboards while she went round with a stencil, putting pink flowers over everything and a trail of them round the top of the walls. She had pictures cut out of magazines of other people's kitchens. It would be sunny and fresh and French. French was the most important bit – French, her heart's desire.

'I can't even look at it.' She looked dangerously as if she was going to cry.

'I think it looks cheerful.'

'What would you know about cheerful?'

That was a bit bald, but he wasn't going to get into a fight with her, not about something trivial like this. He pulled over a chair so that he could embrace her where she sat.

'We can buy more paint,' he said, though it was the last thing he wanted to do. 'I have tomorrow off, and the weekend. Or we could even hire someone to do it.'

'We can't afford that, not if you lose your job.'

'I'm not losing my job. For God's sake, Elizabeth, it's just a temporary suspension.'

'I just feel like nothing's going right,' she said, her voice wobbling.

He held her tighter. 'You've been in this room all day, haven't you? Let's go out for dinner. When we get back, it'll all look just fine.'

15

'Would you not try and straighten up, Father?' said a voice from above. All Timoney could see was two identical sets of trouser legs.

The pain was even worse than the humiliation. The two pall-bearer boys had brought him behind the hearse, which at least formed a screen between him and the relatives at the graveside. 'No, no, please. I've had this before. I can't straighten. My back is in spasm.'

One of the four shoes kicked at the gravel impatiently.

'Do you think you could drive me back to the church in the hearse? In the front of the hearse, I mean.'

'Don't worry, I'll handle this.' The voice of Father Geraghty, booming behind him. His face dipped into the periphery of Timoney's vision, grinning encouragingly. 'I'll drive you back to base, Noel. The car is just nearby.'

Just nearby. It was ten minutes away – ten minutes of crouched shuffling, his vestments trailing the dusty ground in front of him, Geraghty had his elbow in a pinch, urging him on. His back burned with tension, like a rubber band at its furthest stretch.

The bottom half of the car appeared at last in his field of view. He shuffled backwards while Geraghty opened the door for him.

'Just you go round to the driver's side,' Timoney begged, 'I'll see myself in.'

He gripped the door edge with his fingertips and lowered himself backwards, backwards. Please God he would feel the seat under him soon. His fingertips slipped and he dropped, let out a yelp as a part of his spine seemed to shift, delivering a spurt of pure white pain. Geraghty reappeared by his side, helped him lift his feet in one by one and closed the door. Timoney could not help the tears that filled his eyes.

When they reached the presbytery, he couldn't move at all.

'You wait here. I'll get help.' Geraghty's voice was quieter now, almost kind.

He came back with young Jimmy Noonan. The lad's boiler suit was rolled down to reveal a tight, filthy T-shirt. His face and arms were misted with plaster dust.

'Let's be having you, Father,' said Jimmy. Geraghty was leaning in from the driver's door, ready to assist, but the boy was surprisingly competent, slipping an arm under Timoney's legs and another round his back, and he was out of the car in a jiffy, though the sudden lurch sent another bolt of pain through him. He held onto the car door, gestured that he needed a moment.

'Does it hurt bad, Father?' Jimmy asked, his face close.

'He must be lighter than he looks,' said Geraghty.

'Put your hand on my arm,' said Jimmy. 'Take your time.'

And so Timoney took hold of his bare forearm. Skin to grimy skin. The hardness of flexed muscle under his palm. His own arms had never been so muscled, even back in his youth. Health was such a wonderful thing.

136

The journey to his bedroom seemed endless. As they passed the kitchen, the smell of fried bacon came to him, weakened him further. He had not even had breakfast. Through the final doorway and Jimmy helped him down, in a strange sideways collapse, onto the bed. Another wave of pain, then the start of its retreat, the bliss of knowing he could just stay where he was.

He opened his eyes. Jimmy was still looking down on him, and Mrs Noonan was standing at the door.

'It's all right,' he told them. 'I just need to lie here until the spasm passes. It's happened before.'

'Your vestments are getting all crushed,' said Mrs Noonan.

'Never mind that. But perhaps a cup of tea and a little something to eat.'

'What? Here in the bed?'

'Please. I had no breakfast.'

'I'll make you a sandwich. C'mon, Jimmy, you need to get back to your work.'

The door closed. *I had no breakfast.* The horrible after-echo of his wheedling voice. He really wanted some rashers, like she'd just cooked for her son, not a bloody cheese sandwich.

How had she come to treat him with such disrespect? Without God, people are just animals. They sniff out the weakness in each other and exploit it. He'd been too kind, obviously, from the start, too passive. He had not laid down any rules for the house. And he would, just as soon as he was better. He made a quick prayer to God for strength, but God felt further away than he had ever been.

16

Elizabeth was not in the bed when Swan woke. The clock read 9.30, luxuriously late, and brisk piano music flowed through the house. It sounded as though her bleak mood had passed. She was so sensitive to things – to colours and sounds and aesthetics – in a way he could never be. She was still half-mystery to him, but perhaps it would always be like that; even in a marriage there was only so much you could know about the inside of another person's head.

On the off-chance she was giving an early lesson, he didn't disturb her, although the fact that the music was continuous and flowing made him suspect it was just her in there, practising for the pleasure of it. In the vexed yellow kitchen he started to make his breakfast. When he went to the fridge, he found a note pinned there.

Let's go for a walk after breakfast! X

It was nice to be able to say yes to lazy pleasures for once, though writing notes to each other under the same roof brought the MacNamara sisters – never far away – back to the front of his mind.

Shake them off. He had no work to go to, and a walk around the Botanics was preferable to starting on the home decorating again. Enjoy the last of the autumn sun. Elizabeth could name practically every plant in the place, even

139

in Latin. She was smart, she was cultured, and today she was happy.

Buttering his toast, it suddenly occurred to Swan that there might be something significant in her recent volatile moods and in the joyous music she was playing this morning. Perhaps this walk was to be the setting for a long-anticipated announcement. He started towards the front room, desperate to know if his hunch was true, but stopped himself. She would want to tell him in her own way.

They walked through the Botanics arm-in-arm. The park was in a sad state, just one man with a barrow at work, cutting back the withered borders. The place needed some decent funding, but with the economy in the state it was, no one was going to prioritise plants. This was the kind of thing Swan expounded on, nervously, as they walked through the arboretum. He bent to pick up a leaf that was a skeleton, a complex tracery of veins within the outline.

'*Magnolia grandiflora*,' said Elizabeth. 'My mother used to paint them silver for Christmas. Don't rip it!'

He had just been testing, to see how strong the laciness was.

'Sorry.'

'Let's see if the palm house is open. I want to talk to you.'

Were there six words more nerve-racking in the English language? But her pale face looked calm, and she slipped her gloved hand into his bare one to tug him gently along.

They had met at a post-concert drinks reception at the Royal Dublin Society. He had been on plain-clothes duty with the president, and Elizabeth had mistaken him for a fellow guest. She asked him what he thought of the programme, he bluffed by saying he had liked it in parts, and she launched into a passionate defence of Sibelius, a man he had not heard of before that night. Her passion was so engaging that he almost missed the president's departure.

She was too genteel for the likes of him, his father declared, and no spring chicken at thirty-two. Which was rich, given that Swan was five years older. His father's opposition only made him keener, of course. And how lovely she looked right now, turning to smile as she opened the door into the damp warmth of the big palm house, like they were kids sneaking into a palace. There was a chaos of green overhead, and a steady dripping somewhere. Many of the glass panes were cracked, a few missing entirely, and the tall iron pillars were streaked with rust, but the boilers pumped out the heat and the floor tiles were slick with condensation. Old hoses snaked underfoot.

Swan unbuttoned his coat, then pulled Elizabeth to him, started to gently loosen the scarf from her neck.

'I have to tell you something,' she said, and the world stood still.

Was this a moment to remember for a lifetime, here in the hothouse jungle, where he'd learn they were about to be joined by a baby, someone made by them?

'No, no! Not that,' she said, reading his expression easily. 'I would have told you that right away. Oh, I've made a mess of this. It's to ask you something, really. Bobbo Burke rang me this morning from Wexford. They need an accompanist for the opera festival next week. They're desperate.

It's just two weeks, and it's good money. I can stay with my aunts in Enniscorthy – they'd love that.'

'What about your students?'

'None of them have exams right now – they'll be fine. I was more worried about leaving you on your own.'

'Me?'

'Well, with this trouble with your job, the tribunal. I know I'll be leaving you unsupported.'

So she'd already decided she was going. Irritated and disoriented, Swan moved back, and her hand, which she had rested near his heart, fell away. 'I've told you not to worry about my job. I don't want you to concern yourself about me at all.'

'Listen to yourself. Well, if you don't need me, I won't feel guilty about taking the job.'

'If that's what you want, I really think you should go.'

'Good.'

'Fine.'

A warm drip from a banana leaf hit his forehead. He took out his handkerchief and mopped the spot, using it as an excuse to start moving again, pushing along the path through the barring fronds and leaves.

How quickly things could shift between them, from happiness to this awful out-of-tune state. If Elizabeth went away, at least he could put down the paintbrush and roller and return to the MacNamara case, all those beckoning pages. Being part of the festival, back on her home turf, would probably make Elizabeth much happier than acting the *Hausfrau* for him in Dublin. It was a good thing, even if it didn't feel like it right now.

Elizabeth was standing where he had left her, pretending to examine a label.

He called out to her, 'It really *is* fine, Lizzie.'

But she wouldn't look up at him.

17

'Come to my play! I'd love you to come.'

Francesca had been hanging around in Madeleine's flat all day, wrapped in a blanket on her sofa, reading an Iris Murdoch novel she'd found in the bathroom. It had not been an uplifting experience. She knew she should stir herself, get out.

'I'll drag myself together, if you can leave a ticket on the door for me.'

'Okay. It's a good play, really it is.'

It only took a minute, after the lights went up, for Francesca to realise it wasn't.

It was the way the six actors strode out in their identical youth and health and eagerness and took up their marks in individual spotlights. It was the way one of them – the one in the elaborate army uniform – had his hair caked with some white stuff, and wrinkles drawn badly around his mouth and eyes. It was the solemn intensity with which they chorused their first line, not quite in time with each other.

'We are the disappeared. We are the lost ones.'

Oh God. It was going to be one of those plays. Terrible experiences were going to be thrown at her, to shake her complacent existence. God knows, she'd done enough of them herself. At least she'd told Madeleine she would sit at the back, so as not to be distracting. She wouldn't have to look entranced. She did not even have to listen.

But if she didn't listen, she was back to being stuck in her circling thoughts. *My three sisters dead. All three of my sisters chose to die.* Francesca didn't think she had the same impulse, but she sure as hell wasn't going to go searching her psyche for it. She had always been a survivor, and she would survive this too. She needed her share from that house; she needed her share from the bank account. The assets that her sisters left behind would get her back to America, get her financially on her feet. Good things would come from bad.

Madeleine was speaking onstage, the other players in darkness, about the day the soldiers came for her father, how she clung to his leg as he was dragged off, and all she had was a shoe to remember him by. Her tears shining on her cheeks, her hands holding that invisible shoe.

Oh no. They were going into a torture scene. People on their precious nights out, paying for dreadful things to be acted out in front of them. She tried to open her programme silently, check if there was any kind of interval, tilting the page to catch a little light from the stage. Further down the row, a man with a rather patrician profile leaned forward to look at what she was doing. Francesca glared back.

There will be no interval.

Onstage, the lights cut to black and a man screamed in agony.

*

146

Everyone ended up in a pub on Wicklow Street. Francesca had opted for the assessment, 'That was remarkable!'

The young cast glowed back at her, wanting more.

'Really powerful work.'

She let the young men buy her drinks. They were reverent with her, but she doubted they had seen her in anything. It had been eight years since she did that thing at the Gate – they would have been schoolboys.

'Sweet Jaysus, is it a vision?' said a gravelly voice on the perimeter of her group, and the boys parted to reveal her old pal, Hector Lafferty. She slipped off her bar stool to embrace him. He'd started out in the business at the same time she did, but never left Dublin, as far as she knew. But he was a good actor, really good. Not quite leading man in looks, and a bit florid with the drink, but she was surprised how warmly she felt towards him when he squeezed her tight, then held her back at arm's length.

'Aren't you a delicious sight! What brings you back to us?'

His surprise at seeing Francesca meant he hadn't heard about her sisters, or had not made the connection. That was a relief, and she drew him close to her side.

'I'm here for some family stuff,' she said, glancing over to the other side of the room, where Madeleine was drinking with a small and rowdy crew. Hector starting telling the surrounding boys some overblown stories about past adventures they'd shared. Two drinks in, a well-groomed man appeared along the bar and acknowledged Hector.

'Damien, come here and meet the belle MacNamara.'

It was the man who had stared at her in the theatre.

He gave her a conspiratorial smile and entered the group, managing to angle his body so that the younger folk were excluded and their triangle was intimate.

'I have been wanting to meet you for the longest time.'

'Damien Foley, new artistic director at the Sackville – Francesca MacNamara, star of stage and screen.' Hector did it as smoothly as a professional voiceover.

'Oh, I *know* who this is,' said Damien. *Gay*, thought Francesca. Not just the intonation, but straight men in Dublin were never that well dressed. At least that was something that had changed since she lived here. The love that dare not speak its name was starting to flower in its natural habitat.

That made her think of Rosaleen, of explaining to her years ago what gay really meant, and Rosaleen saying, 'But not in Ireland. That wouldn't happen in Ireland.'

Rosaleen had no bigotry in her, but she was criminally gullible. The nuns and then her own sister filled her head with such nonsense – guardian angels, visions, and the terrible anxiety of the holy souls in purgatory who personally relied on her for release.

Damien Foley was boasting meanwhile, talking about their coming season, his big plans – revisiting the classics for today, kind of thing. She listened politely, but then she noticed a jealous, sidelong look from Hector and realised that Foley was trying to reel her in, that there might actually be something on offer.

'How long are you staying in Dublin?' he asked.

'I have some family affairs to sort out – it's difficult to say.'

'I can't believe my luck in finding you here.'

She was thinking of what to say when she was distracted by Madeleine's group.

'Go on, so! Let's see ya,' one of the boys was shouting. It felt like he was trying to attract the attention of the rest of the bar to what Madeleine was about to do. Madeleine was overheated-looking, wild-eyed. Francesca dragged her gaze back to Damien.

'My agent would like me back in New York, but you know, I'm needed here.'

'Would you consider meeting me tomorrow to talk about a role in our forthcoming season? I promise you, I would move heaven and earth to have you as part of it.'

Across the room, Madeleine was wriggling around strangely, seemed to have no arms for an instant, then one hand reappeared from a sleeve opening and dipped into the neckline of her dress to pull out her bra. It was black and lacy, and Madeleine twirled it victoriously around her head. The young ones around her applauded, and Daniel turned round to look, during which moment Hector threw Francesca a goggle-eyed *Get you* look.

Behind Madeleine, two of the boys from the show nudged each other, and one made an obscene gesture. Francesca wanted to go over and slap their stupid faces. Her neck felt hot.

Damien was taking her distraction for reluctance.

'At least come for lunch with me, so we can talk about it?'

She turned her full attention on him, gave him the benefit of her eyes. 'That's so kind. Somewhere nice.'

'But of course. You've made my evening.'

Francesca asked if he would like something to drink, and bought two double whiskeys. She handed one to Hector.

'What are you having?' Damien asked.

'I have to go.' Perhaps he might offer Hector something over their enforced drink.

She walked straight over to Madeleine's group and hooked her niece by the elbow.

'It was lovely to meet you all,' she said in her most formal voice, targeting the two leering boys.

'But I just got bought a drink,' Madeleine pouted.

Francesca moved her hand up to Madeleine's armpit and pulled hard. Madeleine protested all the way across the bar and up the stairs.

'I'm not ready to leave!'

'You're making a show of yourself,' Francesca said, through clenched teeth.

When they reached the pavement, she released Madeleine with a small shove and the girl stumbled and fell to her knees. Madeleine looked up at her, astonished, looking ten years old. Looking lost.

Francesca protested, 'It was an accident. I didn't mean it.'

She crouched down to touch her, wiped the grit from Madeleine's small palms, inspected the hole in her tights. They were both crying now. Passing men made a series of lewd offers while they sorted themselves out and got to their feet. She realised it wasn't just Madeleine who had drunk too much. They stood in a doorway while Francesca found some tissues in her bag.

'Did you leave your bra back there?' she asked.

'It's in my pocket. It was just a laugh, don't be uptight.'

'You've no coat.'

'I think it's at the theatre. I'm fine.'

Madeleine set off towards O'Connell Street and Francesca followed a few paces behind. They skirted the Bank of Ireland in silence. The rain had stopped, but the pavements were slick and shiny, car tyres hissing as they passed. At the lights, she linked her arm through her niece's, and Madeleine allowed it. On O'Connell Bridge they stopped and looked upriver towards the Ha'penny Bridge.

'It's a lovely sight,' Francesca found herself saying, though her eyes kept being drawn to the suck of black water against the sludge-covered walls.

Madeleine's breath was coming in little sniffs. Francesca didn't want her to start weeping again.

'This is what's going to happen. I'm going to move into Rowan Grove, and you're going to move in with me. You need to sort yourself out. You need to think about a job that isn't acting – about making a life for yourself.'

'I don't want to do anything else.'

'You need a good sideline, so. Otherwise you'll have no money, no satisfaction, always insecure.'

'Says the woman who lives like a gypsy.'

'I'm staying.'

'Really?'

'Well, until we get everything—'

'So not actually staying, then.'

Madeleine pulled her arm from Francesca's and walked off towards O'Connell Street.

'Wait!'

Francesca caught up with her at the crossing. Even though there were cars barrelling along, Madeleine was trying to find a gap. Francesca grabbed the back of her dress to hold her.

Her niece shook her off, turned with clenched fists. 'You can't just land back here and lay down the law.'

'Don't you want to live somewhere nicer?'

'My flat's great!'

The green man appeared on the crossing, and they stopped arguing to weave across. Once over, Francesca resumed.

'Your flat is freezing. And it smells. Their house is small and neat, and it's *ours*. No rent. We could – I don't know – make something nice together.'

Madeleine squinted at her. 'You're drunk.'

'Honestly, I'm not.'

'I'm starving.' There was a fancy chipper just ahead of them. 'Let's get a burger.'

Francesca shuddered, took hold of Madeleine again and force-marched her up the road. 'I'll make some spaghetti when we get in. Spaghetti and butter and black pepper.'

The walked on for a minute in silence. Then Madeleine said something under her breath.

'What?'

'It's not a good house,' said Madeleine, articulating every word. 'It's a sad house. And they died in it.'

'We can redeem it,' said Francesca, 'do it up.'

And then sell it.

They passed the Gate Theatre.

'I saw you there when I was small,' said Madeleine, 'do you remember?'

'*Deirdre of the Sorrows*. Tough going for a child. Dull, I imagine.'

'It made me want to act. You were my Auntie Fran one minute, and the next you were like this shining goddess.'

'Trick of the light,' said Francesca, trying to laugh it off, but flattered all the same. They passed the Garden of Remembrance, the statue of the Children of Lir lit up in the dark, the children falling to earth while simultaneously transforming into swans – their souls escaping the world, the leaden world.

'I used to fantasise that you were my mother, not Theresa.'

I know, Francesca almost answered. The way little Madeleine would sit close on the sofa the few times she came to visit; how she would take a hold of a strand of Francesca's hair and stroke it, even press it to her own ginger mop, demonstrating their likeness. She took the girl's worship as her due, just sucked it in, as she sucked in the attention of all around her. She used to believe there would always be plenty of attention.

Maybe she *could* stay in Dublin. Be a bit of the mother that Madeleine had fantasised about, give her the benefit of her own hard-won code. She squeezed her niece to her side suddenly, kissed the top of her head and said, 'Let's just stay up and talk tonight.'

'About what?'

'About you. I want to know all the bad stuff that happened at Rowan Grove. I want to make, I don't know … amends.'

'Just so long as you make the spaghetti first.'

18

Swan nodded sporadically, miming attention. The head of the technical department, Eddie McCarthy, had been speaking for a while now, something about 'security caching' and 'predetermined protocols'. Swan couldn't begin to follow it all. Without looking down, he nudged Rosaleen MacNamara's writings further into a desk drawer, closed it with his knee.

The gist of what Eddie was saying was that something had gone wrong with the information recently fed into the databanks, and Eddie not only felt that Swan should be told about this in detail, but seemed to be edging ever so slowly towards a kind of accusation. But, as Swan couldn't really get his head round what was wrong, he was content that he could not be part of the solution. Something about information not being where it was before, and perhaps not being anywhere any more.

'I appreciate being kept up to date, but I have to make some phone calls right now. Could we resume this later?'

Eddie replied with a series of rapid blinks.

'Much appreciated,' said Swan and stood up. His colleague rose from the seat on the other side of the desk, lifting some daunting computer manuals to his chest.

'I'll have to send a report to Superintendent Kavanagh. I don't have a choice in that, you know.'

'Whatever you think necessary.'

Eddie wouldn't accuse him outright, but he was capable of raising a stink. Swan knew he should try and care more. To be suspended from a second department would be careless indeed. If he got moved off the computer project, he could end up somewhere worse, like the drugs squad. He'd have to wear a bomber jacket and hang out in a van in Ballyfermot, making small talk with boastful eejits. Elizabeth would not be thrilled.

The house felt so different with her gone. He found himself lapsing into daydreams, then jumping like a ninny when some little noise disturbed the new silence. Lying in his lonely bedroom, he often thought of Rosaleen MacNamara in hers, somehow unable to escape it. In the small hours, her words ran through his mind in a loop.

Swan lifted the computer keyboard and tucked it to the side of the beige monitor. He took his file of Rosaleen's writings out of the drawer, together with other documents from the house, things that Considine had copied for him. He hated the idea that this case might slip through the cracks, the ill-fitting details simply ignored because there was no obvious violence, because explanations were not affordable, in a budgetary sense. He couldn't return to argue his case with Kavanagh unless he had stronger evidence of coercion or interference. He had even thought of going to the press with the real details, but he would immediately be identifiable as the source.

And so he carried on studying the elusive pages in snatched hours through his mundane days, especially those pages that seemed indecipherable. He had even been to the evidence lock-up to see the originals and, sure enough, each one bore a light indentation of the page above, so it wasn't hard to perfect the rough sequence of her agony. The most difficult pages were when she must have been blind, writing from memory rather than sight, so the letters formed on top of each other. But if you traced the sequence of loops and lines, rather than what it looked like, you could make a guess at the words. Not that the words always added up to sentences. The final pages were snatches of things, fragments. Perhaps dreams or hallucinations.

Swan worried away at it, transcribed his good versions:

> *trees on fire*
> *burn my eyes*
> *Mary, prayers*
> *His face in leaves*
> *green flame leaves*
> *your hand on me*
> *saviour*

Everything guessed at. It looked like poetry, lined up that way. He could have asked a writing expert, if Kavanagh had given them the resources.

The trees outside her window would have dominated Rosaleen's view. Through her failing eyes they could have looked fiery, the summer sun blasting them. Or autumn leaves turning gold? He let his eyes drift out of focus. From his reading of *The Visions of St Catherine of Siena* he knew the sisters were steeped in stories of apparitions brought about through fasting, the possibilities of summoning the elusive Lord. Their decision to stop eating seemed to be linked to this longing for communion. St Catherine was reported to have fasted for what seemed like inhuman periods of time, and had died from lack of food, taking only the consecrated Eucharist for sustenance during her last weeks. She claimed there was a table in heaven set for her. It was the kind of ruinous fairy tale that made Swan's blood boil. To think that nearly every child's head was filled with utter tripe like that, from the day they went to school.

One page was unlike the others, filled with numbers that appeared to be several attempts at the sum $40 \div 7$ with three different answers: 5, 8, 6.2. None of them right and, in the middle of the page, *1st August* was followed by a string of sequential numbers from one to forty.

Forty divided by seven, he guessed, might be a way of working out the fabled time that Jesus fasted in the desert, forty days and forty nights adding up to five weeks and five days. Rosaleen trying to work out what was fatal, what survivable, perhaps. Rosaleen wanted to survive, of that he was sure.

About some point in the ordeal, though – he guessed around two-thirds of the way through – she stopped pleading her case and entered a helpless place of visions, a world where God appeared in the leaves of trees. He turned a page, started to work on a new scribble. The phone rang and he ignored it.

happy mouth

Happy mouth? That's what it seemed to say. Maybe it was happy *month*. He wrote both versions down. The month could be happy because it was the month she would escape to heaven. Had she become resigned to death in the end?

He reached for the copy of O'Keefe's post-mortem notes. He wanted to look again at something that bothered him. Berenice MacNamara had an estimated time of death between 20th and 24th September. But Rosaleen MacNamara's estimate was between 30th September and 5th October. Both were long dead before the niece came knocking in the middle of October, but what accounted for the difference?

When he had first spotted the gap, he went back to O'Keefe, persuading the pathologist to meet him across the river in Mulligan's. The favour was paid for in a round of Islay malt from a dusty bottle. Smelled like TCP to Swan, but that must be his plebeian nose.

'Many factors could account for the discrepancy,' O'Keefe had said. 'One could have had a naturally robust constitution; one might have had more body fat than the other. They might not have started fasting at the same time. Or perhaps the second sister to die had access to some little nourishment that made the difference.'

Some little nourishment. Swan couldn't help thinking of the sucked paws of that stuffed toy they had found in her bed. *Happy mouth.*

They sat in friendly silence for a while, then O'Keefe tipped the last of his whiskey efficiently into his mouth and said, 'I hope we're going to get the chance to continue to work together, Swan.'

'Have you heard otherwise?'

'Your unfortunate suspension is common knowledge, that's all I meant. I hope it doesn't carry on.'

'You and me both.'

He reached for his coat, 'Got to fly. I've one on the slab.'

'You always say that. I know you're just going home for your tea. Regards to Mrs O'Keefe.'

Swan drew out a photocopy enlargement of the Polaroid of the three MacNamara sisters and Madeleine on the doorstep of Rowan Grove, the one from the album.

Rosaleen MacNamara was on the left of the photograph. She would have been in her early forties, but her hair was worn in a young style, long and straight and held back on one side with a clasp. She had a wide smile, but her eyes slid away to the side. One arm twisted behind her, the fingers clamped around the elbow of her opposite arm, the legs torqued in mid-squirm. She was skinny, the way that nervous people often are.

Berenice MacNamara stood solid in the centre of the grouping, with young Madeleine in front of her. She was looking at the photographer with a certain disapproval, as if he or she was taking too long. Francesca, on the right, was gesturing towards the camera, saying something – it could also have been to hurry up.

It was hard to judge Berenice's weight, with the girl right in front of her, but from what he could see – the full face framed by a dark perm, the wide flare of her calves as they rose from her sensible shoes – Berenice MacNamara was a relatively stout woman.

If anyone had the bodily resources to last longer, wouldn't it be Berenice, not Rosaleen? He made a note on

160

his page of notes – *verify usual body weight of sisters*; he should ask the family about that, or even the priest.

Disastrously, the house keys had been handed back to the family. He had tried to get that delayed, hoping the Technical Bureau would turn up something that warranted a proper search. He had gone back alone one evening, just before he had to hand the priest's keys back. He looked into each of the bin bags. They were stuffed with ordinary household items: clothes, books, kitchenware. The things that must have previously occupied the bare cupboards and wardrobes. He resisted searching them – he could see nothing immediately interesting, and it would have no legitimacy, unless Forensics did the job. He abandoned the bags and wandered from room to room, sat again in that little chair by Rosaleen's bed. He even lay down on the carpet near where she was found – thinking about what impulse had made her hide. If someone had asked him what he was doing, Swan might have said he was waiting for something to occur, for something to be revealed. As if the house that had witnessed those long weeks of suffering could explain what it saw.

Now that the family had access, they would be clearing out the place and there was nothing he could do. He wondered if anyone had warned them about the state they would find the house in. The bodies might be gone, but the disarray and debris remained. Those dreadful buckets of evaporated piss.

He had carried them to the bathroom and rinsed them out; at least he would spare them that.

The harsh ring of the phone interrupted his brooding.

'Detective Inspector Swan?'

'Yes.'

'Una Galvin. I'm your new solicitor for the tribunal. Your files have been passed to me, but it would be good to have a little face-to-face, since the hearing is the day after tomorrow. Not that you'll be called, in all likelihood—'

'Could you back up there a bit,' said Swan. 'Where's my usual solicitor?'

'It was decided – by ones higher up than you or I – that separate legal teams for the detectives would be necessary.'

Swan knew that the commissioner had his own legal team and that Superintendent Kavanagh had another, but this seemed extravagantly over-manned, not to say expensive, for a force so concerned with budgets.

'Are you saying that Hannigan, Murphy and I now have three lawyers instead of one?'

'I don't know all the ins and outs' – Swan heard her shuffling quickly through papers – 'which is another reason we should meet. Here … no. Looks like Detectives Hannigan and Murphy will still be represented by James O'Gorman.'

Swan agreed to go to her office in an hour, jotted down the address. A solicitor all of his own, but he wasn't feeling grateful. Some invisible partition was coming down between him and the other two and, as he hadn't initiated it, he was pretty sure he wasn't on the right side.

A blurred figure appeared on the other side of the frosted door, and he stowed away the photograph of the MacNamaras as the glass shook under a rapping knuckle.

The door opened and Considine's face appeared, with a big smile slapped across it. 'How'ya?'

'Not bad. But I think I may have broken the system.'

'Up the revolution, Comrade!'

'What?'

'Joke, boss.'

She unhooked her satchel from her shoulder and took out some folded sheets of paper.

'These came in. I was going to file them, but I figure you deserve an eyeful first. It's the MacNamaras' account statements for the last twelve months – the bank finally sent them through.'

Swan got to his feet as she spread the pages out. It was immediately obvious what had got her excited. In the 'withdrawals' column was a steady patter of figures – £20, £30, £20 – taken from automatic cash dispensers and stretching back to July. The most recent withdrawal was on 14th October, just four days before the bodies were discovered.

'Someone got hold of the Pass card?'

'Must have. It can't be them doing it. I got the codes to identify the machines. See, in July, you have quite a few withdrawals, some from a machine on College Green as well as the one at Phibsborough Cross, which is the nearest one to their house. At the end of July ...' Considine found the place to show him, 'someone took one hundred pounds out of the machine at Phibsborough – that's the top limit. Then the Northside withdrawals stop completely, but the city-centre ones go on, erratically, nothing too big. Do you think someone was getting out money on their behalf?'

'What had they to spend money on? There was a Pass card in a purse in the kitchen, but it was a joint account – there could be two cards on it.'

'One could have got stolen, but it's interesting that the

activity stops when the bodies are found,' said Considine. 'It might be enough for Kavanagh to get interested again.'

'I'm not sure. It could be legit – one of the family, say. I'd guess the niece.'

'Funny you should say that.' Considine ran her finger down the withdrawals column until she came to the right place. 'This is the only withdrawal that's not from a cash machine – eighteen pounds ninety-nine – an item charged in a shop. I got the vendor code from the bank, and it turns out it's a fancy second-hand clothes shop on Drury Street. Jenny Vander. Popular with the young bohemian.'

'That would fit.'

'Should we take the statements to Kavanagh?'

'I don't want to go to him until we have something really strong, and I'm not sure this is it. We need more.'

'I'm up to my eyes with casework.'

'Well, I've a bit of time on my hands. The computer system is down again for some kind of overhaul. Leave it with me.' Swan unhooked his coat from the wall. 'Is it cold out there?'

'Horrible. Where you going?'

'I've got a brand-new solicitor. We're going to get to know one another at her office in town. So I might go have a casual chat with Madeleine Moone while I'm at it.'

Swan put the files in his briefcase and ushered Considine ahead of him through the outer office. Eddie McCarthy was on the phone. He clamped the receiver to his chest and held the other hand up stiffly, as if stopping traffic. Swan waved cheerily, but kept walking, pointing to his briefcase as if it was some kind of explanation.

19

The teaspoon was furred with dust, some sticky substance beneath. Francesca held it towards her nose and breathed in tentatively. Honey. That unmistakeable musky sweetness.

When she had moved the headboard in Rosaleen's bedroom, the spoon had fallen to the carpet, as if it had been tucked inside or behind it. She remembered this spoon from her childhood. It had a little figure of a bear stamped on the tip of the handle.

She looked over at the black bin bag for rubbish and the cardboard box for items to be kept or sold. She couldn't put the spoon in the box without washing it, but it seemed too good to throw out. It shouldn't be this hard to make a simple decision.

Sharp heels came clipping up the stairs and Madeleine appeared, coat on, hair spiked.

'I'm just going back into town.'

'Are you coming back tonight?'

'Tonight? There's nowhere for me to sleep yet.'

'I'll get the servants to hurry up, so.'

'Don't get at me,' said Madeleine, 'I'm late for a thing.'

She popped up on her toes to kiss Francesca's cheek and was gone, the front door slamming in her hasty wake. Francesca hated how she seemed to have taken on the nagging role of Berenice, while Madeleine reverted to adolescence.

She thought that cleaning her sisters' house would be a ritual of redemption, a way to make order, to annihilate sadness. She had gone at it with furious purpose, hired a dodgy-looking man with a van to take away the worst – the armchair from downstairs, Rosaleen's bed, the mound of bin bags, the stacked buckets. She couldn't be in the house with those things. He had left with room in his transit van. She should have made him take Rosaleen's padded bedhead, and the downstairs carpet. And all that furniture in the upstairs room where Madeleine was to sleep. Perhaps she could sell some of that for a little extra cash.

She had been cleaning for three days now – the immersion switched permanently to 'on', a bill that wouldn't come any time soon. She dragged up carpets and took down curtains. Next week she would be starting rehearsals at the Sackville Theatre, dressed in her New York finery. This week she would play the part of a char. It just needed to be got through.

But she kept finding herself sitting on the floor, or gazing at walls, caught up in a fugue of memory, her goals of order forgotten. The house was the wrong kind of quiet, just weird creaks and clicks and the far-off noise of traffic. When she got her first pay packet, she would buy a radio and have that as company, at least.

Damien Foley had bought her a delicious lunch at the Unicorn and offered her the role of Andromache in *The Trojan Women*. When he first mentioned the 'classics', she assumed he meant O'Casey or Wilde, not classical classics.

Euripides, if you please. And rehearsals started in five days. He was not so much bowled over when he met her in the pub, as having a casting panic, she realised, but he did an excellent job of convincing her this was the best result he could have wished for.

Francesca came back to the problem of the teaspoon. She decided to throw it into the rubbish bag. She'd started to do that with things, and it felt good. If she had asked her, Madeleine would have said it was immoral to throw away anything that someone somewhere might have a use for. Madeleine was better at the theory of cleaning than the practice. She spent her visits at Rowan Grove in a restless mood, gazing out of the windows, or running off to the shops on any excuse. Francesca understood that she had bad associations with the place, but she hoped that would pass in time.

At least Madeleine hadn't been here for the priest's visit. He'd heard she had moved in, he said, and offered to bless the house for her. She let him do it, suspecting that the ritual was as much for himself as it was for her, another kind of cleaning. He was an uncomfortable, stumbling kind of man, asking permission for every room he entered, every scatter of holy water from his silver rattle.

'How's your back bearing up?' she asked.

'Oh, I think it just needs rest. I'm very sorry about the … er …'

He turned puce in the face. She hadn't brought it up to embarrass him, she just thought it would be rude not to mention it.

'You should see someone,' she improvised. 'A good

masseur could sort you out. Swedish massage. I see someone in New York who can work miracles with my shoulders.'

Then she was embarrassed that she'd said 'miracles'. After all this time, the clergy still made her nervous. She gabbled on about backs and remedies.

A few hours after the priest, two middle-aged women came calling, one with a woolly turban, the other clutching a Bible. They said they were in her sisters' prayer group, and would she be interested in joining them one evening to pray for the souls of Rosaleen and Berenice? She would not. Thank you. They whispered their condolences and left. They were probably no older than she was, on reflection, but they were dowdy, aggressively modest. Today there had been no callers. May it last.

She hadn't seen Phil since the funeral, and any time she managed to phone from the pub payphone he claimed to be terribly busy. He said he might be able to take some things to the dump for her at the weekend, but he couldn't promise. Something convenient about the car having gearbox trouble.

During her clearing and cleaning, she kept an eye out for bank statements or a copy of the will, but there was nothing, not even an electricity bill. What if they'd been in those bin bags she let go? Perhaps the police had taken them away. Phil said he thought he had some papers 'somewhere' relating to the finances from the sale of the old house, but didn't seem to be doing anything to find them. She wouldn't admit to him that she was flat broke. Wouldn't give him the satisfaction. At least she'd get paid for this play at the Sackville. Only the Equity minimum, despite Damien's talk of prestige, but enough to sustain life.

Francesca sighed and pulled the elastic from her knotted-up hair, shook it out. Maybe Madeleine would never manage to settle in this place, given its bad associations, past and present. Maybe there wouldn't be a little domestic oasis for them here. But she herself would survive it. She would make this situation work for the short term, until the assets could be realised.

Downstairs, the doorbell rang.

She cursed and tiptoed through to the front bedroom, sidled up close to the window so she could see the doorstep below. A man with dark hair, on his own, shifting about in the cold. As if something had alerted him to her presence, he lifted his face and looked straight at her. It was that detective, his quiet face breaking into a smile.

20

She looked so much like that old film poster. Her hair hanging loose over a pale gown, the curtain pulled to the side. A fantasy creature, and yet just another person. That's what he had to remember. Swan wound in his smile and faced the door, waiting for her to come down. Respect. Politeness. A bereaved person who had no idea about the place she'd occupied in his overheated young mind.

'I'm sorry to bother you,' he started, then stopped, newly distracted by the fact that she was undoing the bow of her dress and letting it fall open. But it was just one of those housecoat things. Not a dress at all. She had jeans and a jumper underneath.

'Come in, come in ...' she said. 'Sorry for the state of things.'

'You've been busy.'

The hall carpet was up, and he could see the armchair was gone from the living room.

'If I could, I'd take a flamethrower to the place. Can I get you a coffee?'

Swan made the usual protestations, but she was already heading for the bare kitchen.

'You got rid of all the bin bags?'

'I wasn't sure if it was your colleagues who left them

171

there or my sisters. In either case, I couldn't live with them. Was there something in particular you were looking for?'

She was filling the kettle at the sink. She seemed so much more approachable than at the funeral, smaller too. He noticed she was in her socks.

'Not in particular, no. It's just that ... well, you know the circumstances of your sisters' death were very unusual. There's no evidence that they were subject to any ... er ...'

'Foul play?' She looked at him over her shoulder, raised an eyebrow. 'Sorry. The only detectives I meet are fake ones. I was a murderess on *Quincy* a few years ago. A black widow.'

Swan had no idea what Quincy was. She took his bafflement for discomfort.

'I shouldn't joke. I'm finding it hard to hit the right note with all this.'

'Of course.'

She handed him a mug of coffee and looked distractedly around the kitchen.

'We've no chairs. Why had they no chairs? Come on into the big room.'

A small sofa had been pulled out to face the sliding glass doors in the back wall and ignore the rest of the room. They settled down on it. The coffee was black and unsweetened. She hadn't presented an alternative. He put it down on the floor.

In front of the shelving unit where Swan had looked through the stack of holy magazines and journals there was a new bin bag, half full and gaping. The shelves had been emptied of everything – books and tracts and rudely cavorting wooden animals.

'You're doing a mighty job.'

She glanced at him briefly, unimpressed. He hadn't meant to sound so patronising.

'If you noticed anything odd in your clearing out, I'd like to know. Anything that would help us better understand what lead up to your sisters' deaths.'

'I thought you'd been through everything. You had this place for long enough.'

'Well, we've documented as much as we could, it's just … you might understand if something was out of place better than I would.'

'I understand nothing. That's the truth of it.'

Swan reached down for his mug, took a quick sip and winced.

'It can't have been easy for you, dealing with what was left.'

Francesca shifted into the corner of the settee so that she was turned to him. He had lost her sympathy somehow. He thought of all the men before him who must have been shrivelled by that cool stare.

'They gave me the impression the investigation was closed. Is this some kind of condolence visit?'

'Actually I'm looking for your niece. No one was in at her flat. I called your brother and he said she was staying here now.'

'Well, she will be, but this isn't homey enough for her yet.'

'So she's still at the flat?'

'What did you want her for?'

Swan watched a tabby cat walk along the top of the fence

separating the garden from next door. He waited until it disappeared over the old back wall before he decided on his answer.

'Someone was withdrawing money from your sisters' joint account – almost up until we found them. There's no report of a stolen card, but one was being used at an automatic cash machine. I thought perhaps Madeleine might have some idea.'

'I'll check with my niece.' Although Francesca's voice was even and gracious, her nostrils flared briefly.

'Thank you,' said Swan, standing. 'Do you still have my telephone number, so she could—'

'How much?' Francesca remained sitting on the settee. 'How much is left in the account after all these withdrawals?'

'I can't say.'

'You can't say. My brother won't say. What a load of crap.'

'It wasn't what I was looking at. I honestly don't remember the exact figure.'

'Ballpark?' The angrier she got, the more American she sounded. She stood up to face him.

'I'm sure your brother, as executor, can get the balance.'

'My brother, *as executor*, can't even find a copy of the bloody will.'

'I think it was a four-figure sum – low four figures.'

'No. There must be another account.'

She bent down and picked up his coffee mug, clashed it together with her own and stomped on soft feet to the kitchen. Swan waited a moment, searching his pockets for another business card. He cupped one in his palm and scribbled his home number on it. When Francesca came back, he offered it to her.

'I've added my home number. I'd like to talk to Madeleine, this weekend if possible. I'm just nearby, I can see her whenever suits.'

Francesca waved it away. 'We don't have a phone here. There was a phone, apparently, but my sisters cancelled the account. The company says I'll have to wait six months. I told them all the wiring is here, all they have to do is flick a switch or something, but they said it didn't make a difference, that there's a waiting list. Every day that I'm home I remember why I left.'

Swan wrote his address under his number. 'Do you know Prospect Square? Beside the Glasnevin side gate?'

'The Gravediggers' pub?'

Swan smiled. 'That's the one. I live across from it. Number twenty-seven. I've a telephone you're welcome to use, if you need.'

'Does that not go above and beyond the call, Vincent?'

'Sure, we're practically neighbours. Do ask Madeleine to get in touch.'

She took the card, put it in her pocket, then pushed her fingers back through the hair, gathered it all up in a twist and transferred an elastic band from her wrist to her hair with a quick snap, like a magic trick. She laid a hand on his sleeve.

'There's a little thing you could help me with.'

She had cleaned out Rosaleen's bedroom. The holy pictures, the frail chair, the bed, the strewn tissues – all gone. Another half-full black plastic bag squatted under the window.

'I was going to let Madeleine have this room, but now she says she doesn't want it, but the third room is so small. And full of old crap.'

A late sunbeam lit up the window and she moved her face towards the light, closed her eyes. He noticed the lilac swipes of tiredness under them.

'I know you were here just after they were found,' she said, holding her face still and blind. 'The priest mentioned it. I keep thinking I'm going to ask you what it was like – what you saw. But then I realise I don't really want to know.'

'I don't think knowing would help. Or that anything I could tell you would make a difference to your loss.'

Francesca took a breath, blew it out loudly and opened her eyes.

'It's this headboard. It should have gone with the bed, but it got forgotten. Could you help me move it downstairs?

'I can probably manage it myself,' said Swan.

Francesca nodded her thanks and left the room. He regarded the headboard for a minute, the last relic of what happened. There were slits worn in the material and a dark stain where a head had rubbed against it over the years. When he tipped it away from the wall, he could see how crudely the material was stapled onto the chipboard beneath. He squeezed the padding here and there, just in case anything was concealed inside. Of course there was nothing, he was clutching at straws. He wrestled it out the door and crab-walked his way downstairs with it.

Under Francesca's instruction, he left it outside on the patio, resting under the kitchen window.

'I'm sorry to use you this way,' she said, beside him. 'Can I make it up to you with another coffee? Or I might have the last of some duty-free somewhere.'

Her face was as open as a friend's now. On the other side of the old wall the big trees hissed as a sudden gust moved through their branches. Francesca hugged herself.

'C'mon in or we'll freeze.'

He should have taken that chance to leave, but found himself watching as she filled the kettle, switched it on, then got out two glasses and poured generous measures of Rémy Martin. She led the way back into the living room, the kettle ignored.

'Did you know there was anything wrong – with your sisters?'

She flopped down on the settee, raising a small eruption of dust that swirled in the light from the window. Swan decided to stay standing.

'I knew they weren't totally happy – I mean, who is? They were none too keen to leave our old house in Fairview, but it was impossible and big, and money was such an issue. It had a huge garden, a jungle by the time they moved out, but sellable as a building plot. This house was practical for them, and not too far out of the old neighbourhood. The money we got was put in a special account, for them to live on. One hundred thousand pounds. A fortune.' Francesca frowned. 'They must have put the bulk of it in a savings account, that would explain it ...'

'Did your sisters work?'

'Rosaleen helped out with a charity when they lived in Fairview, but Berenice never worked. She was capable enough, more so than Rosaleen, but she clung to the idea that our mother needed her. Then when Mam died, Berenice said she was too old to go out and get a job. She didn't want to, or she was scared underneath all her bluster. I used to think the holiness was just a handy barrier against the world.'

'Do you think Rosaleen was intimidated by Berenice? Would she obey her in any circumstance?'

'Rosaleen was soft. Berenice could play her like a violin, so yes – I'm afraid to say – yes.'

Swan felt strangely dejected by her answer. Rosaleen hadn't stood a chance.

'You helped them move into this house?'

She looked at him sharply. 'Don't *you* know a lot? Yes, I packed them up and put them down here. It was quite an operation. And here I am again, moving around the same old stuff. You'll think me very cold-hearted.'

Swan shrugged. 'I'm not your judge, Ms MacNamara. And I've seen grief take many forms.'

'I don't know if this is grief, *Mister* Swan. I think it might be rage.' But Francesca's voice was soft and sorrowful.

He sat down on the end of the settee at last, watched her take out a cigarette and light it. They sat in a silence that he couldn't decide the nature of – companionable perhaps, or awkward. They looked out at the garden, not each other.

'This house is too quiet,' said Francesca eventually and twisted around, craned to see the clock on the mantelpiece.

He took the hint, finished his brandy and stood up. When she opened the front door to show him out, the street lights were flickering on, though it was only four o'clock. An annual surprise, how quickly the dark took over the day.

'Do get your niece to call me.'

She nodded, holding her body against the door edge.

'Or if there's anything more I can help you with ...' he said, and immediately wished he hadn't.

Francesca tilted her head slightly, a flicker of curiosity.

'Appreciated.'

She began to close the door.

'Your sister – Rosaleen – was she quite thin?'

She narrowed her eyes.

'I mean normally, compared to Berenice.'

'Yes, she was thin; always on the go, you know, fidgety. Why?'

'Just ... trying to figure something out. Sorry. I didn't mean to keep you in the cold.'

'Bye, so.'

She closed the door quickly, before he even had time to turn away.

21

The clinic was not as medical-looking as Father Timoney had hoped. It was down in the basement of a building on Mountjoy Square, and the *Executive Health Spa and Sauna* sign by the door was grubby. The window displayed a vase of pink plastic roses and a ruched blind. He looked again at the address he'd written out from the Yellow Pages, clutching the railings to ease some of the pain in his back.

If he turned round and got the bus back to Deerfield, he would have gained nothing. He picked his way down the narrow iron steps.

The reception area was as feminine as the window display. Gilt-framed mirrors all over the walls, bouncing the light around. A woman with a cloud of curly hair and a tight white coat stood behind a counter that was a bit like a cocktail cabinet. He would have felt happier if the place looked more like a doctor's.

'I booked an appointment for my back. A Swedish massage.' He clung to the phrase Francesca MacNamara had uttered, even though he didn't understand what it entailed.

'Lovely, Father,' the woman said. She pointed at an empty row of chairs. 'Claudia will be with you in a minute.'

'Sorry … I was just wondering. Do you not have any

male masseurs?' As he spoke it, the word 'masseur' became suddenly lurid. He should have gone to the doctor, but the MacNamara woman, who seemed to know a lot about backs, told him doctors would only give you painkillers; that what he needed was direct treatment. It had sounded so sensible then. The receptionist was giving him a wary look. He wished now he had dressed in ordinary clothes, but to have hidden his priesthood would have made this whole thing even more furtive.

'Oh, no,' she said. 'Oh no. We don't do that kind of thing.'

He never imagined that being treated by a woman would seem more innocent than seeing a man. But then he realised what she was implying, that to want the hands of a man on your flesh was bordering on the homosexual. He started to sweat. The heating was quite tropical, the window fogged with condensation.

He didn't know if he could make it back up those steps. The spasm in his back was worse than ever. He went and leaned against a wall near the chairs, looked at his shoes, tried to think about Jesus allowing his feet to be washed and anointed by prostitutes. Tried to find some biblical rationale for what was about to happen.

Claudia, when she emerged, was very young, perhaps a teenager, broad in the shoulders and the hips, straggles of blonde hair escaping from some kind of bun. She too wore some kind of tight white overall. She led him to a small room with a high narrow bed in it. Her accent was flat Dublin, despite her exotic name.

'How long have you been, er, treating people, Claudia?'

'I got my diploma two years ago, Father,' she said, cracking a morsel of gum between even teeth. The word 'diploma' calmed him slightly.

'The problem is my lower back. I've been to the doctor about it, a few years ago, and he said it wouldn't hurt to lose a couple of stone, heh-heh … but I'm standing a lot, on concrete floors. I think that doesn't help.'

Claudia did not appear to engage with this explanation, busy folding towels and adjusting the lighting dimmer. She turned on a little cassette player and some warbly flute music ushered forth. His dismay must have shown in his face and she said, 'You don't like it, Father?'

'There's no need for music.'

'Some people find it helps them relax.'

'Very thoughtful of you, dear, but no.'

'Okay, so. You just pop off your things and I'll be back when you're ready.'

She left the room before he could clarify how many clothes he should shed and how she would know he was ready. He took off his jacket, his pullover, his stock and collar, his shirt and, in a moment of bravery, his vest. He would have liked to have kept his trousers on, but realised the belt and all would probably interfere with her being able to work on his sacrum. Not that he had high hopes for this treatment. Her youth, the hair-salon atmosphere of the place. And yet some sense of politeness, or futility, made it impossible for him to leave. He couldn't pick his trousers off the floor even, had to just brush them under a chair with his foot.

He left his underpants on and his socks, wiped the towel

quickly over his sweat-dampened skin and worked his painful way to a lying position on the narrow bed with the towel pulled over him like a blanket. He waited. She would want to get at his back, though. He should be lying on his stomach. When he tried to turn over, he couldn't. He was stuck there, a fat flounder.

The door opened and Claudia came in.

'All right, Father?' she said in a whisper.

'I should be lying on my front,' he said, and found that his voice was shaky. She came close, looked down for a moment, then slid her arms under him. Her face close to his towel-covered belly, which loomed like a hill.

'Try now,' she said, and rolled him over in one quick move. He wiggled into position, but the towel was trapped beneath him. He could feel air blowing over his exposed back and legs. No one had seen his skin since … he couldn't remember. It was so hot in this room.

Claudia was slipping his socks off. The way the material slid over his heels, the feel of her fingers brushing past the sensitive arches, sent him into a whirl of panic. He shut his eyes tight.

Swimming down at Brittas Bay as a seminarian – that was the last time he'd been half naked in front of other people. They had driven out to the coast one Saturday, a gang of them. He forced his mind to go there, to that merrier time, away from this small room with the girl pulling a sheet over his legs and bottom now, but leaving his back naked. Those big waves, and how he and his friends jumped up to meet the peak of each one, the way the water would carry you back until your feet hit the sand again, jumping up into the sun and the diamond spray of water, laughing and horsing around with the lads. Your young body doing just as you bid it to.

There was an odd noise in the room, squelching. He opened his eyes just enough to make out Claudia rubbing something on her hands, some lotion that smelled of lavender. Her clothing brushed his shoulder and her slippery hands came down on his back, stroking over his tired skin, making paths of heat wherever they went. An anointing. She was stronger than he imagined she would be, her palms smoothing long lines on either side of his spine. He tried to breathe, to accept, to calm the rushing in his head. He tried to focus on the memory of the waves at Brittas, rising and falling in their endless rhythm. He felt he was slipping from consciousness.

She moved up to ply the triangle of muscle at the base of his neck, edging into sore places, probing about.

A hiccup rose in his throat, become a squeak. Then sobs, and warm water running from his eyes. And the noise was just awful, his own spasmodic *uh-uh-uh*. Tears softened the blue paper sheet beneath him, turning it dark. It was the most mortifying thing, and he couldn't stop doing it.

'Do you want a little time to yourself, Father?' asked Claudia, leaning forward, her breath minty.

He nodded his head.

The door closed, allowing him to give himself up to this river of self-pity, but no more tears came, just the awful image of the woman in the armchair, the cadaver in winter clothes. It must have been something to do with where the girl had touched him, a cyst of horror hidden in his neck muscles.

Outside in the reception area he could hear Claudia speaking with someone, then muffled laughter.

By the time she came back, he had managed to get most of his clothes on.

'But I've hardly started on you,' the girl said.

'Don't worry, I'll pay the full amount. If you could hand me my trousers, I'd be very grateful.'

'You shouldn't be embarrassed, you know; that kind of thing happens all the time.'

Timoney turned away from her to fasten his cuffs and get his jacket.

'Some people just aren't used to being touched.' She reached for his hand and cupped it in both of hers. She had shiny pink nails, something shimmery under the glassy surface. For a moment he was transfixed by them. 'You're only human, Father.'

'I thought this was a medical place,' he said, taking his hand back. 'I don't need some kind of beauty treatment.'

The girl shrugged. 'Suit yourself. You know where we are, if you change your mind.'

It was only when he was on the bus back to Deerfield that he noticed his back felt much better.

22

Damien had told her that the journalist wouldn't ask about her sisters' deaths, but Francesca didn't trust his judgement on that. There had been next to nothing in the papers, but in Dublin everyone knew things they weren't supposed to, especially journalists. She took a balled-up tissue from her pocket and swiped at the condensation on the bus window, trying to distinguish where they were in the darkness.

If *The Irish Times* interviewer asked, she would say she didn't want to speak about it, that it was too recent. Or she could lead them back to what they should be talking about, by saying that her bereavement brought perspective to a play about catastrophic loss. No. Too callous, it would sound like she was benefiting from her sisters' deaths. Being honest was out of the question; being honest would mean saying that she didn't give a damn for Euripides, but she needed something to do, something to get her out of that house, someone else's words filling her mouth and mind. A pay packet at the end of the week.

She would be as modest as a Quaker with the interviewer, yes. Tell them that she saw herself as a craftswoman, not a star; that she relished riding buses, staying anonymous, observing life at the level of the everyday. Like that man across the aisle in the cheap business suit, drunk and asleep, his hair gel smearing the window glass as he nodded into the night.

She should mention the other women, say how good it was to be part of a strong female ensemble. Two stunning young ones were playing Helen and Cassandra. Flat stomachs, oiled joints. At least she hadn't been offered the eldest role, Hecuba. That was being played with unnerving intensity by Eilís Ni Gríofa, a character actress who looked like an ancient imp. She was currently playing an itinerant matriarch in some important RTÉ drama and was the reason all the rehearsals had to be held at night.

Even with a spot of window cleared, the grime on the outside made it difficult to see out. The bus could be barrelling across blasted plains of the Underworld, down towards the Styx.

But the green neon of the Deerfield Inn appeared through the murk, and Francesca rose to ring the bell, reaching over to poke the sleeping man as she passed. She crossed the car park and walked up Rowan Grove, thinking of the bath she would have, with her script and a brandy. She was surprised to see a light in the front window.

Bags filled the hall, and she had to step over them to get into the living room. Madeleine was sitting on the rug in front of the electric fire, and a young man with a mop of curly hair and very long legs sat on the little sofa.

Madeleine jumped to her feet. 'We've been waiting ages for you. This is my friend Harrison, from Trinity. Harrison, my Aunt Francesca. In the flesh!'

The boy unwound his legs and rose. A fan. She could tell by his unwavering gaze.

'Can I say what a pleasure this is,' he began.

'I'm sure you can, but why don't you let me sit down first – it's been a long day.'

The boy surrendered the sofa, settled at her feet. They really did need to get more furniture. Madeleine went off to the kitchen to make some tea. Francesca made sure not to smile at Madeleine; they needed to have words.

'When I tell my parents I met you,' Harrison was saying, 'they just won't believe it. My mother is such a fan of yours. And it's so exciting to hear you're doing *The Trojan Women*. I wrote an essay on it last term, I'm doing Classics with English.'

'They must be so pleased.'

'Of course there are so few plays with prime roles for women,' he said, his expression sympathetic.

Madeleine came back with three mugs of tea. For a long minute they blew on their mugs and smiled up at her.

'Harrison helped me carry all my bags out here,' Madeleine said.

'I thought I'd be able to borrow my mother's car, but she had other ideas.'

'You must make sure you don't miss your last bus, then,' said Francesca.

'Oh, I don't mind walking.'

'All the same, it is late. But I'd love to talk another time. You must visit us again.'

Harrison, who was obviously a well-brought-up lad, took another quick gulp from his mug, then abandoned it. After whispered goodbyes on the doorstep, Madeleine reappeared.

'I can't believe you were so rude to him.'

Francesca sipped her tea and held Madeleine's eye.

'What?' said Madeleine.

'*I* can't believe that you disappear for days, then just land up here with all your junk, without letting me know you were coming. Manners run both ways, girl.' *Girl*. That's what her mother used to call her when she was in a temper.

Madeleine stiffened and took a step back. 'There's no phone to ring to say I'm coming; what do you expect – a bleeding telegram? And Harrison helped me move my stuff, which you didn't, and then you were really horrible to him. You asked me to come and live with you. I've given up a great flat – and you know I don't even like it here.'

The air between them seemed to shimmer.

Francesca patted the cushion beside her. 'I'm tired. It's been a long evening of weeping and wailing in the ruins of Troy. Come sit down. Let's start again.'

Madeleine sat down, not on the settee, but on the rug.

'You don't get to kick my friends out. You said this would be my home.'

Francesca hadn't handled this well.

'It will be. We just need to sort out some things. I've moved the furniture out of the smallest bedroom and made up a bed for you there. It's a start.'

Madeleine's expression softened, her anger ebbing. She nodded quickly, hugged her mug in both hands. She was still so much a child. Francesca needed to be cautious with the next bit.

'The police were here earlier, Maddy.'

'Do you think there's enough space in that room for

a bigger bed? I hate a single bed now – I like to stretch.'
Madeleine looked up at the ceiling, as if calculating the
size of the room through it.

'Listen. This is something we need to talk about.'

Madeleine's eyes slid back to engage with Francesca, but
her head remained averted.

'They say someone's been taking money out of Berenice
and Rosaleen's bank account.'

There was a tiny giveaway pause before her niece reacted.

'What do you mean?'

'Someone with one of those Pass cards. Taking out
money from cash machines. It couldn't have been your
aunts, for obvious reasons. What do you know about that?'

'Me? Nothing.'

A blotch of red had appeared on Madeleine's pale
throat.

'If you really want to make a career out of acting, you're
going to have to do better than that.'

Madeleine put her mug down. 'You can be a total bitch,
you know.'

'Oh, I know. How much did you take?'

'Rosaleen gave me the card.'

'How much?'

'She was worried about me. She thought it was unfair,
all of you setting up the fund just for them and cutting me
out of everything.'

'They weren't able to make a living. You are.'

'I didn't get much choice. I was kicked out on the street
at sixteen. Anyway, what do you care how much?'

Francesca felt so much like jumping up to shake

Madeleine that she found herself holding onto the sofa arm.

'The money was for them – I don't have a card, Phil doesn't have a card. It's not up to you to decide to siphon it off for your own pleasures.'

'I have nothing. You're well off, and Phil's got his job.'

'Ho! Well off, am I? You've no idea how precarious a real actor's life is.'

Madeleine got to her feet then, holding herself as formally as a tiny soldier.

'You think I can't act.'

'This isn't about your talent. I need to know how much you took. Is it drugs you're on? Is that it?'

Madeleine didn't answer, but stayed standing.

Francesca felt disadvantaged, but, if she stood too, it would escalate further. 'At least tell me how much is left. And I want that bank card back.'

Madeleine nodded her head slowly, knowingly. 'So you can stick your nose in the trough too. Like the way you've taken over this house. *I've made up the smallest room for you, Maddy.* You're really pulling my heartstrings.'

'I'm not sure you have any heartstrings. Not only were you taking their money – you were doing it while they were alone here, starving or sick. Where were you? Why did you not notice what was happening?'

Madeleine's hands were trembling, her face pale.

'Where were *you*? Where was Phil? I'm the only one who noticed!'

Madeleine rushed out of the room, slammed the door, then a thunder of feet on the stairs. Francesca's whole body was flushed with heat. She got to her feet and went into the kitchen, ran the cold tap and took a drink of water. Well, that went well. The conversation she had envisaged was calm and reasoned, with Madeleine tearfully confessing to some minor spending. What if she'd spent the lot? There were tens of thousands in that account four years ago. There should be most of that left, surely.

No further noise came from upstairs. Madeleine had probably thrown herself on the bed in a sulk. Francesca had never seen her in a temper. Had never seen any of the wildness that Berenice used to complain about in the girl.

She took out her script and went over her entrance speech. She wanted it all in her head by Monday. She paced up and down the long room, one ear out for Madeleine's foot on the stair.

When she finally headed for bed, she tripped over Madeleine's bags again in the dark hallway. So inconsiderate. She picked up one, a squashy nylon sausage, and lugged it up the stairs. She flung open the door of the small bedroom and just threw it into the dark, waiting for Madeleine's response, but nothing came. She looked in and the bed was empty, the lovingly arranged covers undisturbed.

Francesca turned and opened the door of Rosaleen's room, but Madeleine wasn't there, either. The moon glinted off the stacked furniture that she had spent all morning moving to make room for her niece. The rolled-up carpet looked sinister on the dusty floorboards, like a wrap for a body. She shut the door quickly, and the bathroom door wavered in the draught.

'Madeleine?'

But she wasn't there, either. Francesca was alone in the house again.

23

Swan was on his way back from the garage shop with a carton of milk when a car door swung open in front of him, blocking the pavement. He stepped back smartly, checking no one was coming up behind, tightening his grip on his front-door keys. But the head that emerged from the car was T. P. Murphy's, and Ownie Hannigan popped up on the other side of the vehicle.

'Jaysus, look at your face,' said Murphy. 'Did you think your time was up?'

'Don't be mocking,' said Hannigan. 'Sure them's the instincts of a fighter, I'd be the same myself.' He clenched his fists loosely in front of his face and boxer-skipped heavily around the back of the car so that Swan was flanked.

'What can I do for you, lads?'

'You could offer us a sup of tea,' said Murphy, looking at the milk in Swan's hand. Hannigan nodded towards Swan's house, two doors down. They already knew which one was his.

'Now's not the best time. Sorry.'

'Oh, say no more.' Hannigan tapped the side of his nose with his finger. 'Young wife, late lie-in. Am I right?'

'I think this milk is starting to curdle. What was it you wanted?'

They moved in closer, Hannigan stretching out an arm to grab an arrow of a railing behind Swan's head.

'Look,' he said, 'you know they've given us separate solicitors, and we just wanted to tell you it wasn't our doing.'

'No, it wasn't,' said Murphy.

'Whose doing was it?' said Swan, keeping his voice mild, unbothered.

'Well, it's the lawyers, isn't it, making jobs for themselves. They're saying that because we were together during most of the interview, and you just came in for a brief spell, like, that our interests are – what did they call it, T. P.?'

'You know, conflict-of-interest kind of thing.'

'I thought a united front was the way we were going,' said Swan.

'Totally united, brother. No question. Among ourselves, of course we are. This is just legal complications.'

They were waiting to see how Swan absorbed this. He reached out for the edge of the car door and closed it, bumping Murphy out of the way with his arm while he did so.

'I appreciate you coming out to explain it. Good to know we're all on the same page.'

Swan walked on, looked back as he turned at his gate. They were standing shoulder-to-shoulder on the pavement, watching. Tweedledum and Tweedledumber. The tragedy was that they thought themselves wily.

'See you in court!' shouted Hannigan cheerily.

Swan put the milk on the kitchen counter, and the cat jumped up to be near it, landing soft and silent. He took a saucer from the cupboard and poured some out. Benny hunkered down and lapped with mechanical enthusiasm.

'What are they up to, Benny? What's the game?'

He put the coffee pot on the gas ring to reheat. He'd had it ready before discovering there was no milk. The house did not run itself in Elizabeth's absence.

If it really had been the lawyers' idea for Swan to have different representation, Hannigan and Murphy would never have bothered to come and tell him. They never did a tap more than the essential. A trip to the Northside on a Saturday morning was exertion indeed. Therefore they had something to gain by the new arrangement. He knew he was isolated within the department, socially speaking, but the ties between Guards were usually strong enough when the threat came from outside. Perhaps he had let himself get too cut off – he couldn't even think of anyone he trusted enough to find out what was really going on. He trusted Considine, but she was new and had little influence.

The coffee started to seethe and bubble. Every little noise seemed amplified without Elizabeth here.

He poured his coffee and brought it to the front room, the room they jokingly referred to as 'the music room', as it was half full of grand piano. It was the room Elizabeth practised in and taught a series of diffident schoolchildren.

It had proved an ideal place to lay out the photocopies of Rosaleen MacNamara's writing – on the piano cover, the long coffee table and over the cushions of the green sofa that no one ever sat on.

Though he hadn't managed to speak to Elizabeth for days, the message she'd left on the answering machine made it sound like she was enjoying herself down in Wexford, her voice hasty with excitement.

He stood and sipped his coffee, surveying the pages. Maybe the space and quiet were not so bad after all. He didn't miss the vague sense of guilt that ran through their usual weekends, either because he was working when she wanted him not to be, or because they weren't making the best of their brief free time when he was there. Too much DIY and shopping, too little running through summer meadows. Out of the corner of his eye, he noticed Benny slip in and go sit on the windowsill to keep watch on the outside world.

He had all day to think about Rosaleen MacNamara. His latest idea was to transcribe everything in the writings that referred to an outside presence – gods, angels, voices, what have you – and try and work out if it was all hallucination or if there was any definite interaction with her sister, or with someone else.

But now his mind was distracted with the question of DeBarra.

Two hours was all he had spent with the man. DeBarra hadn't looked like an obvious thug; he was small, fair-skinned, with sparse hair worn to his shoulders and wire-rimmed spectacles. A bit like a junior university lecturer, not someone who had packed a transit van with Semtex and parked it outside the chip shop in a small Protestant town. When it went up, it took the lives of two teenage sweethearts and the woman behind the counter, along with the British soldier who had come to collect his company's dinner orders.

Usually paramilitaries didn't utter a word during questioning, but DeBarra talked up a storm. Not about the bombing, but about freedom and Marxism, about how his questioners had let themselves become puppets of state oppression. Every simple question elicited a sociology lecture. And DeBarra had not let up even when a Guard brought them cups of teas and ham sandwiches. He wouldn't touch the food, started talking about the ill-treatment of pigs. Mainly to enjoy the repetition of saying 'pigs' in front of two police, Swan had thought. DeBarra was one of those guys who thought himself a bit of a genius. Give him enough rope and he'd incriminate himself. But Swan hadn't taken him for someone who would confess. He should have paid more attention when Hannigan and Murphy had triumphantly produced a signed confession the next day.

If anyone was being worn down in those interviews, it was the detectives, not DeBarra. It was curious, that gesture of forgoing the sandwiches, but consistent with what Swan knew of ideologues, placing themselves above the realm of the grumbling belly.

Wasn't it a similar higher purpose that fuelled the fasting of Berenice MacNamara? People separating themselves from the needs of their bodies, their animal nature. And, having separated themselves, they were freer to do damage.

Two of Rosaleen's most wretched letters had been found among the Bibles and prayer books that lay beside the downstairs armchair … *I don't want to do this any more, please. I find that I love this world, and the God that put me here* … Berenice had known of her sister's desire to live, had read her words and done nothing.

As he reached for a page, he heard the squeak of the gate and saw Benny sit up on his hunkers, attentive. Swan moved out of sight of the window, hovered in the doorway to look down the hall. A slight figure appeared on the other side of the glass panels, an unmistakeable rusty colour to her hair. Even though he expected it, the ring of the doorbell made him jump.

Francesca MacNamara was wearing a long green coat, tight at the waist. Her hair was tied into a bunch at the side of her neck with a trailing ribbon. She looked like something out of a ballad.

'You did say it was all right to call round – I hope you meant it.'

'Of course, come in, you're very welcome.'

'If I could use your phone a minute?'

He showed her to the little cubbyhole beneath the stairs with the shelf for the telephone and the low basketweave stool.

'Cosy,' she said.

'I'm just making some coffee,' he offered, an excuse to leave her alone to make her call.

'That would be wonderful.'

As he opened a new paper filter and loaded it with coffee grounds, he kept an ear tuned to her voice. He couldn't hear the words, but her tone was sharp, turning defensive. The call didn't last long. She appeared in the kitchen before the kettle had boiled.

'Take a seat,' he said, 'and apologies for the mess.'

She flicked her eyes about the newly painted kitchen, the pretty dresser lined with folksy plates and bowls. The oilcloth on the table was covered with crumbs and dirty dishes.

She didn't sit, but drifted over to the back door, looking out of its window at the twiggy shrubs and litter of fallen leaves. She touched the tips of her fingers to the glass and sighed, as if nature depressed her.

Swan cleared the table and swiped a dishcloth quickly across it while her attention was averted.

Francesca shrugged her coat from her shoulders, draped it over a chair and wandered over to inspect an old calendar on the wall. He wished she would settle. She took a wooden box off a dresser shelf and casually looked inside.

'That was my brother I was phoning. He's very unreasonable. Always has been. Do you have siblings, Vincent?'

'No. I'm an only child.'

'That's rare enough in Dublin.' She tilted her head and smiled at him, putting the box back in its place.

'I think there was something – medical – that prevented my mother having children after she had me.' He couldn't credit how quickly they had got on to his mother's reproductive troubles.

'Oh, I'm sorry.'

'Nothing to be sorry about.'

'I guess not. You had all their attention. There were five of us, I suppose you know that. Four girls, then finally the longed-for boy.'

'Where's your other sister?'

'Theresa died in 1969. She got pregnant with Madeleine when she was twenty-one. A much older man. Her first boss. Married, of course. Oh, the scandal. Mam kind of took over the baby, kept it in the family, but never forgave Theresa. She wouldn't let her have any say in Maddy's upbringing. It was impossible for her, so she ran off. Got in with a bad crowd in London. We never established if the overdose was accidental or deliberate. I was in California by then. Phil was gone too. He married young. The only thing we ever had in common was the instinct to leave home.'

Swan busied himself with the coffee-making, letting her talk on.

'Phil's always been conventional; Theresa was the wild one. Berenice was the saint, and Rosaleen tried to keep us as sweet as she was.' Francesca laughed in a slightly forced way.

Swan handed her a mug of coffee.

'And what were you?'

'I was *full of myself*. Sinfully vain, possessing *notions*. Wouldn't you think, though, with all that's happened, that Phil and I could get along?'

She pulled out a chair and sat sideways to the table. Seeing her in his kitchen was very odd. Swan brought a little glass jug of milk to the table, took a seat opposite her.

'How pretty,' Francesca said, touching one of the flowers etched into the jug. 'Is Mrs Vincent about?'

For a moment he didn't know what to say.

'My wife's working in Wexford at the moment. The house is very much her taste. She's here more than I am, so it matters that she likes it.'

'What would you go for, Vincent, left to your own devices – racing stripes and chrome bumpers?'

202

'Gentleman's club, perhaps.'

'Very upmarket.'

He smiled. 'I have my pretensions.'

They sipped at their coffee for a time.

'You've been so kind to me already …' she said, and he knew there was something she wanted beyond the phone call. 'To be honest with you – to be absolutely, shamefully honest with you – I'm flat broke. I was asking Phil there if he could advance me a loan, and do you know what he said?'

Swan shook his head.

'He said he was being generous – *generous!* – letting me stay in the house for nothing. Our family house!'

'I thought you were working.'

'Oh, that. It's just a three-week run. It'll buy a few groceries, but that's all. I really need to know when things will get resolved at your end, so we can move on with sorting their estate.'

'We need to understand what happened.'

'I was told they starved themselves. What more is there? Isn't that horror enough?'

Swan avoided her eyes. 'That's not something that happens. In the normal run of things.'

'Of course, of course. But it's all going to take an age, and I just need to understand … what you said about the bank account – it came as a shock. There should be more money than a couple of thousand or whatever. Was there not another account or – I don't know – shares or something?'

'That's one of the things I want to understand.'

'Surely the police have ways?'

'Our focus is on the forensics evidence at the moment.' He didn't want to admit how little was going on. 'But I'll see what I can do. Personally. Though I'm particularly interested in these small amounts of money being taken out up until September.'

'I've sorted that one for you.' Her voice was bitter.

'Oh?'

'It was Madeleine, but you suspected that already, didn't you? She says Rosaleen gave her the Pass card. I was livid. That account was supposed to last the rest of Bernie and Rosie's lives.'

The balance Swan had seen wouldn't have lasted out the year, no matter how frugal the sisters were. Had someone been defrauding them? He would have to get hold of the bank statements for that whole period since they sold the old house. Follow where the money went.

Francesca placed her upturned hands on the table. It was an odd gesture, and he wondered if she had used it in a play once.

'Please,' she said, her eyes steady on his, 'how much did Madeleine take?'

'What I saw was pretty minor stuff. Around three hundred pounds in all.'

She drew in her arms and blinked. 'That's all? You made it sound worse.'

'I'd still like to talk it through with Madeleine – I could come round and see her now.'

Francesca pushed her coffee mug away in an impatient gesture. 'She's gone back to her flat. We had a fight.'

'About the bank card?'

'It's not about the money, it's about … trust.' Francesca got quickly to her feet. 'I've kept you long enough.'

She swept out into the hall. Swan could feel a headache coming on, pulsing lightly behind his right temple. He followed her. She was turning on the spot, looking for something.

'Your coat,' he said, and went back to the kitchen. As he lifted it off the back of a chair, warm and heavy in his arms, it gave off a dusty perfume.

He carried it out to the hall, but she wasn't there. The door to the front room lay open and she was standing beside the piano, looking down on Rosaleen's writings, her hands clamped to her mouth. He grabbed her and steered her firmly out of the room. She leaned against the wall while he picked up the dropped coat. Tears ran from under her closed lids.

When he handed her the coat, she buried her face in it. He felt he should put his arms round her; he also felt he should do no such thing. He settled for stroking her upper arm, then somehow her face was against his shoulder, her tears dampening his jumper.

'I'm sorry,' he said, 'so very sorry. You shouldn't have seen that. I took them home to work on.'

She said something indistinct into his shoulder. The top of her head rubbed his chin, the evocative smell of her hair.

'I can't hear you.' He said it quietly into her ear. An unfamiliar sensation was starting to run through him, somewhere between arousal and an undulating, lost feeling.

Francesca pulled back and a welcome space opened between them.

'I can't believe there are so many. It went on for so long. Does she say why?'

'They wanted to go to heaven, I think. A lot of it's rambling, like dreams. I don't think—'

He was going to say he didn't think she had suffered, but stopped himself, because that was a gross lie. 'I think she was mostly delirious.'

Francesca swiped at her cheeks. 'I can cry for Rosaleen. But not for Bernie. It's Bernie's fault, isn't it?'

'I'm just establishing a sequence, that's all.'

Gazing towards the light of the front door, she said, 'I got a letter from Rosaleen the same day that I found out. It was an odd letter, more holy than usual, and a bit – you know – muddled.'

'Posted to New York?'

'I think it took a while to get to me. It had the wrong stamp. She asked me to come home. She wanted to talk to someone, she said.'

'Do you have the letter?'

'I think – oh, I don't know. It could be in New York.'

How long could a letter take to get to America? Could it circulate for months without the right postage? As far as he could establish, Rosaleen and Bernadette had not been seen after the first day of August. Two and a half months until they were found. He pressed down the urge to rush Francesca straight to Rowan Grove and make her go through all her belongings in front of him.

'Could you do something for me?'

She gave him a quiver of a smile. 'How can I refuse, now that you have seen me at my watery worst?'

'Have a look for the letter.'

'I'm on my way into town. Rehearsal. I won't get the chance to look until tonight. You're welcome to call round later, see if I've found it.'

'I'll catch up with you later in the week.'

He stood for a while in the hall after he had closed the door behind her. The blood singing in his veins.

24

Father Timoney knew you shouldn't say they were like children, these people, but they were. They had no guile, the demented. *Dementare*, to put out of mind. And they had been put out of society's minds, he reckoned, here in the care home behind the big wall.

Most of them wouldn't know their own names, but at the sight of the shining chalice and the white disc of the Host, they opened their mouths and offered their tongues readily. One woman had kept her tongue hanging out afterwards, the Host stuck to it. He motioned for her to shut her mouth, and she peeled the sodden wafer from her tongue and offered it back. He shook his head and stepped smartly to the side, on to the next poor soul.

After the ones who had stood in line, he went to those confined to armchairs. He still couldn't bend his back, so was obliged to do an odd little bob at the knees to serve them. When he had finished with the residents, he gave communion to the nurses and carers, noticing how closed and private their faces were, in contrast to the old people.

The nun in charge of the home had told him that Father Deasy had never said the Monday mass in the residents' lounge. He'd insisted on using the side chapel, and everyone had to be herded in and out and there wasn't room for the wheelchairs, so some never got mass at all. It was the first whiff of criticism Timoney had heard against his predecessor, and he found it shamefully cheering.

Everyone preferred the informality of the big lounge and a chance to turn off the television. And yes, perhaps a few Protestants or atheists got caught up in the crowd, but it did them no harm. Everyone liked singing the hymns. One cardiganed gent at the back would call out, '*Dominus vobiscum!*' at regular intervals, remembering the old Latin mass.

The final prayers were accompanied by a rising smell of mince and onions. The carers ushered their charges out to their tea while Timoney packed away his travel chalice, altar cloth and box of wafers into their neat leather case. The man who had been shouting in Latin hovered near the table that served as an altar, looking covetously at the objects Timoney was packing up.

'Sorry there, my friend. I have to get these back to the church.'

'*Dominus vobiscum!*' said the man.

'*Et cum spiritu tuo,*' said Timoney, slicing the air with a stiff hand.

He stood in the front porch, waiting for a heavy shower to pass. A wash of evening light was trying to break through the dirty clouds. There were four old people's homes in his area, and he said a weekly mass in each of them, in addition to the daily mass at St Alphonsus and an extra one on Sundays. There were funerals, the odd baptism and visiting the housebound. And still Father Geraghty said, *We must find something for you to do, Noel.*

Before this bad business with the MacNamaras,

Geraghty had even suggested a prison chaplaincy, and Timoney had found himself panicked at the thought.

It was hard to remember now what he had wished for, in making the move to Dublin. There was that young priest the diocese had sent round to discuss missionary work. He was so full of passion, talking about El Salvador, about the radicalism of Jesus and liberation theology. Some of the older priests had muttered darkly about communism, but for Timoney it had stirred up a kind of crisis, awakened him to the uncomfortable certainty that he hadn't had a new thought in years, that he'd become stupefied by same daily round, the same people. The rut that some call peace. He was bored, and his parishioners surely deserved more than his boredom.

In a burst of anxious energy, he had changed everything. A move to Dublin would revive his energies, bring him into interesting conversations with scholarly men, or with young people like the radical priest. Timoney never anticipated that St Alphonsus would be a lonelier posting than the wet villages of Cavan.

The rain was refusing to let up. He pushed open his umbrella and stepped out of the porch, walked down the long drive of Deerfield Care Home, shadows dense under the dripping trees. The pain in his back was better if he moved about, that was the odd thing; it was staying still that made it worse. He made his way along the pavement in front of the pub, picked a place to cross the road. He had to wait well back from the kerb, so the dirty spray from the cars and buses in their heedless passing would not soak him.

At the care home he'd got into conversation with a male nurse about back pain. He seemed to know a good deal about it, said it was an occupational hazard, what with lifting people about the place. Thankfully, he did not mention anything about massage. He said the secret to a healthy back was 'core strength' – a concept that had something to do with weights and gyms – and, really, wasn't it too late in life for him to get into all that? Still, this phrase 'core strength' was going around in Timoney's head. It was the kind of phrase you could spin a sermon from – going from that secular ideal of the body beautiful into a deeper examination: what is our *moral* core strength?

He got to the house and felt in his pocket for the key. The kitchen light was off, but there was a dim blue light shifting and changing in a narrow gap between the living-room curtains. Mrs Noonan must be watching television. If he went in quietly, he could sneak into his room without meeting anyone. Perhaps she had left a plate of food out on the kitchen table, like she sometimes did.

But he still had his mass-case in his hand. He needed to go to the sacristy, transfer the blessed Hosts from the pyx to the ciborium, wipe out the chalice and put the linens in with the laundry. Rites had to be respected, or else … or else what? Or else things fall apart. He always found it hard to keep up his spirits in winter, and this year, in this new place, he could feel himself slipping.

A light had been left on in the sacristy. He supposed he must have put it on when he was collecting his things; the day had been so dark. He hung up his vestments, disposed of the Hosts, checked everything was in order and put away the leather case. He addressed the crucifix on the sacristy wall: 'You know me best, Lord, you see my weakness. Grant me courage.'

It wasn't that God ever talked back, but he used to think of the silence that followed prayer as a soft and infinite acceptance. A silence that was vast, but somehow safe.

Lately it had not felt that way. Lately it felt like prayers went from him and just travelled outward for ever, no landing place. He remembered an amateur astronomer in Ballyjamesduff who had tried to show him the wonders of the night sky. He had handed Timoney some powerful binoculars to view the Pleiades. Timoney had been awaiting new miracles of creation to be revealed to him. He had never expected the bleak feeling that came over him; those cold stars and the silence and absolute emptiness they hung in. Without end.

He awoke from his thoughts and looked about him. The sacristy no longer felt familiar. Beyond the wooden swing door, the dark immensity of the church called to him. He felt a need to see that the sacristy lamp had not gone out, that there was one warm point of light that marked the presence of a greater being. He pushed open the door into darkness and stepped onto the raised concrete of the altar area. The flame was there, just, a fingernail of living light in its cylinder of ruby glass. He had the notion to go down and sit for a while in a pew, just like a simple congregant, and let the sanctuary lamp be priest to him.

He misjudged the depth of the shallow steps in the gloom and the floor met his foot sooner than he expected, jarring his tender spine. He yelled out, and thought he heard an answering sound, a muffled thump from somewhere.

Clutching the kneeling rail, he hobbled down the next step onto the pale wood of the main flooring and lowered himself until he was lying on his back. The pain was excruciating, as if his sacrum might snap with the pressure, but he knew that the flatness would help, if he could just lie and wait.

The extreme angles of the wooden ceiling were spread out above him, like boat keels crashing into each other. As his eyes grew used to the dark, he could make out the damp stains and the warping along the ridges. He found himself imagining that he was looking down on the ceiling rather than up at it – the same reversal he used to play as a boy on bored Sunday afternoons, lying on the parlour rug and believing he was looking down on a pristine white floor, with only a lamp sticking up like a lollipop from its centre, and he and the furniture were attached to the ceiling. What a fanciful child he had been.

Once he had told his mother that Our Lady had appeared at the end of his bed, and she had been thrilled and told everyone, though now all he could remember was the telling and her joy, not the actual vision. It must have happened, though. It set him on the path to priesthood.

His back was not easing. The cold of the floor was creeping into his flesh, making the tension worse. He heard a scuffling sound somewhere below him, something shifting through grit. That was all he needed: vermin in the crypt, to add to his trials.

The sanctuary light flickered suddenly, as if a door had opened somewhere. The shadows reeled about him and hairs lifted on his arms and legs. He had the definite feeling of a presence. What if those holy visions of childhood were about to return? The idea filled him with fear, not awe.

He tried to rise, but could not. With gritted teeth, he managed to roll onto his belly. The cold from the dusty floor felt actively malevolent, something more than the ordinary cold of a November night. He began to whimper. The building was trying to kill him. He always knew it was a bad place, had not admitted it, had not trusted his instincts. He began to pray, but it was not holy grace that visited him, but the memory of Claudia's small hands, smoothing their way over his back. Oh, to be in her warm little room, to be safe and cared for like a child.

He wept luxuriously, loudly, and it seemed, after a time, that the building was weeping along with him, for he could sense a sobbing echo of his own distress. If he didn't pull himself together, he would be sucked deeper into madness.

It's only the wind – the wind makes all kinds of noises.

Timoney crawled up the altar steps and slouched away like an ape into the sacristy, the pain burning like flames, like the devil's own trident spearing his spine.

25

The more tragedy a play contained, the more hilarity behind the scenes. It was a well-known syndrome. Francesca was listening to Catherine and Dymphna, the girls playing Helen of Troy and Cassandra, vying with each other over coffee break.

'There was one guy, he'd, like, call out my name at the end, you know? Catherine, Catherine, Ca-ther-INE! Only you just knew he did it as a *thing*, that the night before he was probably doing 'Sharon, Sharon ...'

'SHA-A-ARON!' obliged Dymphna.

Francesca laughed, tipping her fag ash into the plastic cup that had held her tea. She had taken up smoking again, just for the run.

'It was like he was showing off that he remembered who you were,' said Catherine. 'His little trademark.'

'Eugh, Jesus!' said Francesca.

'I'll tell you the worst thing that someone asked me to do in bed,' said Dymphna. But instead of saying it out loud, she leaned over and whispered in Catherine's ear, pulling back a swag of blonde hair to do so.

'Oh, that's vile!' said Catherine.

'What was it?' Francesca asked.

Dymphna, all wicked eyes, said, 'You don't want to know. Trust me.'

Francesca threw her butt into the cup to sizzle and shrugged them off. 'Better get back to it.'

They had this way of shutting her out. At first she thought it was her age; then she noticed the stage manager was at it too, and realised it was her bereavement they were wary of. People didn't want to tell you anything filthy or wonderful or sad, nothing volatile. She was to be treated with a certain respectful blandness, no stirring up new-filled graves.

Eilís Ni Gríofa was studying her lines over in a corner, mouthing them as she read. As Hecuba, she had about half the script to herself. She never seemed to care what people around her were thinking, focused only on her part and the play, stoking those fires of intensity. She, at least, had not been falsely polite. She deliberately cornered Francesca after the third rehearsal.

'They say you lost your sisters, two at once,' her hand catching the strap of Francesca's bag. Francesca was giving a brief confirmation of this fact when Eilís suddenly said, 'And how *exactly* did they die?'

'They're not *exactly* sure. There'll be an inquest at some point.'

'Terrible, the not knowing.' Eilís's dark eyes raked Francesca's face, harvesting.

A maquette of the stage design sat on a table by the window, showing an arrangement of tumbled columns and broken walls that looked impressive in miniature and would hopefully be convincing in reality. For now, they just had plastic chairs positioned where the war-shattered temples of Troy would be. Francesca took up her position

218

kneeling between two of them. She ran through her lines in her head, while fashioning her doomed baby, Astyanax, out of a few borrowed jumpers:

> *My child! my own sweet babe and priceless treasure!*
> *Our enemies demand your death,*
> *My wretched arms cannot a fortress make ...*

It was past ten when rehearsal finished, and they trooped down the stairs from the high rehearsal room above Abbey Street. They clustered on the pavement, chatting. Having spent hours with each other, it was hard to break free of the group. Catherine and Dymphna were off to the pub, Eilís's husband was parked in a car up the street, waiting for her.

'Sure he loves listening to the radio.'

Damien offered Francesca a lift home, as he often did. On one of these journeys, Francesca had discovered that Damien was not gay, simply camp. It had only been a light pass, the lean-in for a friendly kiss that hovered expectantly for more. She'd been able to brush it off, pretend she hadn't noticed. But a pass it most definitely was. It had given her something to think about. She missed sex. He was attractive. An affair might be fun, but if it went badly, the whole run would go badly.

Now she brushed his lapel lightly and pecked his cheek.

'Thanks, but I need to go and see my niece,' she said, an idea that only formed as she spoke it.

She bought another pack of cigarettes from a newsagent at the top of O'Connell Street and smoked one on her walk up to Madeleine's flat. It had been four days since they argued, and Madeleine hadn't been in touch. Francesca was getting bored of the stand-off, bored and regretful. In her head, she rehearsed a few apologies, all to do with the stresses of their situation, her hatred of any kind of deceit and her lack of skill in living with anyone. She would admit to Madeleine that the whole money question was causing her anxiety. She would suggest that they put the kettle on and talk, like they used to.

If only she hadn't said so much about Madeleine to Vincent Swan. It felt disloyal, now. He was good at getting people to talk, of course he was. And oddly attractive, mooching around in his wifeless house. Then there was that strange incident in his hall, weeping all over him. She had no control over her emotions lately, not in real life, anyway.

Francesca climbed the stone steps outside Madeleine's building and rang the bell three times, until a sash window rumbled open far above her. She stepped back from the door to see. A messy head stuck out of the window – Derek or Dylan or whatever the flatmate was called.

'Who's there?' he shouted.

'I'm looking for Madeleine.'

'Madeleine's moved out. Sorry.'

Francesca took another step back to let the street light fall on her face. 'It's me – it's Francesca.'

'But she's with you. She said she was moving in with you.'

'You really haven't seen her?'

'Swear to God. But you're welcome to come up for a jar. Hang on and I'll throw down the key.'

26

The night was frosty and windless, with a tang of coal smoke. Swan had driven across to Clontarf to go for a late walk along the shore road to empty his head. Being in an office all day, staring at a computer screen, felt like a kind of imprisonment. Night was a fine time to walk, the pavements empty and glimpses of people's lives on show in lighted windows.

He walked across the Wooden Bridge and out along the Bull Wall, a causeway stretching out into the bay. On his left, the grassy expanse of Bull Island was dotted with sleeping geese, their pale bellies just discernible in the darkness. He looked back to the shore, and all the city lights had doubled themselves in the water's still reflection.

It was a long time since he'd been so much in his own company. He ought to go and visit his mother, since he had the time and leisure; that would be the kind thing to do. But he didn't want to break the spell of pleasant self-absorption. He kept walking out to sea.

The asphalt under his feet was damp, but not yet icy. He wandered all the way out to the lit-up tripod with a figure of Mary plonked on the top. *Réalt na Mara*, Star of the Sea. She didn't look out at the sea, though. She was turned inland, towards the city centre, as if Dublin was too untrustworthy to turn her back on. Beyond her, the neat path dissolved into a raw line of boulders washed by the tide, ending in a gassy green light hovering mysteriously in the air.

The hill of Howth rose up black against the grainy sky, its shape suddenly reminding him of another mound by the sea, on the other side of the country, on the Mayo coast. He hadn't thought of it in years. He was stationed there as a young Garda and, one day, out visiting the owner of a caravan site, he had noticed a human skull resting on a shelf in the man's office. Well, he could hardly ignore it. The man explained that some children staying on the site had found it on the beach.

'It came from the famine mound,' he said, and led Swan out to look at a flat-topped hill jutting into the sea. It had been used as a mass grave in the bad years of the previous century, the man said. 'There's been some fierce erosion this winter. The storms back in April. All kinds of bones washed onto the beach. I've had a word with the priest, and he's agreed to re-inter any skulls at the back of the graveyard. On the quiet, like.'

On the quiet, of course. Such things were not spoken out loud then, and the mound itself was unmarked by any sign or cross. It was only in recent years that anyone had thought to raise memorials to the famine that killed a million. In his youth, nobody talked about it, in that way that things that are shameful are not talked about. Shameful because we had let others do it to us. Human skeletons walking the roads of the west, their lips stained green from grass.

When he got back to his house, Francesca MacNamara was sitting on his doorstep.

He checked his watch – a quarter to midnight. She lifted her head at the sound of the gate.

'I need your help.' Her voice desperate.

When he got to the step, she reached her arms up to him. He took her hands in his and pulled her to her feet, casually. He unlocked and opened the door. As the cat slipped out, Francesca slipped in, ahead of him, and went straight to the kitchen, throwing herself into the armchair by the hearth.

The fire in the little grate had collapsed to ashy cinders and a faint orange glow. He knelt at her feet to revive it, making paper twists and a wigwam of splintered wood. He laid three briquettes on it and put a match to the paper. She didn't speak during any of this.

He stole a quick glance. She seemed to be staring at the wall, or at nothing at all. He stood up, brushing his hands together vigorously, foolishly, to break the spell.

'Cup of tea?'

'All this while I thought that's where she was, but they said she didn't come back at all, and no one knows who this Harrison boy is.'

'What are we talking about?'

'Madeleine. She didn't go back to her flat on Friday night, they haven't seen her. It's Tuesday now – four days. Christ!'

He poured two whiskeys while she filled in on more of the story. He pulled a kitchen chair over to the opposite side of the fire.

'We had a row. I mean, Madeleine was really pissed off.

But she left all her bags in the hall, and I thought – I don't know – that she'd gone back to cool off or to teach me a lesson, but he showed me her room and it was empty. She'd given him her keys.'

'This Harrison lad?'

'No! Derek, the one who shares the flat. Harrison is the one she brought to our house, but I don't even know where he lives. I was rude to him – practically kicked him out.'

'Do you want water in that?'

Francesca looked at the glass in her hand, blinked. 'You think I'm overreacting, don't you?'

'Most likely she's staying with friends; maybe she caught up with this Harrison on his way home and went to his. You're not that easy to get in touch with.'

'I suppose.'

'There you go. She couldn't go back to her flat if she'd already given her keys up, right?'

Francesca looked at the fire, nodded, finally took a sip of the whiskey.

'You think she's fine?'

'There's no reason to think she's not fine.'

'It's just with everything ...'

'Of course.'

She smiled briefly. 'That house is grating my nerves. Madeleine didn't like it, either. I knew she wasn't that keen to move in, even before we argued.'

'Oh?'

Francesca leaned back in the chair and stretched her feet out over the tiles of the hearth, the whiskey glass clasped in her lap.

'Madeleine had a pretty lousy time when she was little. I thought I would do my belated bit. We could make a temporary home together – love snatched from the jaws of tragedy. It wasn't a part I could play, turns out. Or maybe it's just the wrong location.'

'Did Madeleine spend a lot of time with your sisters – recently, I mean.'

She shrugged, flicked her eyes away. 'I believe her when she says she didn't know they were … unwell. I have to. The bank-card thing rattled me. It's all such a bloody mess. I went to find her tonight to make peace.'

Swan felt a nudge on his shoe, and looked down to see the toe of her pointed boot parked against his foot.

'Thank you, Vincent. You must have got a fright seeing me on your doorstep again. Did your heart sink?'

His heart had not sunk, but reared, flapping in its cage, and he feared she could tell.

'I just thought something must have happened,' he said. 'I can give you a lift home when you finish that.'

She pushed her lips forward in a little moue.

'It's so cosy here …'

'There's no rush,' he said, but put his own glass deliberately aside. 'Maybe when you get back to Rowan Grove you'll find she's come back in the meantime.'

'Do you think?' Her mind was back on her niece.

They drove out of the little knot of streets where he lived and into the scattered landscape of Deerfield, past the all-night garage, and turned left by the pub car park, where the glitter of broken glass outshone the stars above.

He parked outside the house. The windows were

dark, the curtains open so that you could see through the shadowy interior to the relatively bright rectangle of the back window. A house you could look right through now, though it had hidden so much.

'You were wrong,' said Francesca.

'It was hardly a promise.'

He was immediately annoyed with himself for sounding irritated, for bringing any heat into what must remain an unemotional exchange. 'Look, if you don't hear from her tomorrow, I'll see what we can do to find her friend.'

Francesca threw off her seatbelt and started to dig around in her bag. She picked out a bunch of keys. They had a softened cardboard tag on them that read: *The Misses MacNamara.*

He recognised them as the set the police took from the priest, that first day, when the bodies were discovered. Something occurred to him.

'Does Madeleine have keys?'

She shifted in the passenger seat to get a better view of his face.

'Well, yes.'

'Did she have them already?'

'I guess so. Why?'

He shrugged.

Francesca looked back towards the dark house. 'I don't suppose you want to come in?' she asked and turned to him, her eyes a challenge, so that he couldn't be mistaken.

'I can't.'

'You can, you know.'

She placed a narrow hand on his thigh, pressed her

fingers gently into the flesh. She leaned in closer and he thought she was going to kiss him, but she just leaned her forehead onto his shoulder, which was somehow worse. He kept his hands on the steering wheel.

'Francesca ...'

'Is it your absent wife, or is it some terribly honourable Garda code?'

That allowed him to laugh, to make a joke of it all. 'You're very sure of your charms.'

'Well, they don't seem to be working. I fear my light must be dimming.'

'It's still too bright for me.'

She sighed lightly and retrieved her hand, seemed to curl into herself. 'You know, I've been rehearsing all week with these two stunning girls – my God, the glow off them – and I find myself thinking how I must have been like that once, only I didn't appreciate it.'

'You were a film star, you must have known.'

'I didn't see it in the mirror.'

She looked again at the empty house.

'Look,' he said, 'why don't you stay with your brother or a friend for now?'

'Don't you be making me an object of pity. It's only human to want a bit of comfort, Vincent.'

She searched for the door handle, and Swan reached over her to open it, allowed himself that proximity.

He waited while she unlocked the front door and went inside. She never looked back. He watched the light go on in the hall, then the main room. She pulled the curtains closed, but still he didn't drive away.

A light came on in the front bedroom. Again her silhouette appeared, hair loose around her shoulders now and her movements quick as she drew blackness across the bright square of window. He sat on in his car, thinking, arguing with himself.

Madeleine Moone had her own keys to her aunts' house. Why had she run off to the priest to say she could get no answer, when she could have tried to open the door herself? Granted, the chain was across, but did she already know what might be behind it? Was that what stopped her? And wasn't it just a bit pat that she had turned up again at the priest's house the next day – once the bodies were discovered?

He looked up at the bedroom window and the light went out.

He needed to find the girl, not for her aunt, but for his own sake.

A man walking an old Labrador crossed the empty car park at the bottom of Rowan Grove. The traffic on the main road was sparse now. Beyond, right by St Alphonsus, a pair of car headlights blazed into life, then pulled away from the church, turned towards the city centre. Swan looked at his watch; it was two in the morning. He should be in his bed.

First he made a detour to drive by the low wall of St Alphonsus. There was no light on in the priest's house or church, and no other cars to be seen. It had probably just been a pair of lovers, seeking the shadow of the church.

27

'You're going to be late – again!'

Mrs Noonan was knocking on his door. Father Timoney looked at his alarm clock and saw it was almost nine – half an hour until mass started, and too late to phone Holy Trinity and see if one of the curates could do it in his stead.

He wasn't well. It wasn't just his back problem. He'd lain awake all night, in the grip of a terrible apprehension, then had fallen into blessed unconsciousness as dawn broke. He feared that the old difficulty had come back. It hadn't been mentioned at his interview, and he hoped he might leave that bad chapter behind him. The stay in the 'respite house' – it was nothing as bad as a nervous breakdown. The doctor who treated him said the term was out of fashion anyway, was unscientific, but didn't provide him with another diagnosis of his black periods, just some vague talk of depression. Timoney thought of them more as crises. Challenges from the Lord. Challenges he had overcome in the past and would again.

He managed to roll onto his side, let his feet drop to the floor and then sat up. The pain was dull, manageable. A hot shower and he would be ready to face the morning.

More knocking. 'Are you there, Father?'

'Please, Mrs Noonan. There's no need.'

He got his robe on and shuffled to the bathroom. The door was locked and he could hear the shower running. This was insupportable.

He staggered down the corridor. 'Mrs Noonan! I cannot get into my own bathroom. There seems to be someone inside it.'

She was sitting at the kitchen table with another woman, the small one who never seemed to take her coat off. People off the street seeing him in his dressing gown. His face was hot with annoyance now. Mrs Noonan got to her feet and rushed past him to knock at the bathroom door.

'Jimmy! Jimmy! Get out of there!'

The woman at the kitchen table stared at him with wide, respectful eyes, unaffected by the domestic drama. She had a big stack of labelled envelopes in front of her.

'Good morning, Father.'

He didn't bother to answer. He wiped a hand tenderly over his jaw, trying to judge if he could get away with not shaving.

She persisted. 'Can I do anything to help you?'

'You could stop staring at me, for a start.'

She was grubby-looking. Could do with a shower herself.

'You're not very kind, are you?'

Cheeky strap. He was about to admonish her when Mrs Noonan reappeared.

'Sorry about that, Father; he probably thought you were up already.' She pushed past him. 'Can I get you a cup of tea in the meantime?'

'Is Jimmy actually living here, Mrs Noonan? Is that what's going on? Have I been labouring under some terrible misapprehension that this is a parish house and not some public facility?'

He heard the bathroom door open and looked round to see Jimmy Noonan, with only a small towel around his hips, do a bandy-legged hop down the hall and into the living room.

'Don't get yourself into a state, now,' said Mrs Noonan, pouring out a cup of tea. At the table the other woman – Viney, that was her name – was still goggling at him.

'Mary, I think you should get on now.'

The woman got to her feet and reached for the stack of envelopes.

'No!' said Mrs Noonan sharply, then with a deliberately softer voice, 'I told, you I'll take care of that.'

Mary Viney left the room without fuss or farewells. The housekeeper reached towards him with a full cup.

'Jimmy says the water is broken in his digs, that's all. He'll be gone by the time you're back from mass.'

'I don't want your *tea*,' said Timoney, though in truth he was parched.

The bathroom was steamed up and he had to keep wiping the mirror to shave. He should have been rehearsing his sermon, but instead was composing a speech to Mrs Noonan about how he wanted – no, expected – things to be.

He rushed over to the sacristy with five minutes to spare and Mrs Noonan following with his laundered vestments. He didn't really like having her in the sacristy. It blurred the lines too much between the domestic and the sacred.

'Shall I go turn the lights on, Father? The day is gloomy enough.'

How eager to please she was. He found it depressing that she could not be like this from day to day, that he had to act like a petulant brute in order to have her placating him.

He went to the cupboard to get out the Hosts and to fill the offertory vessels with water and wine. The wine bottle was not there. One of the top cupboards was open, the vases and spare collection baskets pushed to either side. In fact, now that he looked around, the place seemed in more disarray than he remembered it being the previous night. Things had started to slip again, in his head. He'd started drinking in his bedroom, just to get to sleep, hiding the bottle carefully.

The altar wine was on a lower shelf than usual, half empty. Had he drunk that too and blacked out the memory?

Mrs Noonan appeared in the doorway. 'What's wrong, Father?'

'I just hate being rushed.'

'It won't happen again – the bathroom.'

'We'll talk later.'

'Do you want a hand on with your vestments?'

'No, Mrs Noonan, I do not.' He asked God to forgive the exhilaration that filled him as he watched her worried face depart. Things would change around here; yes, they would.

He took a glimpse into the church. Thirty or forty out there, not bad. With the lamps on and the morning light pressing against the coloured glass, all was benign, all demons fled. He picked up the covered chalice and stepped out to face the faithful, his breath clouding in the chill air.

When mass was over, he tidied the sacristy. In the linen cupboard the towels and altar cloths were pulled this way and that. There was dust and wax drips all over the candlesticks. Matt Cotter was supposed to take care of the sacristy, but he'd obviously not done a hand's turn lately. Too busy selling cigarettes and sweets. Everybody taking him for a sap. No, here it would stop.

The first thing he did – the first act of what was going to be a completely new era – was to lock the key cabinet in the presbytery hallway and pocket the key that was usually left in its lock. There must have been a hundred keys inside, some in bunches of ten or twelve: big rusted keys, tiny ones for small padlocks. Only a few were labelled. It was from this same cabinet that Timoney had taken the keys to the MacNamaras' house. Other house keys hung there with similar paper tags indicating to whom they belonged. D'Arcy, Kennedy, O'Toole.

He suspected that Father Deasy was at the root of this lax regime, a trusting innocent. Imagine if someone's house got robbed because of their neglect. Imagine if Mrs Noonan's prayer group, who sometimes met in the presbytery, happened to feel a bit nosy while hanging their coats up, or a passing workman went snooping. It was a disaster waiting to happen. He hadn't made the right start at St Alphonsus at all. He had crept about like a mouse, anxious not to upset, not to disturb. He had let Mrs Noonan take advantage.

This was why the Pope's symbol was crossed keys, he realised. If you had the keys, you had the power. He ran his hand over the closed door – the locked, closed door. It was a start.

There was a little rack of toast and a plate of fried eggs and rashers waiting for him in the kitchen. The day that had begun so badly was turning out surprisingly well. It all came down to simply taking control. Mrs Noonan was over by the sink as she usually was, working away at the surface of a pot. Her back was straight, her rubbing determined.

He salted his eggs, dipped a corner of his toast in the soft yolk before addressing her. It was time to press home his advantage.

'This house is a fairly modest one for the two of us, wouldn't you say? It's just not possible for your children to stay here too. I might need the living room any time of the day or night to see a parishioner.'

She took up a dishcloth and dried her hands before turning. Her expression had lost all its recent meekness. 'Jimmy only stayed on the sofa a couple of nights, Father. Either you want him to be around to fix your roof or you don't. Mostly he stays with his pals.'

The quotations from established building firms had been shockingly high. Father Geraghty said the parish couldn't meet them, suggested they were inflated on account of some gullibility of Timoney's. Jimmy Noonan had offered to do it for half that, and without scaffolding.

'Well,' he blustered now, 'why can't he get a flat like anyone else?'

'He hasn't the money for a deposit, and I certainly don't earn enough to lend him anything …'

A dribble of yolk fell on his shirt front.

'Do you want a wet cloth for that?'

'Yes. Yes, thank you.'

Mrs Noonan came and stood close to him with the blue J-cloth in her hand. He took it from her, but she didn't move away. He looked up into her face. Her eyes were lit with malice. She took a small scrap of paper from her apron pocket, flattened it out on the table beside his plate.

'I was straightening your room and found this on the floor. I hope it is not important, it's all wrinkled.'

Executive Health Spa and Sauna was blazed across the top in red letters. 'Massage £10' scribbled at the bottom. It had been in his inside jacket pocket. For definite. She couldn't have found it on the floor.

'I don't know what that is. It's not mine.'

'That's strange, so,' said Mrs Noonan and returned it to her apron pocket.

He couldn't think of any reason to ask for it back. He dabbed at his shirt with the damp cloth, averting his face.

'Are you finished with this?' The breakfast was only half eaten, but he let her take it away, his appetite gone.

When she was over by her sink again, she spoke.

'I like having Jimmy about. It's a mother's weakness. I imagine not having a family is a terrible sacrifice for a priest – a noble sacrifice, of course, but we're only human, aren't we, Father?'

The way she looked at him. If she had searched his

things so thoroughly, she knew about the whiskey bottle too.

'There is no need to be concerned about me.' He struggled to get up from the table with dignity. His back had started throbbing again.

28

Swan stood on the doorstep of Rowan Grove and rang the bell. It had become a ritual these past few days, to see if Francesca had any news of Madeleine. He had little doubt the girl was sulking, or punishing her aunt deliberately, but she had to relent at some stage. There was also the possibility that she was avoiding him, and any further questions about her aunts' deaths.

Francesca opened the door in bare feet, her hair loose and tangled, her face soft with sleep, though it was already past noon. She didn't speak, just turned and walked back into the house, leaving the door open. She was wearing a big jumper over pyjama trousers, and he recognised it as the one Madeleine was wearing that first night, in the priest's kitchen.

A slanted ray of sun lit up the dust on the floor of the living room. She was over by the shelves, pulling something out of the lone paperback that lay there.

'I'd shoved it into the book I was reading that day.'

She was holding out a few pages of folded airmail paper, and he recognised the handwriting immediately. His pulse accelerated.

'Do you have the envelope it came in?'

'Sorry, no.'

'That's a shame.' He took the letter carefully and placed it in an envelope he had in his top pocket. 'I will get it back to you.'

She shrugged. He noticed she didn't meet his eye more than was necessary.

'Any news?' he asked.

'Nothing. I thought you were going to do something. Look for her, dammit.'

'We will.'

'It's the least you could do,' she said flatly, leaving him to see himself out.

The light on his answering machine was blinking when he got back to the house. He hoped he hadn't missed another call from Elizabeth. But it was Una Galvin, his solicitor. When he called the number that was recited, she answered right away. No receptionist rigmarole. Did someone who answered her own phone have enough sway in the legal world, or had he been sold a dud?

'Where have you been hiding?' she asked. 'We've been given sight of the defence documents, and I'm afraid we need to prepare ourselves for an allegation of assault. I'm looking at a photograph of a scalp wound and some bruising on the kidney areas of a rather unattractive back.'

'DeBarra was in fine physical form when I saw him. The day *before* he volunteered his confession.'

'Well, the whole "volunteering" aspect is what's being challenged here, isn't it?'

'But the timing?'

'They could explain that away by saying the confession

took time to draft and redraft. In the timeline they're putting forward, there was a period on the Tuesday when you were the only person in with DeBarra.'

Swan thought about that. They had stopped the interview briefly when Hannigan went out 'to check on something', which Swan had assumed was a euphemism for using the jacks. He took his time, but no more than ten minutes or so.

'There's a Detective Garda Colin Rooney mentioned, says Hannigan spent time with him, helping on another case. Half an hour. Is that right?'

'There was a short break, yes, but not half an hour. This is ludicrous.'

Swan had actually instructed DeBarra not to speak while Hannigan was out. It had been a glowering competition, with no obvious winner.

'That was fifteen minutes at most, and the interview straight afterwards was a model of dullness. What do my colleagues who took the confession say?'

'Their solicitor won't return my calls. I suspect they are going to say his attitude changed mysteriously during his time with you.'

'That's not even logical. They were with him for hours after I left.'

Hannigan and Murphy were going to stitch him up, they really were. And Rooney too. Swan didn't like the boy, but thought he was better at hiding his feelings than he obviously was. It made him feel foolish, not knowing all this was afoot. Either they wanted to punish him personally or he was the only available fall guy for something cooked up by outside interests. He recalled T. P. Murphy standing up in the Garda Social Club one night, singing 'A Nation Once Again' in shut-eyed reverie. It wouldn't be the first time someone was in cahoots with the Republicans. Was this a scheme cooked up by DeBarra somehow – a way to undermine the Gardaí with false accusations, and promise a dip of the compensation money somewhere down the road?

Maybe Murphy and Hannigan did just hate him. He should go and talk to Kavanagh, or find some allies in the ranks – think smart, for once. He dialled Considine's extension, but Rooney answered, so Swan pressed the hang-up button. He would go into the office in person. See if any plan occurred when he got there.

Ah, but first. He took the airmail from his pocket and walked into the front room. Comparing it to all the others, it seemed to come from a time fairly early on in Rosaleen's ordeal; a similar hand to the letters she wrote to Berenice, begging her sister to talk to her. It was interesting how Rosaleen expressed herself so humbly to Francesca (or Frances, as she was here), in a similar way that she had to Berenice, striving not to offend. *I hope you've got work you like.* Maybe she really was someone who could be kept in her bedroom by mere threats.

There is no one to talk to. Madeleine doesn't come to visit any more.

Well, that put a tin lid on certain theories. If there is no one to talk to and she says she hasn't seen Madeleine in a while, how could he continue with the idea that the niece might have been present, or was directly involved with what was going on?

The end paragraph was tipping into delusionary territory already. *Sometimes it is not Jesus I hear. Sometimes I think it is Satan, lord of lies.*

Satan, Jesus, Mary, a variety of angels and God Almighty himself. These were chimeras, phantoms, not human beings.

And yet. The very fact this letter existed, that it must have been posted at a time when Rosaleen was already pleading with Berenice and feeling the effects of her fast. It didn't quite add up to just the two of them in splendid isolation. If only Francesca hadn't thrown away the envelope.

He put the letter away carefully. He would enter it into evidence later. Meanwhile he made a note to check where the nearest post box was to their house.

Driving towards headquarters through lashing rain, he thought again about Madeleine Moone. It was possible she had simply forgotten her keys the night she raised the alarm. And perhaps it wasn't so suspicious that she would return the next day to ask the priest for news of her aunts. He really needed to track her down, not just for Francesca's sake, but for some better answers to those questions.

The squad office was sparsely populated – weekend hours – and yet his entry created a conspicuous silence. A couple of detectives stopped chatting and returned to their work. Desmond Joyce, the longest-serving of them all, stared openly at Swan as he crossed the room, as if some entertainment might be on the cards. Considine wasn't at her desk.

'Message for you!' Colin Rooney was waving a little telephone slip. 'I wasn't sure where to find you.'

'You have my home number, Colin.'

'Yeh, well …'

What is it?'

'A woman rang from Trinity with names for you.'

Rooney handed him the message with two names and addresses on it. Harrison Todd and Harrison De Courcy Smith.

'Wouldn't you know they'd have two of them,' Swan said. 'I've never met anyone called Harrison in my life.'

'What about Harrison Ford?'

'What about him?'

'Right. Anyway, the admissions lady says the double-barrelled one's away in Florence this term on some kind of exchange. She was anxious that her boys might get the college in trouble, so she was very helpful. I thought you weren't working cases?'

'I'm not.' Swan folded the slip and turned on his heel. As the office door swung closed behind him, he could make out Desmond Joyce starting up on some kind of pronouncement to the room. He could wait and overhear what they were saying about him, what his odds of survival were in the court of his colleagues, but he decided to keep on walking. He might just take a drive over to Harrison Todd's house and have a look. He pulled the slip out of his pocket again, to double-check the address, and bumped straight into a woman coming round the corner of the corridor. She cut a bizarre figure for police headquarters, a knitted beret pulled down hard on her head, so that all her hair was hidden; multiple shopping bags and a big tweed coat of mottled purple. Rain dripped from her bags and beaded on her hat. She stood and stared at him, but it was only when she smiled that he recognised Considine.

'You should see your face,' she said.

'Christ! You look like a lunatic.'

'I'm very hurt.'

They drew into a window bay and she put down her bags.

'You look like one of those women you see muttering to themselves and dragging shopping trolleys around the place.'

'Exactly. I went to the women's prayer group in Deerfield – the Acolytes of Siena. Got some pitying looks, but it's quite restful to be considered harmless. What are you doing in? I thought you were exiled.'

Swan showed her the telephone slip. 'This might be where Madeleine Moone's hiding out.'

'You can't be seen working on the case, remember?' said Considine. 'I'll try and get someone from Deerfield to check it out.' She pulled off the beret and roughed her hair into place with her fingers.

'I thought you weren't on this case, either, yet here you are, working deep cover as a bag lady.'

'Slag all you like, but I found out some interesting stuff. Do you have time for a late lunch?

'We can drive to Ryan's. I've got the car.'

Considine plucked the telephone message from Swan's hand. 'I'll call Deerfield while I'm upstairs.'

'Get them to visit him, not just phone. In case she's there and lying low.'

Considine's car was parked beside his in the lot. The rain had finally let up, so Swan waited between them, jigging about to keep from freezing. When Considine reappeared, she was dressed in her usual black mac and had a slick of lipstick on. She opened her boot to dump in the old coat she'd been wearing, and he noticed two hockey sticks lying on the bottom of it.

'Are you getting sporty?'

She shut the lid quickly. 'They're not mine,' she said, furtive all of a sudden.

'Whose are they?' he asked.

'Friend,' she said, flinging the word away quickly.

They took his car the short distance to 'Bongo' Ryan's, a pub beloved of his department, with multiple snugs that gave a feeling of privacy and intrigue. But the snug walls only went up to half the height of the space, so the privacy was illusory, protecting the eavesdropper more than the speaker.

It was late afternoon, and they found an empty hutch easily enough. Globes of warm light hung from the ceiling. He remembered Christmas would be heaving over the horizon soon, with all its dreadful obligations.

Considine ordered a cheese-and-ham toastie, and Swan decided he'd have one too.

'And a tonic water.'

'I'll have a hot port,' said Considine.

'You coming down with something?'

'I just fancy something soothing, after listening to sanctimonious crap for half the day.'

Swan showed her the letter that Francesca had given him.

Considine took it and read through it twice. 'And has she any idea what these things her sister wanted to tell her were?'

'None. And there's no envelope, so I can't work out when it might have been posted. She said it had the wrong stamps on it – she remembered that. But I don't think Rosaleen could have posted it herself.'

'There's more news. The earlier bank statements for the MacNamaras' account came in. We didn't find any other accounts, but they seem to have spent all of 1981 giving away their money from this one. Starting in April last year, they made gifts of a thousand or five hundred pounds to a whole bunch of charities, not to the niece or any individual.'

'Which charities?' asked Swan.

'A whole scatter of them – Vincent de Paul, the League of Decency, Trócaire, the Knights of Malta, Society for the Protection of Unborn Children – over ten months they disposed of seventy thousand pounds. There were also a few cheques for five hundred pounds drawn on cash, possibly for some local good deeds.'

'It seems perverse, doesn't it? They're supposed to be living on the money and its interest, but they give it away. Like they knew they wouldn't need it.'

'And knew it a long time ago.'

The bartender arrived with the drinks and sandwiches. They waited until he was back at his counter before resuming.

'The family aren't going to be pleased when they hear there's nothing left. Anyhow. What was interesting among the ladies of the parish?'

She stirred the teaspoon in her steaming port, a yellow wedge of lemon whirling through the crimson.

'Unsurprisingly, they were a strange bunch. Not that I've much experience of prayer groups. The room was absolutely freezing, I don't know what holy people have against heaters—'

'Moving right along ...'

'It was all women. They called each other "sister", which seemed a bit strange, since there were no nuns. They weren't very welcoming, but I looked like a harmless eejit, and I said a friend had told me to come. You could tell there were about six of them who were in charge – the top girls – then about a dozen others who played the part of the lumpen congregation, including me. They started with readings and prayers.'

'They just read stuff out?'

'In the beginning, yeah. Prayers to the Virgin type of thing, some I didn't recognise. Then a woman stood up and started to talk about her visions, about seeing angels in the sun, and tiny angels dancing in candle flames. She had this incredibly monotonous voice, though, so she managed to make it sound as fabulous as washing your tights.'

'I'll take your word on that.'

'The priest's housekeeper was one of them, dressed up in her best, and bossy about who got to speak when, but she didn't do any testifying or reading herself. She kept looking in my direction, though. I think she might have recognised me from that first night – I'm not sure. After the woman with the angels finished, a younger woman stood up, dressed in what looked like a kid's duffel coat, slightly greasy hair. I felt like I'd seen her before.'

'There was someone like that at the funeral. Brown coat?'

'She looked ... downtrodden, poor. The kind nobody gives much time to, but the group were hanging on every word. She's got the gift of the gab, starts talking about "journeying to heaven", towers of pink cloud and valleys filled with shining souls, that kind of thing, only better than I'm telling it. So she comes to a crystal hall where Jesus sits with his favourites on a golden sofa – that's what she really said, a *golden sofa* – and someone in the crowd says, *Did you see them?*'

Considine delicately lifted the lemon wedge from her empty glass, sucked it flat and put it back.

'And?'

Considine flashed him a smile. 'And I swear, she looks in my direction for a second and says to them, *I've seen the ones we loved, our dear departed, rocked in Jesus's arms*. And I just knew she was talking about the MacNamara sisters, but why not name them, why be secretive?'

'I'm sure Rosaleen uses that phrase – *rocked in Jesus's arms*.' He reached down and flicked open the catch of his briefcase.

'So they're on this sofa with Jesus, and she says he's holding them tenderly in his arms and stroking their hair – obviously a few spare arms there – and I check out the women around me and they've all got this wistful look on, like they're jealous, not like they're at all upset that their pals have suffered a painful death. It was strange ...

I don't know. I mean maybe they got their grieving over at the funeral and moved on, but this woman – Mary Viney, her name is – keeps going on about this fabulous after-life they're having. Then someone asked about a relative, a dead granny, and whether this woman had seen her up there with them.'

Swan put the heavy file on the table between them. Considine had a distracted look on her face.

'What? What is it?'

She shook her head, pushed her empty glass away. 'It's stupid.'

'Go on.'

'When the woman asked about the dead granny, Mary Viney said she hadn't seen her, but that she did see a man – a young father, she said – horribly hurt in a car accident, but healing in heaven. She described his injuries, how his neck was scarred across and his arm withered. She said he had a lovely smile and a blond quiff and she asked if anyone in the room knew him. She looked right at me, but I didn't say anything, then someone else asked about their dead husband and things moved on.'

'What was it you would have said?'

'My father died in a car accident when I was six. I looked up the accident reports when I was a cadet – a stupid thing to do – and found out he'd been almost decapitated and his left arm crushed.'

'Are you sure she didn't recognise you? This is Dublin. There could be a dozen ways she'd know about your father.'

'Yeah, that's what I thought.' But she sounded unconvinced. 'My round.' She jumped up and went to the bar.

Swan put the file away. He was always cautious to draw a line between the professional and the personal. But Considine had never mentioned anything about her life; he should try to be open to it.

When she came back she was carrying two hot ports. 'You didn't want a tonic, not really,' she said, smiling, normal.

'If you want to talk about anything with me, you know you can.'

She pushed the port across the table. 'Thank you, Sigmund Freud.'

'Don't be like that.'

'The thing is, what I realised at the meeting was that the sisters weren't isolated. They were deep into this Acolytes thing, and the women meet every week. They were part of a community before they disappeared, not some reclusive shut-ins. Their absence would have been noticed. Unless these women knew what was happening, and their disappearance was no surprise.'

'All the parishioners were questioned. No one admitted to seeing them, or having concerns.'

'Yeah, but it wasn't us doing the questioning,' said Considine. 'What if it was Clancy or someone equally dense? He'd think women don't have the brains to lie. But Mrs Noonan certainly has.'

Swan took a drink. The warm port was far too sweet. It reminded him of the hot Ribena his mother used to feed him when he was small and had a cold. An emasculating thought.

'There's so many half-done things,' he said. 'I wish we

could start over. You know, I did some reading on Catherine of Siena – she of the Acolytes. Seems she was famed for her fasting; it brought on her visions. They could have been emulating that in some way.'

'Well,' said Considine, 'I forgot to mention: Mary Viney had her hands bandaged round, both of them. I think she might have been faking stigmata, the old Padre Pio number.'

'Could it just be eczema, something ordinary?'

'Not only that. At the end they were saying a prayer that included *I renounce the world, the flesh and the devil*. The thing they say at baptisms. So Viney's leading this prayer and she's holding out her arms wide. Like a priest would. And I noticed, when her sleeves rode up, how skinny her wrists were – you could see her veins twisting over the bones.'

Swan remembered the woman only dimly. She was small, but hadn't looked obviously thin in her bulky coat. 'You think she's starving herself too?'

'Don't know, but there was something wrong with her teeth, like she had a bridge but it didn't fit properly.'

'Retracted gums, maybe. Renouncing the flesh. Fasting I can just about understand, but starvation is another thing altogether.'

'Don't underestimate the thwarted anger of women. Or their competitiveness. There was some kind of weird fever in that room.'

'Spin me a theory, so.'

'Oh, I dunno. Maybe Berenice was previously the top dog in the Acolytes. She could have got jealous of Mary

Viney and her visions. Starving would have been a way to assert herself as the most saintly. Rosaleen just got caught up in it.' Considine sighed. 'It's all bloody fascinating, but Kavanagh's demanded that the report get forwarded to the coroner next week.'

'What! That's not enough time for all the forensics results, surely?'

'He keeps checking up on me, and when the bank account led only to charitable donations, well ...'

'Next week is not now. We just need to push it.'

'I've heaps of work, as it is. And you're supposed to be concentrating on your artificial intelligence or whatever you call it.'

'Databank. Not any more. My solicitor has advised me to stay home until the tribunal hearing is finished. DeBarra is supposed to take the stand early next week, and I'm supposed to be there.'

'But it's all nonsense, isn't it?'

'Have you seen Hannigan and Murphy about?'

'They're supposed to be working old cases in the archives, but they're mostly hanging about in the office doing feck all, yabbering. Shall we have another?'

Considine had finished her second port, was starting to look shiny and cheerful.

'Thanks, but my teeth feel like they've been flocked.'

'A whiskey, so.'

'Not for me. I need to get going ...'

'What are you up to?'

'I thought I would take in some culture.'

'G'luck with that.'

'Do you want a lift back to your car?'

'Think I'll just sit on here while it's quiet.'

She had a messed-up look in her eyes – something to do with the dead father, perhaps.

Leaving the snug, Swan hesitated. 'They're all fucking charlatans, Gina, vultures on people's losses. Don't you pay that woman any heed.'

29

Francesca followed the progress of the play through the tannoy on the dressing-room wall. Catherine, in her costume as Helen of Troy, was knitting a striped scarf in the other worn-out armchair. Onstage, Cassandra was relaying dire warnings and the chorus were chanting atonal responses. In a few minutes her cue would come. She checked her make-up again – white face streaked with dirt, hollowed eyes. The ASM had tied up the straps of material that held the lifelike baby doll to her chest. Her entire costume was made from artfully layered muslin rags. She met her own eyes steadily in the mirror and got to her feet.

'Knock 'em dead,' Catherine called as she passed.

The translation of the play was a new version, but there was no escaping the ponderous structure of the thing. Hecuba was onstage throughout, wailing and *ochóning* in the ruins with the Greek soldier Talthybius, while Cassandra, then Andromache and finally Helen were wheeled out to heap on more woe. 'Woe!' had become the standard greeting between cast members backstage.

Francesca stood in the wings, one hand cradling her baby's plastic skull. The little light on the SM's desk fell on a script marked over and over with felt-tipped pen. Through a little gap in the flies, she could make out the audience beyond the stage lights, the pale ovals of their faces stacked in the dark. First night, full house. Cassandra began her final prophecy. Francesca's knees were shaking, but she knew that once she stepped out there, they would be still.

If she didn't have this play, well, she wouldn't know what to do with herself. She didn't know how she'd deal with the rage that had been growing within her. Rage at Berenice's insane wilfulness, Rosaleen's weak stupidity, and at Madeleine for running out on her, worrying her. Rage also towards her long-dead mother and the whole aggressively martyred clan from which she sprang.

She felt someone step close behind her and a proprietorial hand slide around her waist. Dry lips touched the back of her neck. Cologne. Damien.

He brought his hand to the doll and prised it away from her costume to check that her breast was exposed underneath.

'There's nothing more vulnerable than one naked breast,' he had said earlier in the week, persuading her into it. They had been in bed for the first time, and he flicked her nipple lightly as he said it, an annoying sensation. He then had to go and tell her that her breasts were 'still remarkably beautiful', a compliment that took away as much as it gave.

He was the same age as her, it turned out, but insisted on treating her as older. She was not sure she liked Damien. But his city flat was a better place to be than Rowan Grove lately, his ticking alarm clock and stuffed-up breathing preferable to her sisters' forlorn rooms, the odd creaks and shifts of a strange house and the lonely sound of occasional cars passing on the big road below. But each morning she returned there as dawn broke, in case Madeleine had come back.

The house felt less homely with each passing day, a coldstore of items that reminded her only of loss. That morning, climbing the stairs to return to her own bed, she'd found a Polaroid photograph lying on the landing. It must have slipped out of one of Madeleine's bags when Francesca had dragged them upstairs, but it was weird that she hadn't noticed it before. The photo was a portrait of Maddy asleep, or pretending to be, her red hair vivid against a green quilt, her skin like milk. Francesca had tucked it into the mirror of the old dressing table and climbed between the cold sheets. It had been eight days now. Why wouldn't the girl come home?

The two actors playing Greek guards fell into step beside her, and Damien vanished. They took hold of the binding ropes tied around her arms. The speakers blasted out some primitive drumming and the noise of tumbril wheels on hard ground, and she was pushed roughly onstage, stumbling forward onto her hands and knees where the light was brightest, raising her face into it:

'*I am herded with the cattle through mud.*
When fortune moves so swift against us
The high heart brought low as a slave's ...'

She found Eilís's eyes, Hecuba's eyes, full of the horror of it all. The audience were not shuffling or dozy; no, she could feel their attention stretched like a web through the auditorium. It was so good to have an audience. All she had to do was lean into the text, pour herself along its channels.

She told Hecuba how she'd just seen her young daughter slain as a sacrifice to the gods on the grave of her husband. Then came the passage she'd struggled with in rehearsal, because it made Andromache unsympathetic, she felt. She had to argue that Hecuba's murdered daughter's pain was not as bad as her own. But as she spoke the words – *To die is simply not to be; Better to be dead than live like this'* – something shifted inside her, filling every cell with its charge.

The rest of the speech came in a torrent, and when she paused for Talthybius to tell her what her fate would be, he did not come in right away. It was like listening to the resonance of a note dying into silence. She looked at Eilís to see if anything had gone wrong and saw that, while her face was set in lines of grief and sorrow, her eyes had a gleam to them, impressed.

A beat, and Talthybius embarked on a long speech about the ways of men and gods, the things that are inevitable and cannot be helped. Francesca clutched her child to her breast, tears – where from? – flooding down her face now, which was dangerous for her make-up, but so be it.

Then came the *coup de grâce*.

'Your son cannot be borne to live, lady.'

The chorus set up a stylised wailing and Talthybius stepped forward, reaching for the child at her bosom. Her limbs began to shake uncontrollably, but all the words were there, streaming from her with no conscious effort. She fought him off, beating at his arms, twisting away, clutching the baby to her.

'He is all I have in this world!'

She suddenly noticed panic in Talthybius's eyes. He was Frank Rodney again, just an actor, like herself. Oh yes, he must take the child – the play said so. She noticed a dotted line of blood rising on the back of the hand that finally clamped on the doll and wrenched it roughly, more roughly than necessary, from its bindings.

An audible frisson ran through the audience as her breast was exposed. She fell to her knees and raised her arms to the auditorium, as if they could save her from the unrelenting horror. One of the pale faces in the dark resolved itself as Vincent Swan. His gentle expression dragged sideways with misery. He had come to see her.

The sight of him just made her cry harder as the soldiers caught hold of her from behind, dragged her across the floor and out into the wings. She would be covered in bruises by the end of the run, but she didn't care.

Hecuba's agonised cries filled the air. Crouched on the floor, in the dark, Francesca opened her mouth and let her death-scream fly.

30

On Sunday morning they found Madeleine.

Swan took the twisting road up to Tibradden, the hills hidden in the cloud, his windscreen wipers swiping at the blur of drizzle. The forestry car park at Cruagh Wood was filled with police vehicles and vans. Gardaí in fluorescent rain jackets moved among them. Two flanked a civilian in a hooded cagoule and matching waterproof trousers, who had a spaniel on a lead. The dog gazing up at its owner, its dripping tail waving slowly back and forth.

'She was found by a dog-walker,' Considine told him when she phoned.

They always said it was the walker, but the dog usually did the finding. Swan spotted Bob at the back of Technical Bureau van, took an umbrella from the boot of his car and went over to offer help. Bob gave him a suspicious look, then nodded at a bundle of white metal rods.

'You can take those, if you're up for it. She's in an awkward place. We're trying to work out how to get a tent over her. This feckin' rain.'

Swan hoped to weave himself into the procedure somehow, before anyone stopped to consider what a suspended detective was doing there. He tucked the rods under his arm and followed Bob up a rough vehicle track, pale clay puddling in the potholes. Rain hissed on his umbrella, the shelter of which Bob had refused to share. As he trudged ahead of Swan, his white suit, tucked under his arm in a plastic bag, was the brightest thing in the landscape. Walls of dark conifers rose impenetrably on either side.

The track branched and they turned out of the trees and along an area of sloping boggy ground, studded with frochan bushes and heather. The ground had been worked for peat at some stage, black lines of turf banks scarring the mossy hillside. Swan spotted three heads over a rise of the land. Considine and Rooney with the lugubrious Desmond Joyce – slow, steady and far from stupid.

There was already a line of bright sticks poked in the ground, and Swan followed Bob along the circuitous route they had cleared to the site.

The three detectives watched their approach. Considine nodded briefly, Rooney frowned. Joyce lifted a hand very slightly and turned away.

'Didn't realise you were back on duty, like,' said Rooney as Swan reached them.

Considine spoke up. 'I asked him to corroborate identification.'

'We don't need that yet,' said Rooney, his mouth petulant.

When the phone had woken him in the muddy half-light, Swan thought first of Francesca, who had been flitting through his dreams, frighteningly distraught, like she'd been on the stage. But it was Considine, her careful, flat tones making no sense to him until she delivered her message a second time.

'They've found a body near the pine forest, a young woman. Short red hair …'

He put on the little plastic overshoes and walked with Considine to a sudden drop, a miniature gorge torn in the sodden bog by flood, or a landslip. A mesh of heather and moss hung down over the raw peat like a curtain dragged from the land.

And protruding from behind this tangle, a pair of white legs, neatly bent at the knee. You would have thought them made of marble or wax, were it not for the chipped red polish on her toenails.

Considine asked Bob to reveal the rest, and he lifted the vegetation back, like a curtain. There was no mistaking her for anyone else. Swan tried to focus on what it might be important to notice, but his mind was hard to bring under control, his eyes skidding between the brightness of her hair, the paleness of her naked body, the darkness of the mud, like snatches he couldn't make match up into a complete image. It was just the pure shock of her being there.

Swan looked to Bob to check if he could get closer, and Bob pointed to an undisturbed section of ground – of mud, really – and Swan stepped onto it. The rain had been so heavy all through the week, he reminded himself, and the ground here so soft and grainy. Unless she was left just this morning, any valuable marks would be gone.

He leaned in as close as he could, tilted his head to see her features. Though she had looked unmarked from afar, he could make out some purple bruising on the cheek pressed into the ground, and the marks that circled her neck and wrists. Her hair was matted with a dark substance at her temple. He thought she looked ill and gaunt, which would have sounded like an idiotic opinion, if he said it out loud.

'Yes. It's definitely Madeleine Moone.'

Behind him, Joyce asked Rooney, 'What kind of name is Moone, now?'

Rooney started to talk about a town called Moone that he knew in Mayo, and Joyce pretended great interest. They would not talk about the case in front of him, that was plain.

Considine was keeping close.

'Did you find anything around?' Swan asked her. 'Any clothes or wrapping?'

'Nothing. He – or they – must have taken it away.'

'Did anyone make a guess at how long she's been here?' Flecks of peat had gathered in the crooks of her body, and he could make out what looked like silvery snail trails on her calf.

'Bob thinks at least a few days. O'Keefe's on his way. At the moment we're guessing she was put in a shallow grave, but that the heavy rains revealed her.'

Joyce and Rooney had ceased talking about the geography of Mayo.

'Gina,' barked Joyce, 'I think we should let Swan get on with his day.'

Swan didn't move immediately. He tried to commit it all to memory. He turned and met Considine's eyes. She gave him a little nod, as if to say, *You can leave this with me*.

He picked his way back across the rough slope as more technicians arrived to help Bob construct the shelter.

Halfway down the track he passed O'Keefe coming up with his old-fashioned doctor's bag.

'Vincent. A sad one, I hear.' Neither of them broke step.

As Swan came towards the car park, the sky lifted and he looked up to see Dublin spread out below him, a toy-box scatter of buildings. A break in the clouds allowed the sun to stream down on the city centre, catching on the corrugated roof of Liberty Hall and the green dome of the Custom House beside it. It looked like a city where good people lived.

He would tell Francesca himself, not allow uniforms on the doorstep to be the first she knew of it.

31

Mr Cotter was busy with other customers, so Francesca flicked through the relevant papers to check the reviews were there, before she had to hand over the money. Yes, there were two. The *Sunday Tribune* had a large photograph as well. Her eye was pulled to her own name in the text, and next to it the tantalising phrase 'a revelation'.

'I hope you're purchasing those.'

'Good morning, Mr Cotter,' she said, flinging the papers on the counter and giving him a poisonous smile. 'And isn't it a gorgeous morning?'

'Gorgeous? It's as cold as a witch's tit out there.' He dropped his eyes to her chest.

'*Such* a pleasure to see you again.'

Outside, she leaned against the pub wall and opened the *Sunday Tribune* properly, folding it back on itself so that the wind wouldn't whip it about. It was the kind of review that featured in wistful daydreams. The critic loved the play, called it 'intelligent and radical'. He praised all of the main characters, but most of all he praised her:

Some of us had perhaps lost sight of the talents of Francesca MacNamara in recent years, diluted by television formats and distance, but this is a performance of unparalleled emotional power, a revelation, and enough to make this critic want to lobby for a civic celebration to mark her return to Ireland. Simply unforgettable.

Francesca clutched the paper to her chest and looked skywards. Tears came to her eyes and ran into her smile. The daily papers had been similarly gladdening, but not as focused on her as this. Christ, it just felt such a long time since anything had gone right, or since anyone said something good about her work. She hadn't realised that she'd given up hope they ever would again.

She'd read the other one at home, she resolved, and set off across the car park, but only got as far as the other side before she had to give in and look at the review in the *Sunday Independent*. Its review was shorter, less fulsome about the production, but it singled out her performance as 'unmissable'.

'Unmissable!' she said aloud, then realised she was at the very spot where she and Madeleine had sat on the day of the funeral, when Madeleine started telling her all about her unhappy adolescence and Francesca had been thinking how she would make everything better. What a mess they had made of it, so far.

She stepped over the wall and headed towards the house. She wanted her good mood back. She would make coffee and spread the reviews out on the living-room floor. She would think about her next move, in the light of this nourishing praise.

Vincent Swan was standing on her doorstep. She gave him her biggest smile. How sweet that he had been there, in the first-night audience, that he could share this triumph with her. But he didn't smile back, and the expression on his face was odd. As she got nearer, he slipped his hands out of his coat pockets as though ready to catch her.

For a stupid moment she was tempted to turn round, walk away from what was coming, but he was beside her now, asking for her key.

Then they were inside the house, and he was talking softly, endlessly. What words he used, she couldn't recall. He held on to her as she lashed out and howled, dry-eyed.

When there was nothing left, they sat on the sofa together, her clenched hands contained in his. She couldn't bear to look at him.

'It must be someone else.'

'I'm sorry, there's no doubt about it.'

'Why would you say that to me?' She turned her face to the back garden. It had started to rain again, the strings of the clothes dryer were beaded with drops, and the beads were sliding into each other, swelling, falling.

'Are you listening to me? Francesca? The Guards will come to tell you about this. They'll be here soon. They'll have to ask you questions. Is there anything you want to tell me before they get here?'

She looked at him then. Although they were locked together, his hands heating hers and their knees bumped against each other, he was not her friend after all. He was just a policeman.

'No. I don't know.'

'Anything about that night you last saw her? Or any-thing from before that, when your sisters were here, before they died – did Madeleine say anything about when she last saw them? It could be important.'

'Shut up. Will you ever just shut up?'

The doorbell rang and he went off to open it.

Nothing made sense.

Low voices in the tiny hallway. Vincent explaining something. A rustle of coats. The Guards came into the room, two tall ones. Different ages but strangely like each other, square-faced and fair-skinned, like actors playing a younger and older version of the same person. And it seemed for a moment that they were all actors together, going through the motions of a scene where bad news is delivered.

'Detective Inspector Swan says he has already informed you of your niece's death,' said the older one, fidgeting with the hat in his hands. 'We would like to extend our deepest sympathies for your loss.' He kept looking over at Vincent, unsettled by his presence.

Maybe the Guard is disappointed, she thought. If you had worked yourself up to tell someone the worst thing they had ever heard, it might be tough to find yourself beaten to the punch – yes, that was it. Then she remembered anew why they were there and closed her eyes.

'I'll go put on the kettle,' said Vincent.

The Guards told her that she would have to come and identify Madeleine's body later, officially. Maybe, just maybe, it was someone who looked very like Madeleine. Francesca jumped up and went into the kitchen, left the two Guards sitting in their chairs.

'They say I have to identify her. That means they're not sure who it is.'

'That's not what they meant. The identification is a formal thing.' He lowered his voice further. 'They shouldn't be troubling you with that. There's no rush.'

She reached out and laid a hand on his tie, just under the knot. Her hand appeared alien to her. She gave him a small, defiant push.

'You don't know it's her.'

Swan put his hand on top of hers. 'Francesca. I'm so sorry. I saw her.'

The older policeman appeared in the doorway and Swan let go of her hand.

'Ma'am, with respect. It would be better if you could come down to Deerfield station with us.'

She asked if Vincent could come with her, but he answered for them that he couldn't; that other people – good people – would be along to talk to her.

'Make sure they drop you home,' he said. 'Or phone me and I'll collect you. I'm at home most of the day.'

In the back of the police car Francesca tried hard to gather herself, but it felt like each minute had become separated from the one before and the one ahead, as if she kept waking up to a different street out the window. She had a bit of paper in her hand with a telephone number on it. She thought Vincent might have given it to her, but couldn't remember why.

Then they were in the Garda station, in an ugly room with chipped lino where two detectives talked to her, asking the same things again and again, only Francesca knew she had already told them these things. One was a young woman she had seen with Swan at the funeral, the other an even younger man who looked pompous beyond his years.

They kept asking about the night she'd last seen Madeleine. What time had she got home? How could Madeleine have left without her noticing? They told her that the boy – that friend from Trinity – had said Francesca had appeared 'very angry' that night. She told them that was ridiculous. She told them to go and ask Madeleine, and they stared at her, goggle-eyed, until she realised her error.

The truth of it, the finality of it, came rushing at her. Her hands curled into fists, her arms withered into her chest. It felt like someone was pulling a cord tight inside her, as if she could disappear inside herself. Part of her was observing this, thinking it extraordinary and excessive. She had no power to stop herself sliding from the chair to the floor, curling under the table.

They tried to get her up, their voices going on and on, their tugging hands. Eventually they called the doctor.

32

Swan woke to the sound of a radio playing below in the kitchen. Elizabeth was back, and the house was a better place for it. He stretched a hand out to her dented pillow – it was cold. She must have been up for some time. Now she was singing along with the radio, and he lay in bed for a few extra minutes, enjoying the sound of her happy voice.

She had even forgiven him for not meeting her at the train station, as arranged. He tried to explain that there had been an emergency, but she brushed it away, full of the events in Wexford, the triumphs of the festival. Over dinner he listened, or half listened, to tales of musicians called Felix or Estelle or the infamous Bobbo, to hilarious mishaps and the compliments people had offered her. He had marvelled at the difference in her.

'Working suits you,' he said. 'Maybe you should go out there and do a bit more.'

'I don't want to desert you, Vincent.'

'I desert you often enough. You don't need to tie yourself to the house.'

'But sometime in the future – soon, maybe – I'll need to be here every day.'

The phone rang, she flew to answer it. 'It's probably Estelle!'

Her absence gave him the moment he needed to realise she'd been talking about children, about the need to be here for a baby. It winded him.

She returned from the hall in a different mood.

'It's your mother. Something about your house guest?' A worrying twist to her mouth.

After he talked to his mother – something trivial about what kind of breakfast an American might expect – he tried to explain to Elizabeth that Francesca had urgently needed somewhere to stay in the wake of her niece's murder. As the word 'murder' came from his mouth, Elizabeth's face darkened. Lines between the rough world outside the door and their home life were being crossed.

'My mother has time on her hands and a spare room. There's no harm. Francesca's not a suspect.'

'Well, that's something. Though your mother might be disappointed by her harmlessness.'

The fact that Elizabeth could shake this off so easily lifted his spirits further, and the evening continued pleasurably. More than pleasurably.

When he was shaved, dressed and ready to leave the house, he located Elizabeth out in the garden, cutting away at yellowed foliage in the vegetable patch, dressed in his old overcoat.

'Cup of coffee for you?' he asked.

'I've had mine.'

'I'll need to get off in a minute.'

'Yes. Don't get fired.'

She looked up and winked at him. *Long may this mood last*, he thought.

*

The cobblestones of Dublin Castle were slick with rain. Drops struck his face in unpredictable spits. Ahead, he could make out the hunched forms of Hannigan and Murphy scuttling into the building. The tribunal had reconvened sooner than anyone expected.

His solicitor, Una Galvin, small of stature and determined of jaw, met Swan in the crowded foyer and led him away to a table where cups and saucers were laid out on a white cloth.

'I don't know what the hell's going on here.'

'Do you mean in general or just with the beverages?'

She frowned up at him. 'I mean with the judge. He's gone off to a side room with the Garda commissioner and a whole lot of other brass. I don't know whether it's a last-minute reprieve or more shit for the shitstorm. Where've you been hiding?'

'There's a difficult case kicking off. A murder. I got your messages.'

'You're not supposed to be working any cases. And it would have been better to meet.'

A trolley appeared around the corner, steered by a sleepy-looking girl. Large metal Thermoses rattled together on the top deck. Una Galvin flapped her hand at the girl to hurry her over.

As well as not picking up Elizabeth from the train station, Swan had missed his meeting with Una because Considine had phoned from Deerfield Garda station to say that Francesca was having some kind of seizure. They had called in a doctor already, but she kept asking for Swan.

She was pale and had quietened when he arrived, sipping

tea in a back room. Her interview was over, but she refused to go back to Rowan Grove and said she couldn't afford a hotel.

'Have you no friends you could stay with. Or your brother?'

'I can't. I just can't,' she mumbled. Her head kept drooping, like it was too heavy for her neck. The doctor had given her a shot of something.

So he called his mother, hoping that the novelty of minding a grieving actress would balance out the inconvenience. Thank God she agreed.

Una Galvin was poking a cup of coffee at him. Swan took it obediently.

'Why did you say *more* shit for the shitstorm? I thought they'd nothing.'

'Well, DeBarra's now got a doctor diagnosing temporary amnesia, and they're using that as the excuse for not entering the photos of the bruising into evidence until now. He'd forgotten they were taken – that's the line we're supposed to swallow.'

'What?'

'I know. Fucking ridiculous.'

She quickly flicked through the contents of her file so that Swan could see the photocopies she had – smudged body close-ups.

'Hard to see in black and white, but it looks like bruising on the originals.'

'They could have been taken any time. Or could be anyone.'

'But once they start discussing it, it leaks into the story, puts us on the defensive.'

'He must have done it to himself.'

'That's not a line I'll be taking. The man in custody beating himself up.'

'What line will you be taking?'

'I'm going for your colleagues' balls.'

'You're very direct, Una, I'll give you that. But if you do, I'll have to leave the Guards anyway.'

'If I don't, I risk you going to jail. You know they both have previous form. Detective Hannigan was suspended in the 1970s for his interrogation *techniques*.'

'Except nothing happened to DeBarra. I saw him leave on the Wednesday, looking fit as a flea.'

A tall barrister in a wig appeared in the corridor, his gown billowing.

'Judge Lawlor will see counsel for the Gardaí right away.'

Una Galvin put her coffee down on the table. 'Developments, DI Swan, developments. Hang tight.'

The foyer cleared of solicitors and their entourages, leaving Swan to face Hannigan and Murphy at a distance. Murphy was bouncing nervously on his toes, Hannigan was sullen. Whatever story they'd concocted, he'd find out soon enough. He turned away to busy himself with pouring another unwanted cup of coffee.

A door from the tribunal hall opened and Superintendent Kavanagh slipped out to join them. He was wearing his full dress uniform, dangling medals and all kinds of gleam. His cap was tucked under his arm.

'Lads,' he said, calling them together. 'Bit of news.

Brían DeBarra has been found in a ditch in Fermanagh. Executed.'

'Yes!' hissed Hannigan, grabbing air with his hand to make a triumphant fist, but quickly lowering as the superintendent cut him a look.

'Not the time or place, Ownie.'

'Sorry.'

'Who's in the frame, boss?' asked Murphy.

'Style of his own side – hands cable-tied behind his back, bullet to the back of the head. No torture, though. Anyway, what do you care? The tribunal is being stood down, and I doubt it will ever stand up again.'

Swan noticed a shine of sweat on Murphy's upper lip. He cared all right, but why?

Kavanagh looked at his watch. 'And in honour of the day being returned to us all, let me buy you detectives a drink. Then you're to fuck off back to your proper work.'

They retired to the back bar of the Clarence Hotel, where Kavanagh's uniform caused unease among the lunchtime drinkers, scruffy Project Arts Centre types. Swan took a whiskey, while Hannigan and Murphy had pints. Kavanagh chose vodka, because 'I'm meeting the Minister for Justice this afternoon.'

It was a stilted gathering, Kavanagh giving his anecdotes about the old days another go-round – all the punches he'd thrown, all the crims he'd outsmarted. When Murphy got up to go to the Gents, Swan excused himself to make a phone call, but detoured after a moment to the jacks. Murphy was not at the urinals, but a door on one of the stalls was closed. Swan went over to the sinks and washed his hands, whistling. Murphy emerged eventually, pale.

'Not feeling so well, T. P.?'

'Just an upset.'

'You know the thing that struck me about DeBarra? How much he talked. A man who talked so much was bound to get into trouble. In his circles. God knows what he talked about.'

'Don't!' Murphy retreated to the grubby towel dispenser, eager to turn his back.

'What was the set-up, T. P.? Were you in it for the cause, or was there a promise of a share of the compensation money?'

Murphy checked there was no one else in the space. 'They threatened me. Threatened my family.'

The door opened and two long-haired youths in parkas came in, scuttling to the urinals at the sight of Swan and Murphy. *We're that obvious*, thought Swan. Murphy took the chance to escape back to the bar. Swan didn't fully believe T. P.'s talk of intimidation, but there was no doubt he was spooked by DeBarra's death and feared someone might come for him too. Ownie Hannigan was probably in just as deep, but better at hiding it.

The superintendent was already on his feet; this would not be a prolonged celebration. Swan went with him, out the back door onto Essex Street East, where a shining car awaited.

'I need to ask you for something, sir.'

'Can you not just have a day's contentment, man?'

'The tribunal took me away from the MacNamara case

at a fairly crucial point. Their niece was found murdered yesterday, as you know. I wanted your permission to put resources back into the earlier case. Proper forensics.'

'What has one to do with the other?'

'I don't know that yet.'

'Your man Colin Rooney reported to me this morning – it's good to see him taking responsibility, he's a bright boy.'

'Gina Considine is very smart, too.'

'I'm sure she's a great help. Anyway, he located a bus driver says he dropped the girl in O'Connell Street the night she went missing. Could be another abduction. Like the one in the summer. She was found up in the mountains, too.'

'There are things we didn't have time to look at before,' Swan argued, 'things that have bearing on the niece's behaviour.'

Kavanagh placed his hat on his head carefully, brushed his thumb along the peak. 'Don't think I don't know what Hannigan and Murphy had up their sleeves today, Swan. I hope there's no truth in it. That you're secretly a violent bastard.'

This was Kavanagh's idea of a joke. Swan was supposed to laugh, but only managed a kind of nod.

Kavanagh looked at him closely. 'Don't go thinking you're special now, Vincent. We stand together or we fall.'

'Sir.'

The driver opened the passenger door for Kavanagh, and the superintendent headed down the steps. Just before he ducked inside he turned back to Swan.

'You can have the resources you need, for now.'

'Thank you, sir.'

Rumours were circulating that the commissioner had fallen out of favour with the minister. The superintendent might be going up in the world. The only thing certain is change. It would be politic to be more agreeable to Kavanagh.

After this case was over, he'd certainly think about it.

33

Father Timoney was dented, but not defeated. He went to the doctor's to get some stronger painkillers to sort out the back problem, but after writing the prescription, the fellow had time on his hands and started to ask clumsy questions about 'anxiety' – *Do you feel you have the support you need around you, Father?* Timoney had noticed a thick file of notes on the table, his own sent on from Cavan, presumably. He dismissed the doctor's enquiries emphatically, almost rudely.

With the help of an extra alarm clock placed in the middle of the carpet, he was no longer reliant on Mrs Noonan to get him out of bed in time for first mass. He had even started to cook some of his own meals. Piece by piece, he would dismantle her *raison d'être*. And he was formulating other plans, too. It was the church that was the problem – the physical church, the building. Those ugly cement walls weighing on him. As winter deepened, the place got colder with every passing week.

In the morning kitchen, after mass, he splashed fat over two eggs in the pan while Mrs Noonan hovered in the background. He could feel her impatience like a vibration in the air.

'Father!'

'Just a minute, Mrs Noonan.'

'Father!'

'I'll be right with you.' He realised he was taking pleasure in the delay, checked himself and turned to her.

'I need the keys.' She snapped her fingers, and he gazed at them pointedly.

'The heaters need to go off in the church – you're just burning money out there.'

As he became more self-sufficient in the domestic sphere, she'd got more interested in the church and its upkeep, making new areas of responsibility for herself.

He sighed and took the pan off the heat, went to the key cupboard, unlocked it and took out the church keys. Perhaps he was slower, more deliberate in this, than was absolutely necessary.

Mrs Noonan took the keys from his hand and stalked out the front door, a certain set to her bony shoulders. He didn't know why he found it so very difficult to be kind to her. Granted, she had rarely been kind to him, but he was the priest, he was the one who should rise above. Young Jimmy had once murmured something inappropriate about his mother's 'time of life', suggesting all kinds of moodiness and irrationality. Though what a young man would know about all that, Timoney couldn't imagine.

When he went back to his eggs they had hardened, the yolks opaque, the whites brown-edged and stuck fast to the pan. He levered them onto his cold toast and put the pan on the draining board.

Mrs Noonan returned as he was eating, put the keys on the table and grabbed the frying pan with a sigh and started scraping at it.

He had looked everywhere for that massage receipt. In her apron pockets, coat pockets, in the kitchen drawers. Even in her bedroom, when she was out doing the shopping. She had made no explicit threat, but he couldn't assume she'd thrown it away. He had to ensure she had nothing to embarrass him with, when the time came to get rid of her.

He coughed meekly. 'I was wondering if Jimmy could give me a hand with the crib?'

'The crib?' she said, addressing the wall above the sink. 'It's weeks till Christmas.'

'Advent starts next weekend. In Cavan we always put the crib up at Advent, the children loved it so.'

Mrs Noonan threw him a disbelieving look. 'Sure there's no children come to St Alphonsus. Not a one.'

'Well, maybe this will bring in some families. And weren't we all children once?'

She just stared at him, her face terrifyingly impassive. 'Jimmy's not around. Better you wait a while. Father Deasy, God rest his soul, he put the crib up for Christmas Eve.'

'I thought Jimmy was working on the roof.'

She shrugged.

'But the storms this time of year – all this rain – it's crucial we get it sorted.'

She dropped the pan into the sink with a crash and turned on him. 'Wasn't it me down on my knees with the sponge and mop, trying to make the place respectable? I know all about it!'

'So when will he be back?' Timoney's fingers had started to tremble. He slid his hands under the table.

'He's on a job.'

'Where?'

'He didn't *say*.' She was screwing up the front of her apron in an agitated way. And he saw that she was not angry with him; she was upset about Jimmy, about Jimmy letting them all down.

Father Timoney got slowly to his feet. 'I'll have to talk to the diocese. I'm sure they can find a reliable builder.'

He went out to the hall and picked his coat from a hook. He didn't know if the diocese would help him, but he had enjoyed sounding decisive. He would call Father Geraghty, but first he would check on the leaks and see if he couldn't get that crib up from the crypt himself. Small steps. *This is how progress is made.*

As he stepped outside, a pale-blue shape loomed up on the church roof and he stopped in shock, only to realise it was just a bit of tarpaulin that had come loose and was now billowing in the wind. For an instant, he had thought it was something miraculous. He hadn't lost his expectation of wonders, after all.

He unlocked the sacristy door and passed into the church. He searched for a good ten minutes before finding the pole with the hook at the end that would open the entrance to the crypt. It was a modest trapdoor to the left of the altar, and he had only been down there once before, part of the extensive tour with Father Geraghty the week he arrived in Dublin. The tour had featured a disheartening amount of pointing out things that needed to be done or mended.

Dark, spiked thoughts were gathering in his mind, ready

to snare him, so he fixed on the idea of the crib again – the wonder he had as a boy, being allowed up to gaze on it after Christmas mass. The plaster figures of Mary and Joseph had been as big as his small self, the sheep the size of little dogs. He felt he could just step in and join them, perhaps lie in the straw-filled manger and feel what it would be like for every eye, plaster and flesh, to be looking at you.

He would find a place to buy real straw. The crib would be a warm, glowing heart in the chill of St Alphonsus. *It is better to light one candle than curse the darkness.*

He hooked the metal end of the pole into a socket in the trapdoor. One pull and it creaked open, breathing cold and vaguely noxious air up into the church. It was dark down there, and he couldn't remember where the light switch was.

Father Timoney went back to the sacristy and fingered the bank of switches there, turning everything on for good measure, but when he returned, the crypt remained dark. He would not fall at the first hurdle; no, even unto the hundredth hurdle, he would not give up. Eventually he found a torch in a sacristy drawer.

The crypt had been intended as a burial place for the new seminary, a place to honour dead priests for passing on their knowledge and wisdom to generations of young men. But young men were no longer attracted to the priesthood. They were too distracted by worldly things they saw on television. Timoney had been part of a simpler world, simple choices. He was glad of that.

He made his way carefully down the wooden steps, following the pool of light thrown by the torch. He couldn't quite stand up straight, but had to crook his neck at an angle. He cast the torch beam in a circle, past the rough brick pillars with their oozing mortar, past various boxes of unknown origin and contents. The crib figures huddled by the far wall, draped in ghostly polythene. At one end the donkey stuck its head out, its pointed ears casting a devilish shadow on the wall behind. If he took it easy, took it slow and sensible, he was sure he could move them upstairs.

As he got closer, he realised that two of the shepherds, or perhaps a shepherd and Joseph – two bearded fellows, in any case – had lost their covers. He shone the torch about, but couldn't locate any fallen pieces of polythene. The ground was covered in a drift of dusty grit, and his torch showed up marks of disturbance, footsteps and swipes. A long, clear drag of something towards the stairs.

He wondered who had been moving things about, or what was stored here that Mr Cotter or some workman might have wanted. While he thought, he flashed the torch about him.

There was a soft lump lying at the bottom of a nearby pillar. For an awful moment he thought it was a body, but looked closer and saw it was only a green quilted sleeping bag, roughly rolled and bundled. He tried to laugh at his own jitteriness, but the smell that rose from the bag was sharp and bodily, like sweat or urine. He retreated, the back of his free hand pressed to his mouth and nose. Had some vagrant found a way into his church and been sleeping here? Had the noises that he thought had come from the spiritual world, that dark night on the church floor, come from some homeless man?

It was possible that he was not alone, even now. He waved the torch drunkenly around the space, but the beam couldn't penetrate the furthest corners. Timoney shuffled backwards, to where some illumination fell through the hatch from the church above, desperate now to find the light switch.

He played his torch over the wall there and at last spotted the grey switch-box with its pipe of cable. As he put his hand out, the beam fell on something beside the switch, on the edge of the brickwork, a glistening smear of crimson brown. Like paint, but not paint. It was just below head height. And stuck to the patch, like fine filaments of copper wire, were strands of red hair.

34

'Honey?'

'Definitely.'

Goretti Flynn offered Swan the chance to look into the eyepiece of the microscope. Transparent beads floating in a golden sea.

'I could pretend I knew what I was looking at.'

'It's very distinctive. The concentration of pollen, you see. And it's not just on the soft toy; there are drops of it on the duvet cover, too.'

The sucked paws of the corduroy monkey had been matted with something more than spittle. Rosaleen had access to some honey in her bedroom – the 'little nourishment' that O'Keefe had speculated about. The awful thought of her soothing herself with the child's toy, nursing on it in her loneliness.

'Rosaleen MacNamara lasted a week or so longer than her sister,' he said. 'The honey could be key to that.'

Dr Flynn, neat as a pin, strummed her gloved nails on the counter. 'Not my area, Swan, you'll need a nutritionist. Were there other traces found in the house: a jar or something?'

'We didn't get to do forensics on the whole house before the sister moved in. Anything is possible.'

They had lost so much. Even with all the resources he had on the case now, he would never know what evidence had been missed.

'There's a spoon, though,' Flynn said, as he moved to go. 'A teaspoon with honey on it, found in a bin bag in one of the bedrooms. Don't want you to get too excited, but the fingerprint guy is working on it now.'

The Technical Bureau had taken all the previous evidence out of storage and brought in more things from Rowan Grove. Goretti Flynn's lab was stacked with brown bags, and two assistants were examining and indexing everything.

With a satisfied nod, Swan took his leave and went to the next-door lab, where Bob Corcoran and Considine were talking intensely, each with an elbow on the counter, like two people arguing at a bar. This lab was virtually empty. While Goretti Flynn had almost too much to deal with, Bob, assigned to Madeleine's murder, had almost nothing. A few photos of tyre tracks in the mud of the forestry car park, some fibres from her mouth and body, a couple of cigarette butts, a ragged piece of plastic caught in roots near the burial, so old it crackled.

Madeleine's body had been washed carefully. She had suffered various bruises and a bad head wound, the cause of her death. O'Keefe did not rule on whether or not she had been sexually assaulted. The most startling finding was that her stomach was empty and she showed signs of extreme dehydration. O'Keefe concluded that she had been deprived of food and had very little water for three or four days before her death.

The investigating team had made little headway, and Considine looked exhausted as she stood there quarrelling. The only steer they had was the bus driver who remembered picking up Madeleine in Deerfield and dropping her on O'Connell Street around 11 p.m. on the night she went missing.

Swan rapped on the open door.

Bob and Considine broke off their conversation.

'Anything?' she asked, in a voice that expected nothing.

'Couple of interesting items Goretti has turned up. But not related to Madeleine. What's happening here?'

'Yeah, what is happening here, Bob?' said Considine.

Bob ignored her tone and addressed Swan directly.

'You'll understand. Most of the fibres we have are from her mouth – generic cellulose fibres from tissue or toilet roll. There are also three clothing fibres from the body – hardly anything – and until we locate the clothes she was wearing, which were most likely to be the source of those fibres, there seems little point in treating them as a priority. I have hopes for the tyre tracks, though. The heavy rain gives us a timeframe.'

'O'Keefe says she might have been in the ground for a week. There could be hundreds of cars parked in the car park in that time,' Gina objected.

'But we're looking at—'

'If you could concentrate on the fibres, then we might know what clothes we are looking for.'

'The samples are so small.'

Swan had the feeling this had been going on for some time.

'I don't want to disturb the work, I just need to talk to Gina for a moment. If you had an extra technician – someone else to work on the fibres – would that help? If you're struggling, that is.'

'I wouldn't say I was struggling …'

'Dr Flynn has some bright young ones helping her next door, and they're getting through things at a great rate.'

'I can do the fibres.'

'Good man. Excellent. We'll talk to you this afternoon, so.'

Swan took hold of Considine's shoulder and turned her in the direction of the door. 'Thanks again!'

Considine walked ahead of him to the end of the corridor. He noticed the back of her neck turn pink as she walked, so it wasn't a surprise when she wheeled round on him.

'I could have managed that myself!'

He held up his hands in contrition. 'All I could see was you with your heels dug in, and Bob doing no work.'

'He was refusing to examine the fibres.'

'And now he's examining the fibres. That was what you wanted.'

'Because a man told him to.'

'No, because I suggested that Goretti was better at the job than he was. And whatever persuasion I have comes as much from my rank as my manliness.'

'It all adds up to the same old shite.'

'Maybe it does. I don't care as long as we have progress.'

She scowled for a moment longer, then shook her head. 'Sorry.'

They made their way down to the unit office, and she brought him up to date with Madeleine's case, keeping her voice low.

'We can't find anyone who definitely saw her in the city centre after she got off the bus. We've even had bodies hanging round the stops at last-bus time, asking passers-by, and nothing. There's a boy says he thought he saw her on Wicklow Street at midnight, but he's not certain. She's hardly the only girl with short red hair in Dublin.'

'What about Harrison Todd?'

'He's not changing his story – he left her at the house with the aunt. And the bus driver, Willie Ward, says he's sure she was alone.'

'And he's certain it was her?'

'He was emphatic. And gave a really clear description.'

They reached the office and Considine pulled her chair over to Swan's desk, frowning.

'Any other ideas?' asked Swan.

'I don't know. I went back to Rowan Grove early this morning and managed to get those two bartenders – the next-door neighbours – out of their beds. It was bothering me that I hadn't met them, only read the notes from the Deerfield detective – Sergeant Clancy, you remember.'

'I remember you were not an admirer.'

'Anyway, one of them says that he saw a guy standing at the end of the road, looking up towards the house when Madeleine was knocking at the door, creating a distur-bance. He said he got the impression the guy was waiting, but he didn't see them together or anything, he just noticed him standing and watching. He also said Madeleine mentioned that she forgot her keys. So she wasn't hiding the fact that she had keys.'

Something was niggling at Swan. 'What was the bus driver called again?'

'Willie Ward.'

'I know that name. I'm sure I typed it into that bloody computer during my exile.'

'You think he's got a record?'

'I can't remember. It was mostly organised crime and armed robberies that I was detailing, but his name was in there somewhere.'

'Could be another Willie Ward.'

Swan pushed back from his desk. 'Leave it with me.'

He knocked on the door of the computer department before entering. Politesse would be necessary, given how he had left things. Eddie McCarthy swung round in his chair. Lifted his eyebrows in an exaggerated way.

'Well, well.'

'I know your system isn't up and running fully, Eddie, but I thought you might be interested in a small test for it.'

'You certainly gave it a test last time,' Eddie said, with a prissiness that matched his knitted waistcoat. 'We've only just patched it up.'

'See, there was a name I remember *inputting*, and I was wondering if it would be difficult for you to retrieve it for me.'

'That's what the system is for, Inspector Swan. Or did you not pick that up?'

'The name is Willie Ward. William Ward, if we're feeling formal.'

Eddie sighed, but pressed a button on one of the metal boxes lined up behind him, so that a line of little red lights sparked up and winked. Once the lights had stabilised, he turned to his monitor and started tapping away at the keyboard. The machine began to generate flickering lines of text across the screen. After scrolling through them, Eddie extracted a sharpened pencil from a drum of sharpened pencils, wrote a number on a telephone slip and handed it to Swan.

'What's this?'

'The case-file number.'

'What – I still have to go down to the archive and search for file boxes?'

'You're not in a sci-fi film, you know.'

'There must be some more information than that. Can you not search that case number and see what other names come up?'

Eddie jutted his sharp little beard at Swan. 'Well, maybe your time on the databank wasn't completely wasted.'

Swan came round to Eddie's side of the desk and stood behind him, as further lines of text started to type themselves out on the black screen. Dashes, slashes, sequences of numbers, and embedded among them ordinary names and addresses, but no indication of who were the accused, the victims or the witnesses, until the name Don Zanotti joined the ranks at the end of the alphabetised list.

'The Zanotti kidnapping,' Swan murmured.

Zanotti was a well-known Dublin businessman who'd been abducted in Dalkey by an IRA gang in 1979 when there had been a spate of such things, a ruse for raising money for arms, though Swan suspected much of it got siphoned off along the way. Since he had worked the case himself, he knew that Willie Ward was not one of the kidnappers, so he must have been a suspected associate or even just a witness.

With that thought, it all came back to him.

'Gotcha!'

He gave Eddie a quick whack on the back. Intended as a friendly gesture, it produced a bout of coughing, but Swan was already out the door.

He ran into Considine on the stairs, coming to find him.

'Willie Ward,' he said, 'is a liar.'

'I know, I've just got off the phone with the dispatcher at the Islandbridge garage. Ward wasn't on, the night Madeleine disappeared. It was the night before.'

'Do you remember the Zanotti kidnapping? Willie Ward was the witness who said he saw two men struggling in the back of the car near Finglas. It sent us in the wrong direction completely.'

'Jesus! What's his game – looking for attention? You'd think he wouldn't try the same thing twice.'

They moved apart to allow two Guards to pass down the stairs between them.

'As far as I remember, Ward never got charged for misleading us, and he didn't appear in court, so yeah, maybe he's still desperate for attention.'

'… or he's involved somehow.'

'Or Madeleine was on his bus the night before and he's got his days wrong. You're going to bring him in, aren't you?'

'Too right,' said Considine, but she didn't move. Something was bothering her.

'What is it?'

'If he's lying, or innocently *mistaken*, then we've nothing to put Madeleine in town. I suggested to Joyce that we cover Deerfield anyway, but he didn't take up my suggestion.'

The last sighting of Madeleine, before the bus driver supposedly picked her up, had been in the house at Rowan Grove.

'I'll go talk to Francesca MacNamara again,' he said.

'I should come with you.'

Strictly speaking, Considine was right. It was her case.

'She's at my mother's. She's not well. Let's keep it informal for now.'

Considine gave him a sceptical look, like she'd known him a hundred years.

35

It was a beautiful poached egg, a pillowy white oval with a shining yellow dome. For two – or was it three? – days now, Vincent's mother kept appearing through the bedroom door with trays, urging Francesca to eat. Vegetable soup, a lamb chop and green beans, eggs on toast. A folded white napkin and shining cutlery beside. All so thoughtfully simple and kind. It made her weep. The stupidest things made her weep. Francesca admired each offering as you would a picture, but she couldn't swallow any of it.

Eileen Swan had given her a room up under the roof, with a high single bed and a little skylight over it. And in that room Francesca had given herself over to her illness, her grief that was her illness, and the woman just let her be. Didn't try to shush or comfort.

Any time she fell into sleep, Francesca would dream of Madeleine, always the same dream – Madeleine with a light in her eye, laughing at her, telling her it was only an act, or that yes, she had been dead, but now she wasn't any more and to stop gawking like that.

Today Francesca was trying to hold everything very still and quiet and shallow. She thought about God, specifically whether she should start believing in him, because what random universe could deliver up this excessive toll? Maybe it was the devil she should be believing in.

She got out of bed carefully and pulled on the heavy checked dressing gown she found hanging on the back of the door. Down in the hall she dialled Phil's number.

'Yes?' He answered straight away, sounding annoyed.

'It's Francesca, Phil. I wanted to say I'm sorry.' She heard a sigh, or perhaps just a breath. 'I'm sorry you had to go and identify Madeleine. After having to do it before. I should have done it.'

'You'd got yourself into a state. Where are you, anyway?'

'I'm … with a friend. I'll give you the number.'

'One of your theatre friends?'

'No, I'm actually—'

'Well, I'm glad you found somewhere. If it wasn't for Mairead's mother coming up from Cork, you would have been welcome here, you know that.'

'Sure.'

'My manager's signed me off work for a week. I didn't want him to, but he made me. It's like *I've* done something wrong.'

'It makes people feel awkward,' she said.

He didn't reply.

'Look, Phil …'

She wanted to have a different kind of conversation than they normally had, but as she searched for words, her nerve failed. 'Let's keep in better touch, eh?'

She gave him Eileen Swan's number and hung up. It took all her strength to get up the winding staircase and back into bed. She hoped sleep would come again, because dreaming about Madeleine was better than thinking about her, about how frightened she must have been at the end. She couldn't stop thinking about the conversations they had had, sitting up late in Madeleine's freezing flat, drinking cheap Hirondelle while her niece told her tales of adolescent wild times. She thought they had all the time in the world to get to know each other.

There was one story especially that bothered Francesca, that kept skipping through her mind.

It had started innocently enough.

There was this boy I was crazy about. He was only fifteen, but real tough and swaggery, like, went out of his way to show that he didn't give a damn about anyone. I was convinced he secretly liked me, but the more I followed him about, the more he had to show all the others that he didn't care. One night we were in the grounds of the care home, y'know, over the wall. We were playing Injuns – throwing sticks for tomahawks and whooping around. He caught me by the hair and dragged me away from the others. I thought, 'Here's my big chance.' So I start to kiss him, and he rips my shirt off. And I thought, 'Slow down there, Tonto!'

Madeleine had been sitting on the floor, knees up to her chin, laughing and glugging wine, like this was the most hilarious story, while the back of Francesca's neck went cold. She did try and say something, like 'That's awful' or 'terrible', but Madeleine just batted away her protests with a swipe of her arm, cigarette end glowing.

And I'm trying to hide my tiny tits, so I can't stop him from dragging me further away, then he takes this washing line from his pocket – Ha-ha! – and starts tying me to this tree. Seriously. And maybe I'm getting a little scared about what he's going to do now, and I'm worried about being more or less naked, like; and doesn't he just disappear, the little shite, like for hours. I mean, I know he would've come back, only Bernie comes and finds me first and, well, you can imagine. Shocked rigid, she was.

So that was it. That was why I got sent to Phil's. I mean, I know it looked bad, but nothing had happened.

That's what she said. Nothing had happened. Did Madeleine not even know what danger looked like?

When Francesca woke again, Vincent Swan was sitting on the end of her bed, looking down at her. She flicked the sheet over her face, embarrassed.

'How long have you been there?'

'Not long.'

She drew back the sheet and raised herself up, rubbed her eyes.

'Sorry to wake you.'

She shrugged. She had no vanity left. He rubbed the back of his neck quickly and she thought about putting her own hand there, of pulling him to her, his mother in the kitchen below. His hand was lying on the blanket now, near. She picked it up and gazed for a while at her fingers entangling in his. She knew there would be no sudden, obliterating, erotic moment. He was not the type. She tried to catch his eye, but he also seemed mesmerised by their joined hands, as if they were some separate entity, a manifestation he had no control over.

'I need to talk to you.'

'Official talking?'

'That kind.' He managed to draw his hand gently from her grasp. 'My mother's in a mood with me for disturbing you. You have her feeling protective.'

'She was very good to take me in.'

'She's enjoying it. Humming away to herself in the kitchen.' He looked towards the door.

'What is it?'

He sighed. 'We're not sure, now, that a bus dropped Madeleine into town. The driver got the night wrong. If she didn't go back to her flat, or to friends … was there anyone she would go see in Deerfield?'

'I don't think so.'

'You never saw her with anyone?'

'No. But she used to hang out with the local kids when she lived here. They used to get up to the usual delinquent things.' An image of Madeleine tied to a tree in the dark lit up her mind. She wouldn't tell him that. She wouldn't humiliate Madeleine that way.

'I'm sorry to be asking more questions. Are you all right?'

She nodded quickly.

'Any of this gang still about?'

'I don't think they were close friends, do you know what I mean? She mentioned the Cotter boys from the newsagent's, and the Noonans. There may have been others, but I'm sure they've grown up and scattered to the winds by now.'

'The first time I met Madeleine was in the priest's house. His housekeeper is Mrs Noonan. Any connection?'

'I don't know.'

He looked irritated, like her answer wasn't good enough.

'I was in America!' She felt tears fill her eyes, which was so frustrating.

He seemed to be looking in his jacket pockets for a handkerchief.

Francesca reached for a tissue from the pile on the bedside table and pressed it to her eyes. 'Every time I think I can hold steady, I'm proved wrong.'

He was staring at the bedside table, at the Polaroid of Madeleine sleeping, which had been concealed by the tissues.

'Is that recent?'

'It's nice, isn't it? I found it in the house after she ... after she ...' Hot tears were rolling down her cheeks so fast now that she needed to mop them with a sheet. She could not recognise herself these days.

He was asking if he could borrow the photograph, and Francesca shook her head.

'Please, I'll return it as soon as I can.' He reached over her, took a tissue from the pile and lifted the photograph with it, wrapping more tissue around it. 'Thank you.' He was looking at her with such sympathy it made her frightened.

A knock came on the door.

'Vincent!' His mother didn't open it, had made no sound on the stairs.

Francesca watched him shift his gaze to the wall somewhere above her head.

'A Detective Considine was on the phone. Needs to talk to you urgently. You're to meet her at St Alphonsus.'

He was already on his feet, moving away.

36

A steady *plip-plip* of water fell from the church ceiling into a yellow plastic bucket far below. The drops fell with such gathered force that a halo of spray glistened on the wooden floor around it.

Detective Joyce and young Rooney sat in the middle of one hard pew. Rooney's hands were loosely joined between his knees in a semi-prayerful gesture, while Joyce took an ostentatiously secular pose, legs crossed and an arm stretched along the pew back, as if relaxing on a lounge-bar banquette. Swan and Considine sat in the pew in front and twisted round to affect the necessary huddle. In front of the altar, white light radiated up from the crypt entrance where Bob was working.

'We have enough to assume it's her,' said Rooney. 'The hair's a good match, and we're near where she was last seen. We should have a blood type within the hour. The mark is consistent with the wound to her head.'

'But there's no sign of her clothes or the shoulder bag we think she had with her,' Considine said.

A volley of flashes issued from the hatch in the floor, silhouetting a rising form. The shape resolved itself as Bob Corcoran's hooded head and shoulders. He was carrying a puffed-up paper bag the size of a pillow.

'Sleeping bag?' called Joyce.

Bob came towards them, the bag resting on his forearms.

'Urine definitely. Faeces too. Stains on the floor beneath it suggest she was there for a while.'

'Can I have a look?' asked Swan.

Bob opened the mouth of the envelope. The bag was green and quilted, a perfect match to the one in the Polaroid of Madeleine that he had taken from Francesca. The photograph was already at the labs, already being processed for fingerprints and leads to paper stock or particular cameras. They didn't yet know how it had appeared in the house at Rowan Grove.

The detectives sat on for another minute in the pews, a heaviness in their shared silence.

'Can we see the sacristy?' Swan asked Desmond Joyce.

'Can we see the sacristy?' Joyce asked Corcoran simultaneously.

'On you go. Dr Flynn is *within*.'

Swan hadn't entered a sacristy since a brief and mortifying stint as an altar boy when he was ten. His mother had wanted to give him confidence, she told him recently. What she'd given him was two years of petty assaults from his classmates.

This sacristy was very different from the Victorian one in his old parish church. The modern wardrobes and cupboards were on a domestic scale, like fitted bedroom furniture, and lined the walls on three sides. A small door led into a kind of scullery with a steel counter and sink, where another halogen light on a stand blared a dazzling light. The four of them gathered around the door of this

306

inner room. Goretti Flynn was squatting under the sink, scraping out the gunge of the sink trap into a plastic basin. She stood up and moved smoothly into presentation mode.

'It's all been washed down, but we found what look like traces of blood on a sponge that was here, and traces on the floor all the way in from the altar area. We think she might have hit her head on the pillar because he was carrying her, or there might have been a struggle.'

'Perhaps she was trying to escape,' said Considine.

Swan noticed the two women hold each other's eyes for a moment, as if resting in this slightly more comforting version of events before moving on.

'Perhaps,' said Goretti. 'In any case, he brought her here after it and cleaned up the traces in a very methodical way. This counter was covered in vases when we arrived.' She indicated a collection of glass vases gathered in a corner, green squares of foam stuffed within. 'No prints on anything.'

'I wonder why he bothered to wash her,' said Rooney. 'If she'd stayed buried, we might never have found her.'

'He might have had knowledge of forensics,' Swan said. 'Or maybe the washing was part of it in some way, part of his pleasure.' He thought about the wiped switches in Rowan Grove. It felt like a connection, this assiduous attention.

Swan regarded the long metal counter that ran seamlessly into the sink. Madeleine could easily have been laid out on it, with room to spare. 'He would seem to be pretty organised.'

'He's not as clever as he thinks. None of them are.' Flynn stooped to the pipes again, her jaw set.

The door that led from the sacristy to the outside world was only half a dozen paces from the room with the sink. Swan remembered the night he sat in his car outside Rowan Grove, inert with indecision after Francesca's attempted seduction, and the headlights that he saw flare into life beside the church.

'Can I go out this way, Goretti?' He pointed at the door. Dr Flynn nodded. 'It's clear.'

He stepped out onto the tarmac, closing the door behind him to discourage the others from following. He could see across the busy road and the pub car park, through the bare branches of the cherry trees to the MacNamaras' house. Yes, the car he saw had been parked right here, next to the sacristy door. In one way it was a brazen choice, so visible from the road, but the dazzle of the headlights effectively hid whatever happened behind them. And from this position, all you could see of the priest's house was the blank gable of the end wall.

He hadn't seen any detail of the car or its driver, but he saw it at a particular time and date. He counted. Five nights ago. O'Keefe had estimated that Madeleine had been dead for less than a week. It fitted.

He walked round the side of the building and re-entered the church by the main door. Joyce, Rooney and Considine were standing in the central aisle, deep in talk.

'You're blinded by conditioning,' Joyce was saying. 'Not only did he supposedly "find" evidence in the crypt, he also "found" the dead MacNamara sisters, and entertained the niece in his house. He's new to the area, and people have him down as a bit odd, a bit on his own. He had access to the church and to the MacNamaras' house. If he wasn't a priest, he'd be top of our list.'

'Lots of others had access too,' Considine countered. 'Lay helpers, workmen, the other priests from the parish ...' she hesitated. 'I mean, he's quite old.'

'Quite old? Thanks a bunch, sweetheart. He's no older than I am.'

Swan joined the argument. 'How would he have got her to the Dublin mountains to bury her?' He has a bad back – he was crippled with it at the funeral.'

'That can be faked,' said Joyce.

'He doesn't even drive,' said Considine.

Joyce made an exasperated noise. 'I don't think the initial investigation went deep enough.'

Swan let that one go. No one had been interested in the deaths of the MacNamara sisters at the time, least of all Desmond Joyce.

'Have you spoken to the housekeeper's son?' asked Considine. 'Jimmy Noonan was doing work on the roof, according to Father Timoney.'

'He's not in Dublin any more, according to his mother,' said Rooney.

'Exactly!'

'I'll tell you what,' said Joyce, 'you and Vincent are welcome to turn up any other suspects. Me and Einstein here are going to shake down the priest. They're keeping him at the station for us.'

After they left, Considine turned to Swan. 'Joyce is very fixed in his vision.'

'He's never got over that case – a priest accused of

abusing some kids. Nothing was proved, but it sort of turned his world upside down. He'd been quite holy before, but his kids, you know, they're little gods to him.'

'You hear rumours that kind of thing happens more often than you'd imagine. But killing is a different matter.' Considine started to rub her hands together, trying to warm them.

'I've been thinking about Jimmy Noonan too. I think Madeleine knew him from the neighbourhood, back when she lived here. What if it was him watching from the end of the road that night? I always wondered why she turned up at the priest's house again the following day, rather than just phone him. Maybe there was some connection between them? Do you remember, the first time in the priest's house, there was another person there we didn't see – Mrs Noonan cleared someone out of the living room before Colin and I talked to Madeleine there.'

'I didn't see anyone,' said Considine.

'I think Jimmy was there, though. How did we miss him?'

'He might be some innocent dolt. But he had the strength, and the access to this place.'

'And I believe he knew Madeleine.'

It was only mid-afternoon but, despite the lights, the church was gathering gloom. The cellar-like smell of the place seemed particularly strong.

'Remember the funeral?' asked Considine. 'There was a workman on the roof, pinning down a tarpaulin or something. I thought it must be an emergency, because they hadn't asked him to stop while the mourners gathered. That could have been Jimmy.'

'What was he like?'

'A shape against the sky. Nothing more.'

Swan went over to the crypt opening and called down to Bob.

'Has anyone looked up on the roof or in the tower?'

'Do we have reason to?'

'There was some recent work going on up there – could be a good place to conceal something. Like her clothes, say.'

'It's a bit dark now.'

'It's still the working day. Indulge me.'

Swan and Considine emerged from the church into the slightly warmer temperature of the outside world. The light from the priest's kitchen spilled a yellow glaze on the damp ground. Through a haze of condensation, they could just make out two figures at the kitchen table, heads bowed.

'Let's go talk to his mammy,' said Swan.

Mrs Noonan answered their knocking, looking strained. She bobbed her head out of the doorway to check who else was around before she would let them in.

A stale smell of cigarettes pervaded the house, and the patterned vinyl seemed grubbier than before. Mrs Noonan opened the door of the bleak living room and flicked on the overhead light.

'We can just sit in the kitchen – we're no one special,' said Swan, ducking round her and heading down the hallway.

A hanging layer of smoke bisected the kitchen. The chairs around the table were empty. One had a brown coat slung over its back. A couple of mugs, a full ashtray and

311

a set of black rosary beads sat on the chipped Formica. But the visitor hadn't departed, she was standing by the refrigerator in the dark part of the kitchen, staring out as if afraid of being caught.

'Hello there,' Swan said. He recognised her immediately – the strange prophetess of the prayer group. He could sense Considine draw close behind him, alert.

Mrs Noonan dodged in front of them, snatching the dirty mugs from the table.

'We'll continue this later, Mary,' Mrs Noonan said.

'Are we interrupting something?' Swan asked, a harmless smile fixed on his face.

Mary Viney took a step forward, her eyes locked on him. 'We're praying for Madeleine.'

She was wearing an odd dress with puffy sleeves, patterned with flowers the size of plates. It looked like some cast-off, practically down to her ankles and hanging loose over her thin frame.

'You knew Madeleine?' he asked. She took another step. It wasn't just her teeth that were odd. The irises of her eyes were such a dark brown that they blended with the pupils, making them look deadened, like a shark's.

'We all knew Madeleine,' Mrs Noonan interrupted, thrusting the duffel coat into the smaller woman's arms. She tried to mask it with her body, but Swan saw her give Mary Viney a shove towards the door.

Mary paused as she drew level with them, saying to Considine, 'God sees everything. You can't hide your doings from him.'

To Swan's surprise, Considine's face went a sudden

subtle pink, though maybe it was annoyance rather than – what – embarrassment? He'd never heard Considine utter the slightest holy thought, but she seemed to be vulnerable to this woman's nonsense. Mary left the kitchen, and he listened for the sound of her departing steps and the front door closing.

Mrs Noonan started turning on taps and banging the kettle against the sides of the sink.

'No, no,' said Swan, 'we don't need anything, just a quick chat while we're passing.' He pulled one of the chairs out from the table. 'We'll soon be out of your hair.'

Reluctantly, Mrs Noonan sat down opposite. Her fingers scrambled over the table to find her cigarette packet.

'Father Timoney is still at the station,' Swan said, 'he's been very helpful.'

No reaction. No anxiety for her employer, no pride in his helpfulness, either. He moved on, asking bland questions to get her talking. How long she had lived in the house, how many children she had and what they were up to. Maeve, Donal and Jimmy were all a credit to her, apparently. Maeve was married in Canada, Donal was in Liverpool.

'I understand Jimmy was doing some work at the church.'

'They already asked me about Jimmy,' she said curtly.

'Yes. I was just thinking, when I was in the church there, that it's an awfully big job, the roof, even for a skilled workman.'

'Father Timoney's a cheapskate.' She sparked up her lighter and dipped her cigarette into its flame.

'And Jimmy stayed here sometimes, did he?'

313

'Do you have children, Mr Swan?' She squinted at him.

'Not yet,' he said, surprising himself.

'Why wouldn't he visit the odd time with me, his mother – isn't this my home too? Hasn't he been getting himself up on his feet, trying to make a life here and no one to help him, and unemployment the way it is.'

'Where is Jimmy now?' Considine asked. 'Is there another address in Dublin he uses?'

'He's on a job in the Midlands. I told them, I don't know where.'

'Does he keep any of his things here, his tools, his clothes?' asked Swan.

'I don't see it's any business of anyone ...' She started to stab out her cigarette in the ashtray. It crumpled and she burned her fingertips on the embers, snatching them away and wiping them quickly on her skirt.

Considine came in with her conciliatory voice. 'We weren't wanting to bother you at all, honestly. If you prefer, we can ask Father Timoney to allow us access.'

There was a nerve-shredding scrape as Mrs Noonan thrust back her chair on the tiles. 'Is there no end to this?' she said, and headed off back to the living room.

There was a white door in a corner that Swan hadn't noticed before, and this was what Mrs Noonan opened for their inspection. It was a walk-in cupboard, piled with cardboard boxes, bags, assorted bits and pieces.

'Is there a light?' asked Considine.

'There is not,' said Mrs Noonan, with no effort to conceal her satisfaction.

'All this is Jimmy's?'

314

'It's little enough. It's his life.'

Swan leaned on the jamb and looked further inside, willing his eyes to adjust to the dark. There was a loosely rolled sleeping bag on top of the other things, though different in colour from the one found in St Alphonsus. There was also a dusty toolbag with a partially open zip. He could just see the dull glint of spanners inside – perfect to get some prints from.

Behind him, Considine was trying to soft-soap Mrs Noonan, talking about the slovenly behaviour of sons and the work they generated for women. She usually had a good instinct for setting the right tone, but the housekeeper was too annoyed. They needed to play down what they had found, so that Mrs Noonan would not try and dump it, the minute their backs were turned. He needed to be careful that his inspection appeared cursory. Just as he turned away, he noticed a small teak elephant on the floor of the cupboard, like one of the set in the MacNamaras' house.

'Isn't he lucky to have you, now?' he said.

Mrs Noonan answered with a sniff, and they moved back towards the kitchen. Halfway down the hall, the housekeeper stopped suddenly and opened another cupboard door set into the wall. Swan thought he was about to be shown more of Jimmy's belongings, but there was just a thick wedge of hanging coats, and beyond them a metal wall cupboard.

'That's where we keep all the keys. He locked it. More than a week ago he locked it, and he refused to give anyone else a key.'

'Jimmy?'

'No! Not Jimmy. Father Timoney!'

Swan stretched past the coats and played his fingers over the rim of the locked cabinet door.

'Father Deasy never had cause to lock it. I have to ask Father Timoney to get out a key for me whenever I need to. I don't know what to think of that. It's suspicious, isn't it?'

'Has there been anything else odd about Father Timoney's behaviour?' Considine asked, her voice low and sincere.

'I wouldn't know where to start.'

They returned to the kitchen table to hear her out. Mrs Noonan reached for another cigarette, but Considine insisted she take one of hers. Swan observed them, Mrs Noonan visibly relaxing as she launched into her criticisms of Father Timoney.

'Well, there's the keys. And he spends time alone in the church, talking to himself. I didn't want to tell Father Geraghty about it, but now I feel guilty that I didn't. Father Timoney says he's been troubled with this back of his, you know, but I think he could be putting it on. Using it as an excuse.'

'An excuse for what?'

She shook her head slightly to indicate her reluctance to say, but the way she cocked her cigarette was pure Bette Davis.

'I found ... I hate to say this ... evidence that he was seeing prostitutes.' Her mouth puckered.

Swan could feel Considine tense beside him. Perhaps Desmond Joyce's suspicions were well founded.

'What was this evidence?'

''Twas a receipt from a *massage parlour*.'

'You sure?'

Mrs Noonan jumped up to fetch it from somewhere, giving Swan and Considine a moment to swap an incredulous look. She was back in an instant, holding the rectangle of paper in front of Swan's face so that he could see the biro scribble – 'Massage £10' – written in a big, looping hand. The address was Mountjoy Square, but the Executive Health Spa was not a place he was familiar with, although these establishments tended to come and go. The price was cheap, and the very fact there was a receipt was not in keeping with what he knew of brothels. He was tempted to put it to Mrs Noonan that this might actually be a receipt for a massage, plain and simple, but it was politic to go along with her version for now. How she must dislike Father Timoney, to hang him out to dry in this way.

Considine slid a fresh envelope from her bag and opened it, so that Mrs Noonan could drop the receipt inside. The housekeeper seemed momentarily reluctant to surrender it. Then she parted her finger and thumb, and it dropped into the envelope with a dry whisper.

They made their goodbyes and said they'd be in touch in due course, making it sound a long while away.

'And I hope young Jimmy has luck with this new job,' Swan added, just as Mrs Noonan let them out. 'Where was he before?'

'What's that?'

'You said he was trying to make a life here now. Where was he before?'

'England.'

'Oh?'

317

'Birmingham, mostly.' Her expression hardened. She was greatly disappointed with them for mentioning her son again.

'At least it wasn't America,' Swan cajoled. 'My own brother went to work in America – construction. He has a great life now, but my mother misses him still. Goodnight now.'

They walked to Considine's car and stood for a while there, looking back at the house.

'Do you miss him, too – your brother?'

'There is no brother.'

'I knew it!'

As they watched, Mrs Noonan re-entered the kitchen and went to the sink. They waited until she settled at the table with a mug of tea.

'Right,' said Swan, 'we need to get the warrant extended to the presbytery and call for some Guards from Deerfield as back-up.'

Considine opened the driver's door. 'Are you staying here or coming with me?'

'I'll hang about, in case she tries to get rid of the stuff. Or on the off-chance that Jimmy shows himself.'

He cast his eyes around until they came to rest on the neon pub sign. 'I'll be over there,' he nodded. 'I doubt Jimmy was a stranger to his local – might find out something more.'

'I'll get someone to put a call in to the Birmingham police while I'm at it,' Considine said. 'The Met, too. Jimmy mightn't have a record with us, but there could be a reason he came home.'

She slipped into the driver's seat and was gone with a roar. Swan saw Mrs Noonan raise her head at the sound of the car leaving, but she didn't move from the table.

He took a turn around the outside of the church, enjoying the last glow of light on the horizon. When the presbytery came back into sight, Mrs Noonan was still in position, head bowed. He thought at first she was praying, but then saw the pale flash of a newspaper page being turned.

It felt safe enough to go over to the Deerfield Inn. He could keep the presbytery in sight from one of the windows. He dashed across the road in the shadow of the pedestrian bridge, following the scuffed paths through the grass verges where people preferred to cross.

37

The Deerfield Inn was a suburban, soulless kind of pub. Passing the windows, Swan could see the lights of the gambling machines winking in an empty lounge bar. A young fellow was shining the bottles above the optics. As Swan pushed the big gilt handle to open the porch door, he scraped his brain for some innocuous sports news to begin the chat with.

She was standing in the middle of the lobby, as stiff as an Irish dancer waiting for her cue. But her face was full of anticipation, those black eyes almost bulging.

'Miss Viney.'

'I knew you'd come find me. I saw you cross the road.'

'That so?'

'Swan is a lovely name. But you don't look like a swan.'

'I'd hope not.'

'You look like a … Pharisee. A lover of rules. Blind to the light.'

She sounded excited, thrilled to be giving him cheek.

'Perhaps you'd join me for a drink?' he said. 'You can tell me more.'

'I don't drink.' She pushed a hand into the neck of her dress and pulled out a key on a string. Sharing the string were three crucifixes of different sizes and elaboration.

An uncomfortable bunch to wear close to your skin, but perhaps that was the point.

Mary Viney pushed the key into a little metal circle in the wall, opening a door that had been all but invisible before, matching, as it did, the rest of the dark panelling in the pub entrance. The open door revealed a dirt-spattered staircase leading up to the next floor.

'We can go up there to talk,' she said.

'What's up there?'

'I live up there.'

The stairs led to a big open room, crowded with furniture. Mary turned on an overhead light and removed her duffel coat, hanging it on a hook that already supported six or seven hangers with garments on them.

The space was chilly. There were stacked pub tables and chairs and what looked like bits of a disassembled stage filling most of the floor area, but narrow pathways had been cleared to the front and back windows.

'You live *here*?'

'I do.' She walked off into a side room and closed the door. It might have been a toilet, so he didn't attempt to follow.

Instead he squeezed his way to the front window and looked out towards the presbytery. Even at this distance, he could see that Mrs Noonan had closed the venetian blinds in her kitchen. On the far side of the church, two men from the Tech Bureau were setting up a long ladder against the bell-tower wall, while another held a torch on their work.

There was a single mattress laid out near his feet, in a gap between some dark wood tables and the wall. It was stacked with neatly folded blankets. Stuck to the wall above it was a collection of holy pictures, the kind you would tuck in your missal. It reminded him of the pictures stuck above Rosaleen MacNamara's bed. Beside the mattress was a row of chairs with a collection of shopping bags on them. A plastic phone with its cord wrapped around it stuck out of one. It was an odd, provisional way of living.

He moved to the back window and was treated to a clear view of the terrace at Rowan Grove. Mary Viney was certainly in the catbird seat here, with all the landmarks of the MacNamaras' lives in plain view.

He could hear water running behind the closed door. He went and knocked politely.

'Yes?'

The door opened into a scullery, a dirty place full of glasses and crates of empty bottles. A seatless toilet was on view in a dark space beyond. She was pouring orange squash into two smeary half-pint glasses full of water.

'How long have you been staying here, Mary?'

'They let me stay for nothing, if I clean the pub.' She said it with a broad smile, as if she couldn't believe such luck. 'And I can use all this furniture, if I like.'

'Have you just moved here? I noticed you don't have many things of your own.'

'Things are not important. People get that wrong. There's a glory to nothing, to being nothing.'

She handed him his orange squash. Her hands were bony and reddened, her fingernails bitten to the quick, but he could see no sign of any marks on her palms, or reasons for the bandages that Considine had noticed her wearing.

'So you've been here a while?' he persisted.

'A year or two. I don't know. I don't pay much attention.'

'Have you family, Mary?'

'I have my sisters. Do you want to sit down?'

'I'd like that. There's things I hope you can help me understand.'

He led her to the front window, wanting to keep watch on the presbytery and church while they talked. He took two chairs from a stack and placed them close together.

'So ... I saw you were praying with Mrs Noonan. It must be difficult for all of you, these deaths. Were you close to the MacNamaras?'

'I was honoured to know them. Such faith. They're in a better place now.' Her voice was dull, matter-of-fact.

It was difficult to tell whether she was putting it on, this holy-fool act. Every now and again she would get a sharp light in her eye, which made him wonder if she was playing him. Thinking what to say, he glanced to the side and his eye fell on a box half filled with yellow pamphlets that he recognised as *The Visions and Revelations of St Catherine of Siena*, the home-made magazine of Rowan Grove. The other half of the box had a sheaf of A4 pages, the top one with the headline HALLELUJAH!

He looked back at Mary, who was watching him closely.

'May I?'

He lifted the page, a bad composite of typing and crooked Letraset. The headline below the large *Hallelujah* stated: 'They Have Gone Before!!', and below it:

God is ALL-powerful and he gathers the faithful into his arms. Make ready for his harvest. Be pure of heart and pure of body. For he says onto us COME TO ME.

Our sister Acolytes Berenice and Rosaleen have shown the way to slip the bonds of earth and enter the heavenly light. We renounce the flesh that leads us to sin with lust and gluttony. We do not let the world enter our mouths. Without CORPUS we are PURE SPIRIT.

It is not those who can inflict the most, but those that suffer the most, that will triumph.

Under this, a PO box number, easy to trace. But he doubted he would even have to go to that trouble, as Mary Viney was sitting a foot away, eager to oblige.

'It's a statement to the world,' she said, 'so others can be inspired. But now I'm not allowed to post it to the press, in case we get into trouble. But the words are from Berenice, and no trouble can reach her.'

'But you put this together?' A nod. 'You knew they were starving? All of you *Acolytes* knew?'

'I was the only trusted one. It was important that there was no interference.'

'When you last saw Berenice and Rosaleen, was it in their house?'

'Yes.' Her eyes fully engaged with his.

'Were they alive?'

'Yes,' she answered, but her expression wavered and she looked down at her lap, brushed something invisible from her knee.

The unplugged phone in the shopping bag suddenly made sense. The missing telephone from the Mac-Namaras' house. Mary had brought him here to see these things.

'And nobody else except you knew it was happening?'

'Berenice is an extraordinary woman. She knew that weaker women would try and stop her. Even in her physical difficulty, her mind was as resolved as an arrow.' Mary Viney leaned in closely to him, so that he could smell her breath. An odd metallic odour. 'I have that strength too, and I long for home.'

'So who is stopping you sending out this important statement? Is it Mrs Noonan?'

She nodded her head quickly. The downy hair on her cheeks caught the light. He remembered what Considine had said about her being skinny. Mary took an eager gulp of her sweet orange squash. But there had been no signs of food or its preparation in the scullery.

'Well, I'd like to hear about it. When did Berenice give you this statement?'

Mary Viney straightened her spine and turned her head towards the window in a self-conscious manner. Her moment had arrived.

'Mrs Noonan was worried. She didn't know they had started, that it was actually happening, but they weren't at prayer group, so she kept telling me to go and check on them. She kept at me. I went up there one night and I called in the letterbox. Finally Berenice opened the door. She was very changed. She let me in, but I had to promise I wouldn't try to influence her mind or Rosaleen's. She said she wanted to say something to the world, so that people might know and understand their sacrifice.

'I sat and took down her words. Then she told me that when they left the world, I was to be joyful – that's why I put "Hallelujah!" at the top. "I want you to glory in our strength," she said. Then we prayed together.'

'What about Rosaleen?'

'That time, Bernie said she was asleep upstairs and I was to speak quietly. But when I went out to the hall, I heard her call, "Hello, hello", but Berenice said I wasn't to go to her. When I went back again—'

'When was this?'

'It took me a few days – I had to buy Letraset and wait to use a typewriter and copying machine they have in the library. Berenice didn't answer the door that time, but I knew to get the key from the presbytery, with no one seeing. I wanted her to see the announcement, to be pleased with it. She wouldn't wake up; she was breathing, though, she wasn't dead. Then I heard Rosaleen from upstairs – "Mary, is that you?"'

Swan felt a sick jolt of realisation. Rosaleen's letter to Francesca had included the line "I've been begging Mary to help me", and mentions of Mary had been sprinkled liberally, along with Jesus and God, and he'd never thought it was anything other than the Holy Mother being invoked.

'She was so pleased to see me. I sat with her and we prayed. And I agreed to post her letter to America, though I didn't send it too quickly …' She trailed off, uncertain.

'Did you not think to help her, Mary? You know she didn't want to die.'

'It was very hard on me, too. She'd come so far, she was

almost there. It was only the hunger was making Rosaleen say things like that.'

'So you left her there.' He was having difficulty keeping his tone conversational.

'I struggled. I prayed and prayed for God to help her, to show me a way to help her. I shouldn't ever have doubted he would.'

'What do you mean?'

Mary Viney stood up quickly and went over to pull one of her holy pictures from the wall. She came back and offered it to him. It was of an angel. Not the winsome nightgowned kind, but a virile archangel with muscles and a spear, wearing something like a Roman centurion's costume, a writhing serpent at his feet.

'He sent an angel.'

She was standing under the bare bulb and it shadowed her features deeply, her eyes disappearing into their sockets. A disquieting stiffness had taken her over again. It seemed that an icy breeze whispered through the room.

'He arrived in the midst of my trouble. He just – materialised in Rosaleen's bedroom. From nowhere. And he said to us, "Don't be afraid." I asked if he had come to take care of them, and he said he would. When I looked at Rosaleen, her eyes were shut and she was quiet, and I knew he would carry them home. And I was free to leave.'

'And he looked like this?' Swan tapped the little card.

Mary Viney snatched back the holy picture. 'You don't understand anything of the spirit. You're a small man.'

'You might be right. But I'm trying to understand, I really am.'

'Jesus did not come in full array. His glory was too magnificent. He came as a man.'

'This angel came as a man?'

Mary Viney huffed impatiently. 'He borrowed the form of a man, so that only I would know him.'

The room jumped into sudden sharp focus.

'Did God choose the form of Jimmy Noonan for this angel?'

'The boy who arrived back from England wasn't Jimmy, he was a messenger. Mrs Noonan cries for him, now that he's gone again, but he wasn't her real son. She doesn't understand that there's a whole world beyond the surface of things.'

'What did he do with them, Mary?'

'He watched over them.'

Mary walked to the window, right up against it, so that the pane almost touched her nose.

'I went back the next day to talk to him. I wanted to ask him something. Berenice had departed this life, and he was sitting right beside her. I was glad he was, it was a tender thing. No earthly man would do that. I asked him would he do the same for me – carry me over? He said he would, but he had to stay for Rosaleen, that I should wait for him. But nothing happened. Then they were found and buried, and still he didn't come to me. Many days I saw him on the church roof and he would look over here. I thought he was telling me I must wait.'

Swan got up to stand beside her, to better imagine her watching Jimmy on the roof. He noticed her eyes move to the bus shelter outside the shops.

'I wanted him to take me with him. But he took her.'

Her finger shook as she raised it to the glass.

The blood was ringing in Swan's ears, and he struggled to keep his voice calm. 'Do you mean Rosaleen?'

'No, she was long gone. He left the priest's house one night and was walking from there,' she indicated the presbytery, 'to here.' She pointed at her chest. 'It was finally my time. But she called to him, and he went over.'

Swan looked down at the bus shelter, the empty space lit by an ad for perfume.

'"Is that you?" she said, and he went to her. He caught her wrists in his hands and she looked like she was trying to escape, twisting about, but she was laughing too. Then they went off together.'

'Mary? Who was at the bus stop?'

She tilted her chin up, blew a circle of brief mist on the window pane.

'You already know who. Madeleine. The little red one.'

38

Swan waited down in the car park for Considine to return, cursing himself. It was plain that Mary Viney was touched by madness, an unreliable source for anything that would hold up in court. And he had stupidly supplied her with the name Jimmy Noonan, not the other way round. All that stemmed from this – her account of him magically beaming into Rowan Grove, his tending the dying, even his abduction of Madeleine – could be nothing more than fantasy: a way to deflect attention from the fact that it was Mary who had been in the house and abetted the sisters' dying.

And yet he did believe that bitterness in her voice, when she said she'd seen Jimmy with Madeleine at the bus stop. They had known each other as adolescents, it wasn't so strange that she would go off with him. Swan glanced up at Mary Viney's front window, could make out the dark shape of her, still looking out into the night. He moved closer to the pub wall, out of sight.

Once Considine arrived with the warrant and back-up, they could take Mary Viney into Deerfield for some kind of statement. He trusted she wasn't the type to flee; she was enjoying her confessions too much. The single light still shone in the presbytery kitchen. Nothing moved in or around the church. The forensics team appeared to have packed it in, their ladders gone from the tower, their van too.

Something was nagging at him – if Mary had been in the house when the sisters were weak and dying, or even if the 'angel' Jimmy had taken over her watch, as she claimed, how had there been a chain hooked across the front door? Did Berenice use her last strength to stumble into the hall and put it in place? But Mary implied that she had seen Berenice dead. Either it was all nonsense or there was another route for someone to get out.

He found his feet leading him to the old stone gateway to the side of Rowan Grove. *Deerfield Care Home* engraved in white on a slate plaque. Maybe he'd have just a quick look while he was waiting.

The old house at the top of the drive was well lit, with a side conservatory full of empty armchairs. Swan veered off the drive and headed between the shadows of the trees, the autumn leaves turned to slick black shreds on the mossy lawn. He reached the line of horse chestnuts that formed the view from Rosaleen MacNamara's window.

It hadn't been apparent from the house how high the ground was here. Standing beside the trunk of one tree, he could see right across the old wall on a level with Rosaleen's window. Anyone could have kept watch on her movements from here.

The ground fell away steeply from his feet, down to the wall that separated the nursing home from the small terrace. The wall was as tall on this side as in the Mac-Namaras' back garden – eight feet it looked like, or even nine. A drift of old leaves and weeds hid its base.

Jimmy Noonan was a handyman, would have easy access to ladders. He must check if Jimmy ever did any work for the nursing home, had a valid excuse to be wandering here.

Swan lifted his face to regard the tree, and there it was. A horizontal branch, black against the purple sky and thick as a rugby player's thigh. It stretched all the way to just above the wall, before it forked into smaller branches.

The tree would have been covered with leaves all through the sisters' ordeal. *His face in leaves – green flame leaves.*

Maybe Rosaleen had seen him watching. Jimmy Noonan could have known of their starvation plan from his mother, or overheard it discussed in the presbytery. He had observed them, been drawn to this place. The MacNamaras' keys would have been available to him at his mother's, but why risk being seen at the front door, if he could come in this way and use the open back door?

Swan felt his way around the trunk, looking for a way up. He found a low scar, a socket where a branch had once grown. He inserted the toe of his damp shoe and took hold of a branch above his head. One pull and he was off the ground and in the tree, breathing hard but moving methodically, shifting one arm or leg at a time to a new hold. He experienced a giddy boyhood lift to his spirits as the branches swayed under his weight. He soon reached the big limb that pointed towards the garden wall, pausing on the cleft where the big branch met the trunk.

It stretched away from him, sturdy, but too narrow to chance walking on. Had Jimmy Noonan tripped along like a tightrope walker? The boy would be used to heights.

Swan thought about climbing back down, about explaining his theory, and Considine sending some young Guard here to try it for them. She was probably waiting for him at the presbytery now.

He slid down to a crouch, leaned his weight on one arm and freed his legs to sit on the branch, feet dangling. But instead of climbing to the ground, he found himself starting out along the limb in a shifting side shuffle that would probably wreck his trousers. No matter. The branch dipped with each foot he gained. By the time he reached the wall, it had bent so low that his toes scraped the top of it. The MacNamaras' house was completely dark, as were the houses on either side. The empty rental next door had all its curtains closed, but the MacNamaras' windows were uncovered, naked to the night. He could even make out the shapes of the furniture in the downstairs room, where they'd moved it aside during the second search.

Swan tried to ease himself slowly onto the wall, but the limb was under so much tension that, as he shifted his weight, it whipped up his back and knocked him sideways into the garden. The ground banged up to meet his hip and arm, and his head ricocheted off the earth with a thump that rattled his teeth.

He was sure he'd heard something rip inside him, some fibrous tearing, and lay for a moment waiting for the real pain to come. His ears rang, and he could taste blood in his mouth where he had bitten some part of his lip or cheek. Out on the main road a motorbike roared in acceleration, brought him back to the wider world. He wriggled his fingers and moved his ankles about. The body functioned, though with a strange rubbery quality. He pressed his hands against the earth and got himself sitting, then standing. If he breathed too deeply, there was a stabbing feeling.

He looked up to see the branch, way out of reach now, trembling back to stillness. Bollocks! He ran his hands over the blocks of the old wall, looking for toe holds and hand holds. The wall did not oblige. Still, he hooked his fingertips into some little dips and scrambled the toes of his shoes against the surface. Useless. If Jimmy Noonan used this wall as an exit as well as an entrance, he had some kind of superpower.

Swan examined the wooden side fences – too difficult to climb, too well anchored to break. He turned and swept his eyes over the garden again, as if a miracle object could appear – a ladder in the grass, say. But there was nothing, only that rotary dryer and a split plastic dustbin. There was no way out except through the house.

He turned the back-door handle, but the door didn't give. Deep down, he knew it wouldn't. Because the door had no key, his colleagues would have padlocked it after they finished, to secure the house. He squatted down to examine the door crack and could just make out the gleam of a metal bar across it.

Fuck! He turned the handle again, rattled the door, even though it was futile. He went over and tried the sliding patio door, with no success. His pager buzzed in his pocket. Considine's name and a local phone number. She was probably phoning from the pub, wondering where he had got to.

'If I could phone back, I would,' he said to the kryptonite

glow of the screen. He hoped that Mary Viney was still sitting in her flat, had not made an escape or, worse, gone to tell Mrs Noonan that her son had been discussed with the police.

He was cold now, headachy-cold. He could die out here of hypothermia and humiliation, or he could do something.

'Ah, for fuck's sake.' There was a solution that he had been blind to. A messy solution, but elegance had gone out the window the minute he started climbing that damn tree. He went over to the rotary dryer and flipped the metal catch that allowed it to collapse like an umbrella, then pulled it out of its socket. It wasn't exactly aerodynamic, but it would do the job. The patio doors would be made of some reinforced stuff. He decided he would aim for the big kitchen window over the sink.

Swan lifted the stringy metal bundle onto his shoulder. A foot of shaft protruded from the end. Averting his face, he butted it into the window. Just before the glass shattered, it seemed to bend, distorting the shapes behind it and reflected in it. The glittering crash ended abruptly. A calendar on the kitchen wall riffled slightly in the breeze, but there was no other sound.

He plucked some shards of glass from the bottom of the window frame, enough to get through without further injury. He fetched the bin and upended it, the split side jammed to the wall where it might hold for the instant his weight would be on it.

Swan hopped up onto the ledge and stepped through the window frame in a crouch, onto the sink drainer, slithery and crunchy with glass. He decided to leap and ended on his arse, of course, a sharp pain in the base of his palm as a shard lodged there. The street lights at the front of the house cast a dirty glow down the hall towards him. He stood and carefully extracted the bit of glass from his person and brushed himself down. His pager buzzed again in his pocket.

They better not have padlocked the front door too. He walked quickly along the hall, checking the space beneath the stairs as he passed. The catch of the door was within hand's reach when he heard a faint but distinctive creak upstairs. The thought of Francesca occurred to him first, but no, of course she was at his mother's. He dropped his hand and listened, and as he listened, he looked up the stairs. There was a hatch into the attic that he couldn't remember noticing before, and he only noticed it now because it was a square of deep black – open.

It could be that his colleagues had searched the attic and left it like that. The house was perfectly quiet, but he started to move stealthily up the stairs. A voice in his head reminded him that he needed to get back to the presbytery, that Considine and the Deerfield Guards were waiting.

There was a small stepladder on the upstairs landing, like the ones the Tech Bureau used. He wondered if they had found something so interesting up there that they intended to return. He climbed the ladder and was just putting his head through the hatch when the blow came – a hard kick to the side of his skull that sent him flying off the ladder, tumbling down the staircase, battered by walls and those hard wooden treads, trying to curl his arms to protect his head as he felt himself upended, then nothing.

When he opened his eyes he was in the middle of the living-room floor. His coat was off him and something was wrong with his arm. Very wrong. It felt cold and didn't move when he told it to. He wanted to look at it, but couldn't take his eyes from the young man in dirty work overalls who stood over him, a foot on either side of Swan's hips, bending forward to stare at him closely in the half dark.

'You the Guards?'

'Jimmy, is it?'

'You tell me and I'll tell you.'

'I'm from the Guards, yes.'

'Only ya don't look terrible scary. Bit fuckin' clumsy an' all.'

He lifted a booted foot and placed it on the wrist of Swan's already injured arm, and pressed his full weight on it, rocked his boot back and forth until it seemed the bones rubbed together and a strange noise scraped from Swan's throat. The young man bent his face closer, his expression alert, but his mouth hanging obscenely agape, wet lips, his breathing deep. Was it this face that Rosaleen was hiding from, that taunted Madeleine in her terrible last days?

'Who knows you're here, piggy man?'

The pain was coming in waves, while Swan kicked his feet uselessly.

A shadow flitted past the front window and the attacker jerked his attention away. They both heard the sound of running feet on the road. Swan gave as loud a roar as he could manage – *HERE!* – all the pain and shame and outrage powering its volume.

The young man glanced towards the back of the house, then down at Swan, deciding whether to run or hurt.

A voice shouted, 'Police!' and the front door shuddered in its frame.

Suddenly his tormentor was gone, feet thundering into the kitchen, the sound of glass cracking under them. Swan wrenched himself up and caught up with the man as he was halfway through the window. He made a wild grab for the man's leg with his one working arm. He managed to grasp an ankle and haul hard enough to make him lose his balance. The man fell across the sink and window frame, glass flying everywhere, kicking and kicking with his feet, but Swan determinedly hung on. Whoever was trying to batter the door down was making slow work of it.

Then the blessed sound of the door crashing against the wall, and voices in the hallway. The ankle in his grasp had stopped kicking. There was a stuttering explosion of light as someone turned on the kitchen's fluorescent tube.

He hadn't expected so much red. The draining board covered in blood, blood dripping from the window frame, down the line of yellow tiles, the shards of glass practically floating in it. But it was the sliver of glass that protruded an inch from the young man's neck, where he lay across the window frame, that explained this mystery.

Considine was at Swan's side. She covered his hand with her own and removed his fingers from the man's leg. 'I wasn't sure where you'd got to. Someone heard glass breaking.'

He took a step back and watched her reach into the window to feel for a pulse. Her fingers on the man's punctured neck, pressing futilely. The kitchen was filling up with people. Detective Joyce was there, and Colin Rooney, and the sergeant from Deerfield, crossing himself.

'Ah, Jesus, what have you done?' Joyce said, and turned to Swan, disappointment and a certain malicious pleasure fighting it out in his eyes. 'Could you not have waited for us? I'll have to call this in now and clear the scene.'

'Is it him?' said Swan. 'Is it Jimmy Noonan?'

'You don't even know?' Joyce said. 'Dear God. Kavanagh's going to love this.'

'It's him,' said Considine softly. 'Mugshots were faxed through from Birmingham. He was well known there. What's wrong with your arm?'

She was looking down at Swan's right hand, hanging by his side. It was dark purple and the palm was facing outwards. As he tried to move it, a watery, nauseous feeling came over him. Detective Joyce backed off. Considine urged Swan towards a chair in the living room, but he shook his head and leaned against the kitchen wall instead. He needed to think.

If only he had removed all the fragments of glass from the window frame, Jimmy Noonan would be handcuffed now, ready to be brought in for questioning. This was disastrous. There might not be enough evidence to link him to Madeleine's murder. And the chances of connecting him to the deaths of her aunts were probably slimmer. Already the puddles of blood around the sink were cooling, the surfaces losing shine.

'Not good. Not good at all.' Detective Joyce was talking to someone in the next room, as Swan found himself slipping down the wall into beautiful darkness.

39

He was lying in a small room, but the floor was rocking. Two men leaned over him, swaddling him in blankets and belts. It wasn't a room, it was an ambulance. When he looked down his body, past his feet, he saw Considine's tense face approach the open door.

'Can I go see him?' she asked some out-of-sight person.

'Why don't you just go with him?' Desmond Joyce's voice. 'Nothing else is going to happen here for a while.'

Considine squeezed into the vehicle, crouched on a little seat, and the doors banged closed. 'This is exciting, I suppose.'

'I'm all right,' he tried to say. He did better on the second go.

The ambulance lurched into motion, and she grabbed the bars of the stretcher thing they had him tied to. He felt floaty, intoxicated, and realised they must already have put various drugs into him. Considine was telling him something, her voice battling with the enveloping sound of the siren.

'What?' he mouthed.

'They found photos on him. In his pocket.' She mimed the location. 'Rosaleen and Berenice. He was there. You were right.' She smiled. 'Understand?'

He indicated that he did. But he felt no satisfaction, only turmoil. He'd caused a death, held a man down while he bled. Perhaps he was dying too, all this rush and emergency. The ambulance slowed, swerved and stopped. It was a short distance to the Mater Hospital, a fact he felt suddenly grateful for. He really did not want to die, he discovered.

They were pulling his trolley out of the ambulance when he remembered.

'Gina!' he called.

Her face appeared briefly in his field of vision, bobbing along beside him.

'Mary Viney. Lives above the pub. Get her arrested. She knew about Jimmy.'

He hoped she had heard. The world was turning kaleidoscopic, a spooling reel of ceilings and faces and strip lights, the smell of antiseptic and rubber, then unconsciousness coming to claim him again.

They kept him for a week after his surgeries. Elizabeth sleeping in a chair next to him that first night, her head and arms stretched across the end of the bed, a supplicant for his survival. He thought she would be angry with him, getting himself injured like that, but she surprised him again.

'We're going to get through this,' she said several times, smiling and determined, as if the danger was not to him, but to both of them. Which was true, when you thought of it that way.

His right arm was quite messed up, several breaks and a

chipped elbow. His skull had suffered a fracture, a delicate white line running down the moon of his head X-ray. Some ribs were broken, but all the rest were just bashes. His face was an ever-changing palette of bruising. He didn't know which injuries had been caused by his fall down the stairs and which had been inflicted later by Jimmy Noonan. There were many questions he would never have complete answers to.

Considine filled in a lot of the gaps for him. It turned out that the keys to the empty house at the end of the terrace had also been in the presbytery key cabinet – vouchsafed to the old parish priest by some previous tenant and forgotten. Jimmy found them, though, made a little home for himself there, accessed from the back garden. A bed of cushions on the floor, an ashtray and a line of beer bottles around the skirting, some pornography. Staying occasionally at the priest's house, storing his stuff there, was a decoy – a way to give his mother the impression he was moving about, that he had friends.

Probably this was how he became aware of his neighbours' suffering. Those thin, jerry-built walls couldn't have contained the sound of Rosaleen crying out constantly for her sister. The rest could be seen from the trees in the nursing-home grounds. At some stage Jimmy found out that the attics between the houses connected, that the builder hadn't managed more than two courses of breeze block between the properties before deciding to cut another corner. This was what enabled Jimmy's 'magical' appearances, and why no chain or high wall could keep him from his visits to the dying women.

Some days Swan had no stomach for the progress reports provided by Considine. The details of Jimmy's previous assaults on young women in Birmingham – alleged assaults, that is, for none made it to trial. No corroboration, a lack of evidence. Jimmy had always been careful, it seemed. One day she showed him the copies of the Polaroids they'd found in Jimmy's pocket. He knew she was trying to assure him that he should have no regrets over Jimmy's death, that no one could have qualms over such a sadist. Swan turned them face-down on the green honeycombed blanket, images he could not un-see.

Jimmy Noonan had a particular appetite that Swan hadn't encountered before; an intimately cruel and voyeuristic streak. How he could look so closely at suffering and come away, wanting more. How he tended his victims with such concentration – the washing of Madeleine, the sitting with Berenice's body – in a hellish perversion of care.

But there would be no confession, no court hearing in which the crimes of Jimmy Noonan would be listed and weighed. No hearing likely, either, for Mary Viney, handmaiden of hunger, now committed to a psychiatric hospital. Not that answers could change what had already happened. Someone like Noonan did the things he did because he wanted to; and maybe, in court, your psychiatrists would line up and trace the diagram of childhood trauma or damaged cerebellum or psychopathic delusions. Some of them would be very convincing, and people might get the idea that understanding what went wrong would some day prevent other wrongs. Some day.

Swan persuaded Elizabeth not to stay overnight at the

hospital, now that he was out of danger. But then he could not sleep at all. The moaning and snoring of the other men in the ward, the lack of darkness. He lay and he thought about what might have been. If they had properly investigated the deaths of Berenice and Rosaleen, could they have found trace of Jimmy earlier? An unwiped fingerprint in the many places he'd lurked: toying with those animal ornaments, using the bathroom, sitting and watching – that slackened face – as their light faded from the world. If only Swan had paid enough attention to the right things, if he had credited the involvement of harmless-looking women like Mary Viney, there was a chance they might have caught Jimmy Noonan before he found Madeleine. Or before she found him.

How many times had Jimmy visited her in the crypt before the stumble or push that caused her death? O'Keefe's report that she might have been given 'a little water' in her final days, just enough to keep her going. How long might he have kept her there, barely alive? There was no solution to these questions, and yet Swan kept following them round and round. Or he thought of Francesca. He worried about how much she understood of what had happened. Did she realise that the Polaroid he took from her bedside had been taken in the crypt, during Madeleine's imprisonment? O'Keefe said she was still alive when it was taken, as she had no mark on her temple. But whether she was unconscious or sleeping, he could not say.

When it got to around 4 a.m. Swan's eyes would start to close, and there would be the images from the other Polaroids hovering behind his lids. They were both of Rosaleen

– one of her lying in her bed, skinny hands clamped to her face to ward Jimmy off, or to cancel the sight of him. The other showed her head and shoulders with the yellow light of the flash bouncing back from inside her pupils, like an animal caught in headlights. Her skull showing through her skin, mouth open for the spoon that entered the frame from below, dripping with golden honey. Beads of it shining on her collarbone and chin. Noonan had kept Rosaleen alive with sweetness; her purgatory extended for his whim.

Swan couldn't stop imagining the terrible resolve it must have taken for her to drag her bones from that bed and squeeze herself away underneath it, out of reach of his taunting and feeding, with only her rosary beads for protection, and her prayers for company.

40

Timoney got his suitcase down from the wardrobe. The old one, made of some kind of shiny cardboard substance, that his mother had bought when he left home at seventeen for the seminary. Bursting with pride, she was – she kept stroking it in lieu of stroking him.

He flipped open the catches and started to empty the contents of the wardrobe into it – a worn black coat, three black suits, various grey jumpers.

Father Geraghty appeared in the doorway. 'I can get someone to do that for you.'

'Nonsense!'

Geraghty looked at his watch, a glint of gold. 'Maybe I should have come later.'

Timoney folded the jumpers with a care made delicious by Geraghty's impatience. He was moving to the big parish house, a bedroom had been made ready for him. Mrs Noonan had resigned her job following her son's death, naturally enough. She had been *cooperative*, Geraghty told him. Nobody knew where she had moved on to.

Geraghty was altogether more considerate these days. It wouldn't last for ever, but Timoney had come to realise that his proximity to tragedy and violence, and the consequent interest of police and reporters, had shifted the ground between them. Why should he benefit from such tragic goings-on? It wasn't his place to question the workings of the Lord. He was an innocent. Culpably innocent, in that he had not recognised the evil that lay in Jimmy Noonan's heart. Timoney had even thought him gentle that day Jimmy helped him into the house, when his back had gone out. Supported by his strong young arms.

'Noel! Are you even listening to what I'm saying?'

He came back into the moment to find he was holding empty woollen sleeves out in the air, an action suspended.

'Sorry.' He bundled up the last jumper roughly and added it to the case, then went to empty the chest of drawers.

'I was saying, Noel, that the bishop phoned again. He's of the opinion, after consideration, that your comments about bulldozing St Alphonsus, while intemperate, may have been useful in the long run. Planning could look more favourably on a development plan for the site, in the circumstances. A way for the parish to move on and get some financial return. You're very lucky, Noel, that the bishop sees it that way. He has a great distaste for the melodramatic.'

Timoney had happened to be in the church when the RTÉ news crew arrived. There seemed no reason not to talk to them, or show them around the blighted building. They had an energy about them that woke him from his morbid reflections, their lights and cases and bustle were fascinating. They stood him outside the front porch with its warped canopy, and a lad with a camera on his shoulder the size of a bale of peat briquettes told him to speak directly into the lens. A huge dark eye, glassy and unblinking. It asked for the truth and he told it. This church was an evil place. Unredeemable.

Now it seemed that everyone agreed with him.

Father Geraghty carried his bags out to the car, partly in deference to Timoney's bad back, mostly to hurry things on. The smell of Mrs Noonan's cigarettes and bad cooking still hung around the bungalow. He felt only relief to take a last glance and cross over the threshold. Relief, then a stab of pain near his sacrum, as he stepped too heavily onto the tarmac. Geraghty's car was already puttering exhaust fumes into the cold air.

Maybe he should go and see that Claudia girl again. Actually submit to her small hands this time. Did Christ not have his feet dried by the hair of the Magdalene and anointed with oil? He needed to get healed. How could he serve God well, if he was not well himself?

41

'Give it here.'

Swan had been twisting a sugar sachet in his good hand, hoping to bully it open. Francesca pulled it from his fingers, tore it and spilled it into his coffee. She reached for the spoon.

'I can stir it myself, woman.'

She rolled her eyes and looked pointedly away. He wished he hadn't said *woman* that way, hoped he could pass it off for a joke. Behind her, beyond the plate-glass window, a 747 took off. Christmas carols jangled thinly from a speaker somewhere.

It had seemed the right thing to do, to accompany her to the airport, to bring things to a formal close between them, but she was acting high-handed in a way he recalled from his very first meetings with her. His own irritability confused him too.

She peered up at the monitors hanging from the ceiling.

'Can you see – are they boarding yet?'

He looked at the list of flights, though he already knew the answer.

'No. You've plenty of time.'

'You shouldn't have asked for the cab so early.'

Not being able to drive with his arm in plaster, he'd

hired a taxi. When he arrived at his mother's house to collect her, Francesca was ready to go, standing in the hall between two suitcases. His mother came and folded her into her arms for a long embrace.

'You mind yourself, girl.' Both had tears in their eyes.

Now Francesca was looking over at the bar, a reproduction Oirish pub with a papier-mâché side of bacon hanging from a rafter, and ironmongery placed around its fake windows.

'We should have a drink,' she said. 'Take the edge off the day.'

'It's a bit early.'

'Doesn't count in airports.' She shoved some banknotes at him. 'Have to get rid of these anyway.'

He pushed them back, and went up to order two small whiskeys. Maybe it would change the mood. There were no trays, so he had to bring them back one at a time. When he put the glass in front of her, she hardly raised her eyes. They sat in silence, pretending to be listening to a distant announcement.

'There was a newspaper photo we came across during the case,' he said, 'of you out there, on the steps of a plane. I think you were being waved off to the States by fans. That must have been quite an experience. I do miss that open balcony on the old terminal. I used to cycle out here with my friends when I was a lad – watch the planes come in and out. That was our idea of a great day out.'

'It's hard to be reminded that your glory days were so long ago.'

'I'm sure there's more glory days to come.' He said it too quickly, too pat. She flicked her eyes at him impatiently.

'Francesca. All I meant was, this is a particularly dark time. Things will change. The sunshine will do you good, for one thing.'

She shrugged, stirred the air with her drink.

'And you have work to do, your television series back on the box …'

She threw back the last of her whiskey. 'I think I'll just walk to the gate now. If you don't mind.'

He'd expected that they would hug, at least, or that he would allow himself a chaste kiss on each cheek, a moment's physical contact. But somehow she was already walking away, and she didn't glance back. He followed her bright head as it weaved through the duty-free shop, then she was gone. He would probably never see her again.

Swan waited for a pang of something to hit – sorrow, regret – but it didn't arrive.

As he passed back through security, flashing his badge, there was a young athletics team going through the other way, girls with ponytails or short hair wearing identical green tracksuits embroidered with harps. They were excited, chatting to each other, laughing through the metal-detector gate, giving cheek to the security guards.

It made him smile. He wanted to shout *Good luck!* but didn't. He was feeling surprisingly well all of a sudden.

Tonight he would take Elizabeth out to dinner, celebrate their little news. She said he couldn't tell anyone – not even his mother – for another month or so, not until the pregnancy was safely established. This seemed overly cautious to him, but there was no harm having some time to get used to the fact that his world was about to tip on its axis.

Swan went down to the arrivals hall and bought a coffee, took a seat near a baubled tree. He was on suspension again, until the report into Noonan's death was complete. He wouldn't go home just yet, though. He'd watch people waiting for their friends and family. He loved that moment. The doors swishing open. The arrivals looking so innocent and lost behind their trolleys. Then the change happening in their faces, the smiles breaking out. The tears.

42

Fuck them all. The dead and the living. Fuck kindly Vincent Swan, the big man buying her a too-small drink. Fuck his one-armed chivalry. Fuck the whole country. She was damned if she was ever coming back. The engines roared down the runway.

Francesca opened her eyes as the plane lifted, the market gardens of north Dublin falling away, the white edge of the sea. Everything tilted as they spiralled upwards. Then an annihilation of cloud.

He could have come for her. Vincent admitted that he'd been right next door all along. Jimmy Noonan. She remembered him now. A pup of a boy at fifteen, that time she'd moved them all into Rowan Grove. She chased him down the lane behind the shops after he'd stolen Madeleine's new camera, the Polaroid she bought her in the States. Just a nasty skinny boy.

She caught up with him at last by the walled-off end of the lane, grabbed the hem of his jumper. What was she going to do? Beat him? She wanted to. He spun round and laughed in her face, slid a hand over his crotch, thrusting his hips at her.

'Do you want a bit of this, you old slag?'

Astonished, she loosened her grip and he tore away, jeering. How does a nasty boy become a monster?

Every night she runs down that lane again after Jimmy Noonan and imagines killing him. She has held imaginary knives, guns and wire garrottes in her aching hands. She has no doubt that he was the nameless one who tied Madeleine to that tree years ago, the boy Madeleine thought would come back to release her.

Ping! The seatbelt lights go off. The plane emerges into sunshine, a pure world of white cloud banks and blue sky. A nice place to get off, she thinks, just step outside. She picks her handbag off the floor and checks again that her sleeping pills are all in there.

The police found Jimmy in Rowan Grove. Had he been waiting for her return? The thought that she might have been killed, too, somehow relieves her guilt.

An air hostess looms above her.

'Something from the trolley?'

'Bloody Mary, please.'

The hostess pulls down her seat table for her, places a tiny vodka bottle, a plastic glass of ice with lemon, a can of tomato juice and a small packet of dry-roasted peanuts on it. She points out the folded blanket on the seat beside her.

'It's got slippers in it too.'

Francesca thanks her in an unsteady voice.

A glimpse of sea appears below, navy-blue crêpe broken by one uninhabited rock. Ireland is behind her now, America ahead. Escaping is her real talent.

She pours the vodka and raises her plastic beaker. A resolution would be the thing – an oath to live on for her sisters and for Madeleine, to try and relish the world they have been ousted from. But she doesn't even know if she will make it through the flight.

ACKNOWLEDGEMENTS

I want to thank all those who supported me with advice and friendship through the making of this book, especially Jonathan White, Merlin James, Jane and Menno Verburg, Alison Stirling, Caroline Barbour and Denise Mina.

It has been a real pleasure to work with my editor, Miranda Jewess, and I'd like to thank the whole team at Viper and Serpent's Tail for their enthusiasm and support. Thanks also go to my agent, Jenny Brown, for steady steering and great kindness. I'm grateful for timely financial support from Creative Scotland's Open Project Funding, and to Cove Park, the Scottish Book Trust and Moniack Mhor for residencies worth their weight in word-counts.

Final credits go to the Slaughterhouse team for the morning coffees, Bridget for the walks and Ruth Clark for everything else.

ABOUT THE AUTHOR

Nicola White is a writer, former curator and documentary maker. She won the Scottish Book Trust New Writer Award in 2008, and in 2012 was Leverhulme Writer in Residence at Edinburgh University. Her novel *The Rosary Garden* won the Dundee International Book Prize, was shortlisted for the McIlvanney Prize and was selected as one of the four best debuts by Val McDermid at Harrogate. She grew up in Dublin and New York, and now lives in the Scottish Highlands.

@whiteheadednic